The Nature Notebooks

Other Books by Don Mitchell

HARDSCRABBLE BOOKS — *Fiction of New England*

Raymond Kennedy, *Ride a Cockhorse*

Raymond Kennedy, *The Romance of Eleanor Gray*

Lisa MacFarlane, ed., *This World Is Not Conclusion: Faith in Nineteenth-Century New England Fiction*

G. F. Michelsen, *Hard Bottom*

Don Mitchell, *The Nature Notebooks*

Anne Whitney Pierce, *Rain Line*

Kit Reed, *J. Eden*

Rowland E. Robinson (David Budbill, ed.), *Danvis Tales: Selected Stories*

Roxana Robinson, *Summer Light*

Rebecca Rule, *The Best Revenge: Short Stories*

Catharine Maria Sedgwick (Maria Karafilis, ed.), *The Linwoods; or, "Sixty Years Since" in America*

R. D. Skillings, *How Many Die*

R. D. Skillings, *Where the Time Goes*

Lynn Stegner, *Pipers at the Gates of Dawn: A Triptych*

Theodore Weesner, *Novemberfest*

W. D. Wetherell, *The Wisest Man in America*

Edith Wharton (Barbara A. White, ed.), *Wharton's New England: Seven Stories and* Ethan Frome

Thomas Williams, *The Hair of Harold Roux*

Suzi Wizowaty, *The Round Barn*

The Nature Notebooks

a novel

Don Mitchell

University Press of New England

Hanover and London

F

Published by University Press of New England,
One Court Street, Lebanon, NH 03766
www.upne.com
© 2004 by Don Mitchell
Printed in the United States of America
5   4   3   2   1

Library of Congress Cataloging-in-Publication Data

Mitchell, Don, 1947–
The nature notebooks / Don Mitchell.
    p.   cm.—(Hardscrabble books)
Includes a reading group guide and questions for discussion.
ISBN 1–58465–357–4 (cloth : alk. paper)
1. Women naturalists—Fiction.   2. Creative writing—Study and
teaching—Fiction.   3. Natural history—Authorship—Fiction.
4. Ecoterrorism—Fiction.   5. Sabotage—Fiction.   6. Vermont—Fiction.
I. Title.   II. Series.
PS3563.I75N38 2004
813'.54—dc22   2003025340

For Jay and Louie Howland
with love

"What are you doing now?" he [Ralph Waldo Emerson]
asked. "Do you keep a journal?"—So I make my first
entry to-day.
                    —Henry David Thoreau
                    October 22, 1837

... as I said to [Edward] Hoagland: "It is no longer
suffcient to *describe* the world of nature. The point is
to *defend* it." He writes back accusing me of trying to
"bully" him into writing in my manner. Which is
true, I was. He should.
                    —Edward Abbey
                    Journal entry, May 30, 1979

Contents

Author's Note

This is a work of fiction, and its characters and events are inventions of the author's imagination. The novel's situation is based, however, on two ongoing circumstances affecting Vermont's highest mountain.

Since 1997, public access to Mount Mansfield's "Nose" has been restricted because of radiation emitted from one of several broadcast towers located there. A solution proposed in the spring of 2003 involves building three new towers on the mountaintop to broadcast high definition TV signals.

In the autumn of 2003, Stowe Mountain Resort was poised to begin a major expansion of its facilities on Mount Mansfield and adjacent Spruce Peak. The master plan includes a mountainside "hamlet" of four hundred luxury condominiums, a new hotel, a retail plaza, a golf course, six new ski lifts, many new downhill trails, and ponds impounding 175 million gallons of water for snowmaking.

These circumstances lie at the heart of the novel's world.

The Nature Notebooks

Foreword

Erin Furlong

Well over a year ago, when I first began facilitating a workshop for nature writers at Burlington's Fletcher Free Library, my goal was to compile a book examining how a group of typical Vermonters came to see the world around them in a whole new light, thanks to taking on the discipline of "nature writing." That would have surely made an interesting volume, but the present one is rather different from what I had planned. After the tragic events of last autumn on the heights of Mount Mansfield—events that most readers will be already familiar with, thanks to media attention that shed more heat than light—it made sense to set the record straight by compiling certain passages from the nature notebooks kept by three particular members of my writing group. From the journals of Lauren Blackwood, Marianna Finch, and Rachel Katz, I have chosen those portions that document the history of each woman's interactions with Kyle Hess. There were half a dozen other talented writers who participated in our group and kept observation journals, but this trio of women comprised the members most affected by my friend Kyle's all too brief visit here.

If Kyle showed up on my porch again today, flashing his boyish grin and staring with those bright green eyes, I feel certain I would open the door again. I saw there was so much he could offer to my writing students, and he never once complained about the time spent working with them. Trying to help strangers forge a stronger bond with nature, then hammer language till it rang out with their new awareness. Kyle was both thoughtful and adept at helping people do that. And he was accomplished, too, at doing it himself.

Kyle made my students feel they were taken seriously—and they surely were. He showed them how the words they selected to express themselves were deeply important, and might truly make a difference. Also, he was straddling—with seeming comfort, and at times with striking grace—the ragged boundary that too often separates those bent on appreciating nature from those bent on fighting to defend it. I think of Kyle as a man of courageous action, not just another self-absorbed wordsmith. Words and deeds—one without the other was, for him, mistaken.

I want to let these notebooks speak for themselves–*they do*—but just a quick note on how I've chosen to arrange them, and the briefest effort to mention certain features in the actual journals that the reader cannot see. I've placed Lauren first because she's focused on terrain, and the physical geography of Mount Mansfield underscores all that happened during Kyle's five weeks here. What I wish could also be revealed in print is how traces of Lauren's daily labor on her farm—which backs up against the mountain's western slopes, near Underhill—make their way repeatedly onto her notebook pages. Streaks and smears from hands that were often literally dirty. Fingers painted with fresh earth. Leafing through her journal entries, I can see her digging in the soil, helping make things grow.

As for Marianna, I wish there was a way to show how her journal also is a scrapbook of the flowers, leaves, and insects that she chose each day for contemplation. Raw stuff for her efforts at descriptive craft. Also, I wish the printed page could reveal the delicate precision of her elegant handwriting. Far more compelling than mere penmanship, each word bespeaks a woman taking real joy in setting forth her inmost thoughts. Her notebook functions as a multilayered work of art.

Finally, in putting Rachel last I hope her voice will show the feisty and determined spirit that made her Kyle's match. What cannot be shown here are the series of detailed sketches that decorate the margins of her well-worn notebook. Wonderful depictions of rock walls with crags and fissures, thanks to her perspective as a climber scaling dizzying heights. Some of these are rendered with such skill, they seem to leap right off the page and come to life in three dimensions.

So—with great humility and deep respect for these three writers, I present their nature notebooks.

Lauren Blackwood's Notebook

September 6 – October 12

Friday, September 6

Paraglider

Blue wings drift against a bluer sky . . .
Old dream of flight now seems too easy.
Modern-day Icarus soars fearless, does not trust in wax.
Puts his faith in Dacron and aluminum and Velcro.
My side of the mountain was not meant for this excitement, though—
These extreme sports, extreme sportsmen. And I hate
Seeing the Stowe, Inc. carnival, year-round circus, spill down
Into Pleasant Valley's peace and
Quiet. Now he's coming right this way, suspended in
mid-air, reck-
    less bird
      man

Saturday, September 7

 He came out of the clouds in late afternoon on one of those end-of-summer days that feels like autumn, and I watched him swoop and soar for a good twenty minutes in his blue paraglider, nylon wing the color of a robin's egg. Behind him stretched the rocky corrugations of Mount Mansfield, and beneath him lay its steep and thickly forested flanks. Since I farm the nearest open fields in his flight path, after a while as he kept losing altitude I started feeling certain that he'd touch down in my pasture. That's when I ducked inside to change into a skirt and put the kettle on.

 By the time I stepped back on the porch, the guard dog was going crazy. That's Vasilis's job, though. "Good boy," I called to my fluffy white puffball of a barking Great Pyrenees. The man aloft was circling overhead, in easy earshot and decidedly wary. "Will he bite?" he called down from directly above me. The sheep were already scattering away, and the llamas ganged together in attack mode, getting set to spit.

"I don't think so. Long as you don't land near the animals."

"What's the dog's name?" I liked this freelance flier's voice, a little nervous and modulated under the circumstances. I liked the way he made it carry without shouting.

"Vasilis."

"What kind of a—okay, Vasilis." He had found where he would land. "Good dog. Down, boy."

"Vasilis means the king. In Greek."

"Let's be friends, your majesty." And with that, his feet were on the ground. The bright wing sagged, and my drop-in guest began extricating himself from his nylon harness. The dog bounded forward to draw an imaginary line in the dirt between the sheep and this perceived intruder, but the intruder backed away—they always do, when challenged by 130 pounds of canine.

"It was the llamas that attracted me," he said as he flopped his gear across the fence and climbed over the stile. He was lanky, broad-shouldered, and his features seemed curiously small and understated, overwhelmed by his shaggy head of curly golden hair. Not what I'd call a devastatingly handsome face, but likable enough. His eyes were inquiring and a lively shade of green. Intense. "Sorry for the interruption. Kyle Hess." He stuck a hand out. "Wow—that was some ride."

"You took off from the ridge?"

He nodded, pointing to a place along the mountaintop that is known as Frenchman's Pile—a stone cairn marks the spot where, by legend, a Quebecois explorer got zapped by lightning during an electrical storm. These can arrive in a matter of minutes, up there. Frenchman's Pile is midway between the mountain's Nose—a stark promontory stabbed with several prickly broadcast towers—and the true summit of the mountain's Chin, Vermont's highest point at 4,393 feet. "Hell of a mountain," my Icarus said cheerfully. "Heck of an updraft." He looked around him, wide-eyed. "I really like your llamas."

"Thanks," I said. "The llamas are a long, happy story. What happens now to you—have you got a chase team? Need to use my phone?"

"Just need to get back to my van, over in Stowe. Parked by the gondola." He laughed. "I didn't lug this rig the whole way up the mountain."

"Stowe's a long way back, by highway. Twenty miles—up through Jeffersonville, then down through Smugglers' Notch. Long way around the mountain."

"I can hitchhike. Wondering, though, if I could leave my stuff here. Grab it when I swing back through."

"Put it on the porch," I told him as he bent to fold his bright wing and roll it up. "Do you want some coffee, tea? There's water on."

"No, thanks. You don't need to go to any trouble for me."

"No trouble—actually, you couldn't have dropped in at a better time." We were on the porch now, and I picked up my nature note-book—*this* one—and waved it at him. "I go to this writing group, in Burlington. For nature writers. And our workshop leader has us jot down everything we see for twenty minutes every day. All our obser-vations. So I was sitting out here, watching, and I wrote about you."

He waved into the middle distance, where the sheep had settled down and now were back to grazing. "You seem to have a lot of na-ture to observe."

"Yes, but a paraglider dropping in is hard to beat. Everyone will be impressed."

"Actually, I do some writing myself. In the nature field."

"Do you?"

He unzipped his nylon shell and rummaged in a pocket. "You know how when hot-air balloons land in a field, they're supposed to give the farmer champagne?"

"No, I didn't know that."

"Well, I carry this to give." He handed me a slender, evidently self-published book—*Prayers on the Wing,* it was titled. On the back was a picture of this Kyle Hess soaring at Yosemite, with Half Dome in the background. The biographic note said that he lived in California.

"You're a long way from home."

"Oh—that's out of date. I'm on the move, these days. But I like New England well enough. And I *love* Vermont."

"What brought you here?"

"An old friend." He pointed to my notebook then, spread open on the porch chair. "So, can I read what you wrote about me?"

"It's a poem," I said, a bit defensive because I don't write a lot of poetry. But I picked up the journal, folded back the page, and showed him. I could see his lips mouthing the words as he finished reading— *reck/less bird/man*—"That's where I stopped," I told him. Inside, the kettle whistled.

"Not bad. But you pegged me wrong—I'm not involved with the madness at Stowe."

"I just meant—"

"Make a revision." He smiled. "Anyway, it's late. I should get a move on."

"You don't want a hot drink?"

"Maybe later, when I grab my wing. Point me toward the highway?"

I got him aimed toward Pleasant Valley Road, and told him what he had to do to make it back around the mountain—back to the gaudy and upscale Stowe side. Next thing I knew he was heading down the driveway, half-turning once to wave a long arm back at me. I sat on the porch leafing through his chapbook, and once he was out of sight I found myself impressed, somewhat. He had a strong, easy style. A way with words. I hoped I'd get the chance to talk more with him, later . . . but his paraglider gear was still sitting, rolled up on the porch, when I went to bed. That must have been around 10:00. And in the morning it was gone. I don't recall the dog barking more than usual, and I never heard a thing.

I've left *Prayers on the Wing* on my night table, right next to *Walden* and *Walking* and *The Maine Woods.* Imagine, having nature writing fall on me out of the sky.

Sunday, September 8

I have spent the morning battling weeds, but the weeds are winning. What I like to call the breeding pasture, in particular, has really gone to hell this year with burdock, purple thistle, and a recent, full-blown onslaught of obnoxious stinging nettle. None of the grazing animals I try to raise will go near these invasive species, so they bloom and multiply . . . they prosper. Oh, and did I mention that the burdocks get embedded in the sheep's wool, damaging their fleeces? All this will get worse, I know, until we get a killing frost.

Until then, it's up to me to keep the weeds at bay. I keep thinking how upset my dad would be if he could see these fields that he used to care for. I never had much respect for the way he farmed—he'd overgraze a field down to bare dirt, then goose the sod back with a fertilizer cocktail—but I can't recall the pastures ever looking this rank when he was in charge. And since I've made the choice to raise meat organically, it's not as if I can just spray herbicide to get on top of things.

One bright spot is my acre of pick-your-own along the highway, a gold mine that runs itself with a cash box and an honor system. That plot of soil, thanks to ample mulch and sweat, is weed-free . . . but no way could I put that kind of effort into these upland pastures where the livestock make their living. Or at least attempt to.

I've been doing balance sheets, now that the growing season's coming to an end. Incredibly, the seven breeding llamas on this farm will make more money this year than one hundred sheep. I have nagging doubts, though—llamas may just be a fad. These past couple years, they have become the hippest rural pet. Wait till supply catches up with demand, though. And a lot of llamas are downright nasty—visitors who get too close are apt to be attacked. Not to mention having to wipe stinky spit from off their faces.

Plus, at the A&P I see they still have lamb chops in the meat case. I've never seen a leg of llama sitting there.

Okay, I've been reading more of Kyle Hess's chapbook that he left when he landed here. Twenty-five short chapters that, collectively, become a manifesto for a new way of seeing nature and our role within it. For example, he writes that

> any change that matters must begin—we know this in our hearts—with the profoundest expression of humility. Recognizing that *humans are nothing* in the cosmic scheme. All human history is nothing but a meteoric streak across the ageless sky. And from that humility ought to spring compassion for the whole of creation that's embarked on this adventure with us. Equals. Every choice we make should then affirm the right of all things to exist alongside ourselves. To coexist. Nothing should be sacrificed on the altar of our "progress," or endangered by our greed. When we exploit and manipulate nature, we exploit *ourselves*—as individuals, and as a species.

And then he goes on to say why we should save the last whales and the rainforests, care about the plight of spotted owls and monarch butterflies. He's the kind of writer who can watch a pair of bugs making out, and nearly have a breakdown. Although he certainly describes them with precision.

Funny how he fell out of the sky and whipped this book out at me. I used to wrestle with a lot of his concerns, but now I'm realizing that I've made a kind of peace. Not that I am cool about the redwoods getting shipped off to sawmills, but I just don't buy the "nature is a groove" idea. So Californian . . . and so out of touch with how I actually live. When I walk that weed-strewn field where I want to breed the ewes—where there should be, by October, thick clumps of clover to shake down next spring's crop of lambs—and when I see it going by to plants the sheep won't look at—well, I could do with some species extinction. If I got to do the choosing.

I know I shouldn't say that. I should maybe bite my tongue.

When my dad was dying—can it be four years ago, already?—he told me he didn't think I should keep the farm. He knew that the march of suburbs north and east of Burlington was bound to bump up against Mount Mansfield, setting me up nicely. And it still might come to selling house lots, it might. But I've come to realize that Dad never knew I am as stubborn as he always was—and I never knew it, either, till the farm was in my hands. And farming *does* require nature to be exploited. It's an unceasing project of manipulation.

Now I see the dog is barking because the stud llama, Mister Rogers, wants to steal his food. This is why I keep the dog, to raise guard llamas in a way that gets them used to working with a canine. But not this way. Stand your ground, Vasilis—damn. My dog is getting creamed. Out-manned and—yes—exploited by a big manipulator. Got to go sort this out, bring peace to the neighborhood. So— I'll try to write more later.

Monday, September 9

A drawback to returning, as a grownup, to the place where you grew up is that the place names hold no magic. You just take them all for granted. When I lived with Jason in Milwaukee, right after college, looking at a highway map could be like reading poetry. Chippewa Falls, Spring Green, Fond du Lac . . . each name held a hidden meaning that would pique my interest. Same thing here, I guess, for furriners—I realized this talking with that Kyle Hess the other day, giving him directions to get back around to Stowe. He was so curious—asking why we call it Smugglers' Notch and Pleasant Valley, Jeffersonville and Frenchman's Pile. I take all these names for granted since I've known them all my life.

Even "Mount Mansfield" gave him a point to make. He said it was arrogant—and didn't I agree?—for humans to name a mountain after themselves. Asserting their so-called dominion. Man's Field. As if nature's purpose was to be our mirror.

That's not accurate, I told him. What happened is that pioneers looked along the mountain's spine—three miles of bumpy rock— and saw the outline of a human face there, staring skyward. Forehead, Nose, Lips, Chin—these names refer to specific features on the mountain. Even some of Stowe's famous ski runs play with these same names: Nose Dive, Chin Clip. Double black-diamond trails.

But he had been reading up. He told me that before the English got here, the Abenaki had their own name for the mountain: *Moze-o-de-be-Wadso*. Mountain-like-the-head-of-a-Moose. And just that simple contrast said so much about the difference between Native American perspectives on the natural world and our own.

I said that it couldn't be that simple, but I was impressed that he'd done this homework. Not many visitors passing through would make the effort.

"Names are key," he told me. "Names record how humans see the world."

Funny—I don't think we talked for more than ten minutes, Friday. And yet Kyle Hess made a strong impression on me. As I read through the slender book he left behind, it's like I'm involved in an extension of that conversation.

Moze-o-de-be-Wadso. Sure.

Tuesday, September 10

With foliage coming, I've been thinking about opening the cottages again. Dad built three of them, scattered along the winding drive that connects the farm to Pleasant Valley Road; each of the cottages is named for the apple tree that sits in its front yard. One, though—Golden Delicious—has fallen into such disrepair that I use it just to store the llamas' tack. But the other two, Jonathan and Winesap, could be gotten into rentable shape with just a few days' work. Each of them has views of Mansfield's summit and the valley's long, dramatic sweep down to Underhill. When the leaves are at their peak and gawking out-of-staters cruise the back roads, burning gas, I could rent those babies for a hundred bucks per night. Each.

The cottages were one of Dad's schemes to keep the farm solvent, once he realized the dairy business was heading south. I still can hear him railing about how hardworking Vermonters like himself were serving as unwitting caretakers to a landscape that outsiders forked over big bucks to see. But there was no money in caring for the land,

and the tourist dollars were not winding up in farmers' hands. Having cottages to rent was supposed to change all that. Visitors would pay to milk a cow, he thought, or feed a calf or lend a hand with haying. "Nature's what we've got to sell," Dad would say with confidence. "Why wouldn't city people pay to get a taste of nature?" He was certain this was a market he could tap, and that families would return here year after year, using their vacations to live and work like dairy farmers.

Trouble was—God, there were so many kinds of trouble. The insurance problem. The water and septic issues. The matter of having to remortgage the farm . . . but the biggest trouble came from finding out that "agri-tourists," once Dad had courted them, wanted to see only a nice, clean, prettified version of nature as presented on a farm. Dealing with manure was not a popular attraction. Nor were the heifers who kept humping each other, or the cow who'd learned to suck her own teats, or the one whose bag was purple with mastitis. Not to mention breach births, stillbirths, prolapses—hey, all these various forms of shit do happen. But we had to keep our customers from finding out.

When the farm came into my hands, I kept the dream of marketing nature to tourists alive for a brief time. Then I let it die a slow but gratifying death. The problem is, a farm like this is up to its neck in nature—no, up to its eyeballs—but the agri-tourists want to stick in just a toe. They test the water, and there's always something "off" about it. This is a disconnect that I should keep my mind on. Same thing with most of the others in our writing group . . . even Erin Furlong, our semi-famous leader who lives in a brand-new split-level by the lake. I'm not saying that I am right and the others are wrong, just that we shouldn't paper over how we may have different things in mind when we talk about "nature." Based on different life-histories, different kinds of projects.

Still—working back to where I started with this entry—I think for a small investment of time, I could make the cottages rentable for leaf-peepers. And with winter coming, I could certainly use the money. Have to think this over, see if it sounds like a plan.

Wednesday, September the Eleventh

(Promise to myself: I will never call it 9–11 again. I'm going to say and write it longhand, rather than in code. Not to forget what happened, but to show that time does heal.)

This may turn into a rant, but someone's screwing around with the mountaintop. *Moze-o-de-be-Wadso* is about to get trashed again. All morning long I've watched a mammoth helicopter ferry machinery to the Nose, piece by piece. I asked Stan about it down at the general store, and he says they're getting set to build three new broadcast towers so we can all have better TV reception, and less static on our cell phones. I remember hearing about this a while back, but thought they couldn't get a permit. Guess I was mistaken.

This is so offensive to me. That ridgeline is home to an arctic-alpine ecosystem. Rare, fragile tundra plants. Hikers are requested not to step off the trails so as not to crush the flora. And yet the TV stations get okayed to bring in all this gear and stomp around, doing anything they want. And when they've had their way again with the mountaintop, we'll get to stare at a ridge defaced by yet another phallic monstrosity. Check that—a trio of them.

Incredibly, the state university happens to own the mountain's ridge—thanks to a purchase made in 1859—and it's officially a "Natural Area." What's up with that? UVM collects fat rent checks from those broadcasters—way into six figures a year, I read once in the paper. This is what the TV stations pay to beam their signals from the state's highest peak. And, because the university is always strapped for cash, the trustees want the money bad enough to compromise their deed restrictions. "Natural area," my ass.

This is starting to make me very angry. Man's field, all right—a field of antennas. Maybe I'm sensitive because the mountain is part of my daily bread, always in my field of vision or just on the edge of it. Many times a day, I lift my eyes up and expect to feel fed. Refreshed. Maybe I don't place the right value on the social good of high-def television and static-free radio, bell-clear voices on the cell phone. But it seems to me that people start to mess around with something like that mountaintop—a natural feature of overwhelming beauty and obvious fragility—and they don't know when to stop.

Kyle Hess writes, toward the end of *Prayers on the Wing,* that

> I am always praying—also pleading, from the depths of Spirit—that we'll learn to use the greatest gift we have as humans: our compassionate intelligence, our wisdom based on empathy, self-consciousness, and love. And use the special vision this amazing gift confers to show us when we need to draw a line in the sand. Prohibiting our species from indulging our worst instincts. To say, *That's enough. No more. We cannot go on torturing the planet.*

I looked up that passage and read it aloud when the helicopter droned up Maple Ridge for the umpteenth time. And I think the author's right. I've never been a big activist about the day's environmental issues, but I'm thinking I should maybe speak out this time. Try to make a difference. Maybe write a letter to the editor about how the mountain's being *tortured*—yes, he chose the perfect word. And turned into a pincushion. Maybe I can craft words with the force and grace that he comes up with. Maybe I can say something to change people's minds.

Thursday, September 12

At night I hear the coyotes and by day I whack the weeds, but real trouble, when it comes, arrives from out of nowhere—or at least from a quarter where you'd least expect it. My dear Roman-nosed ram, Caligula, was lying on his side this morning like a ewe in labor, and when I helped him up he strained to squeeze out a few painful drops of pee. Then the tip of his penis peeked out, red and swollen, from inside its woolly sheath, and a weak stream of blood and urine started dribbling from an orifice that looked not only blackened but necrotic. And this is the stud who I was counting on to breed one hundred ewes in a few short weeks. I'd say I'm in trouble, here. And my ram is, too. Big time.

Jackie Johnson, my unflappable vet, is an expert at these matters and she showed up within forty-five minutes of my calling her. From a certain dry perspective it was almost funny—two grown women fooling around with this big guy tipped up on his butt, each of us taking turns to probe and poke and help extend his sickly-looking member. "Looks like he stuck this into someplace that he shouldn't have," Jackie joked, which made me laugh and tell her that's exactly what I said to my ex-husband. Though it hadn't seemed the least bit funny at the time, backed to the wall in Wisconsin in a bitter winter, warmer days a long way off.

Number one concern, of course, was urinary calculi because a ram's urethra plugged with little crystal stones can burst a kidney quick, after which there isn't much that anyone can do. So we jabbed a catheter into Cal's sad-looking, shriveled-up urethral process and fed the tube into his belly—seven long inches—then Jackie coupled a syringe to the free end and gave whatever might be lurking there a thorough irrigation. But more likely, she decided, was that the old boy had come down with a virulent urinary tract infection. She said this after his rectal temperature came in at darn near 108 degrees. So now we've got him on a massive regime of antibiotics, twelve cc's twice a day jabbed into his neck—which is already looking lumpy, stuffed with penicillin G. A drug I'm not even supposed to have on the premises. With luck, after a week of this he ought to come around. So much for trying to be an organic shepherd . . . but no one's going to be eating Caligula. And as for farming with a strict ideology, every person has her limits.

I am writing—trying to, at least—about "nature." Not the kind the others in our writing group are into, though. This is a nature that I damn well need to manipulate, and have my way with. To manipulate as best as I know how.

If I lose Caligula, I'm not completely naked as we head into the breeding season—even though it's late to go shopping for a ram. I still have a pair of flashy bucks that I held back from last year's crop of lambs, hoping to find someone who would purchase them as breeding stock. They're young but well grown, and between the two hard to build an independent life. Not because I dislike men, but to prove to myself that it can be done. That a person in my situation still can do that.

He said: "Try me out, why don't you? I want to do something useful for the mountain, and being close to it—physically—means a lot. Besides," he added, "I could maybe help you with your writing."

"Help me—you're so sure?"

"Well, I do have contacts. You know—editors. An agent, even."

I guess I'm embarrassed to admit this may have tipped the scales. And I am already dreading that I will regret it, but— okay, I told Kyle to come by tomorrow and we'll see if we can work a deal. This is giving me a late-night headache, but I gave my word. Probably I'm taking an unreasonable chance, but we can call it my contribution to 'the movement."

P.S. after visiting the barn: Caligula is back on his feet, and his glassy eyes look bright with medication. Also, his molars have stopped grinding like they were this morning. All due thanks to Jackie's wisdom and her wonder drugs. I've got a hunch that the old boy's going make it.

iday, September 13

Busy day.

When he showed up around noon, evidently all of Kyle's worldly ongings were crammed into his rusty van—which seemed a bit sumptuous, until he told me that he'd never really settled in at 's. What we worked out is that he's going to live in Golden icious—the oldest and most dilapidated cottage, which I've been g mainly as a storage shed—and set to work immediately fixing he other two so I can make some money on them when the leaves turning. He's going to give me twenty hours a week, as long as he keep his mornings free to do his writing . . . actually, this may set d example for me.

en he proved, in just a few short hours, how good with his he might turn out to be. Using some weathered boards stored

of them I'm thinking they could do Cal's job. But they are his sons, and I hate the risk of birth defects if I let them breed their sisters and their cousins and their aunts—not to mention their own mothers, who are out there, too. This is just the kind of hasty management decision that can take the flock downhill.

Also, it is painful to see animals suffering the way that ram is now. Straining so hard to pee, and coming up short. If Cal has a genital infection—well, I can relate. I remember what that felt like, and how furious it made me that my husband was the culprit. A sickness that kept spreading till our marriage had been laid to rest.

I have to leave now for Burlington—it's Thursday night. Looking at these last few pages, most of what I've written lately seems too rough and personal to share with the others. I may have to pass, when it comes my turn to read aloud. Maybe the grand heights of style come out of just staring at a leaf or flower, or watching clouds drift by. Maybe my problem as a wanna-be nature writer is the daily burden of an all-too-practical engagement with the subject. Maybe I need greater distance—that, or something new and strong to shake up my perspective.

Quick shot of penicillin G for Caligula, and then I'm off to town.

Late—Just Home from B'ton

So we're sitting in our circle at the library—the nine of us who Erin is teaching to be nature writers—and who walks into the room but Kyle Hess. Looking somehow skinnier and shorter without his wing, and with his blond hair darker and all patted down, slicked back from the shower. I sit forward, startled, and then Erin *introduces* him—it turns out that our workshop leader and this paraglider guy go way back. Then my hard drive kicks in and I realize, as Erin starts giving us his bio, that he's not just the author of a chapbook of reflections on biodiversity—he's the author of *Leaves from Mendocino*, the journal of a California forest activist. This is a book I've heard of, by a real author in the nature writing field. Almost on the A-team. So now I'm looking at the man who landed on my farm in a whole new light.

Is he "relocating" to Vermont? Marianna asks—she works in real estate and doesn't miss a trick. Kyle says he doesn't know about that, but he's pretty sure he's more than passing through. He says the state has "a great rep" in West Coast environmental circles, that we have the kind of culture to support creative activism on the Earth's behalf . . . or words to that effect. The thing is, he doesn't have a lot of money just now and he's badly in need of a place to stay. Erin has been letting him crash in her study, but it can't go on much longer—she has kids, a husband, and no extra room to speak of.

I start thinking, then I ask aloud exactly when Kyle blew into town. Ten days ago, he tells us. First I'm thinking, what a fantastic coincidence, this old pal of our writing group's facilitator drops out of the sky on me . . . then I'm thinking, wait a minute, there's no way what happened Friday afternoon could have been a mere coincidence. Erin must have told him where I live—the sheep, the pick-your-own, the llamas. He went up the mountain, scoped out my place, and used it as his target.

I look across the room and try to catch Erin's eye, but she's a sphinx. I remember how she said, though—she wrote this in a note on my manuscript, two weeks ago—that she thought my writing was a bit too solipsistic for a thirty-something woman with a pretty face, an athletic figure, and a ton of energy. That it wouldn't hurt to get more people in my life . . . and, by extension, into my journal entries. Even Henry David Thoreau, she said—Thoreau's the author she thinks I should model my own writing after—even Thoreau hung out with Channing, Alcott, Emerson, when he spent two years at his cabin at Walden Pond.

But I do not live and breathe under Erin Furlong's spell, I don't jump to get in step with each suggestion she comes up with. No, like Henry David, I have my own drummer to attend to. The thing is, though, now it seems obvious that Erin was setting me up with this Kyle Hess. Trying to, at any rate. She knows all about the empty cottages on my place, knows that I have room to spare. What a meddler—I suppose I ought to feel flattered, but instead I'm kind of ticked.

Afterward, I walked with Kyle down to get some coffee Church Street pedestrian mall. The night was warm; the ha teenagers were out in force, flaunting their various pie tattoos. We sat outside of Borders, and I came straight to t "You can't expect me to believe your 'dropping in' the othe an accident. Why couldn't you just come up the drive normal person?"

He laughed. "First impressions matter. And I wanted t the lay of the land, so to speak."

"What is it you want from me? What does Erin want t

"Erin wants to help me bring a dose of West Coast ac movement in Vermont."

"The movement—you mean, for the environment?"

He nodded. "Mount Mansfield's a great place to visible symbol. Fragile ecosystem. And it's under se from developers. You happen to live there, and with— I peeked inside the cabins."

"Those cottages are not for rent."

He smiled disarmingly, showing off perfect teeth wonder if he really was my age, or several years you said. "Because I can't afford to rent one."

"Oh, you were thinking I'd just let you stay for fr

"I can work. And you could use the help, fr someone to hack down those weeds that are takin out the barn. Or put a new roof on that cabin th Winesap, was it?"

"Golden Delicious," I corrected him. "But t cabins."

He gave me a blank look. "Whatever. I coul lots of skills."

"I'll bet you do," I said quietly, right on the e this was heading, see it from a mile away. A standpoint, I have to admit that Kyle Hess se man, a person with whom I might enjoy sp thing *off* about letting him move in, though,

behind the farm shop, he turned the old milk house at the barn into a new tack room for the llamas' stuff . . . and it's more convenient having their leads and halters right there, close at hand. When it came time to make the obvious gesture of inviting him in for dinner, Kyle said he understood I was "a private sort of person" and he wanted to respect that—he was happy just to live here without making impositions on my space, on my routines. And I thanked him for that, then insisted he come in and have a plate of moussaka with me. I even rummaged around down cellar and found a bottle of retsina to wash it down with.

A nice thing about his being new to the area—and new to farming, too—and yet being a writer, is that Kyle has a knack for asking leading questions . . . and questions that, since I happen to know the answers, make me sound intelligent and feel like I actually might have a lot to say. Like when we got into the differences between a first-rate guarding llama—the kind I try to raise here, to sell to livestock farmers who are getting creamed by coyotes—and the more even-tempered, people-centered packers that carry heavy loads on wilderness treks. How you almost never get both sets of aptitudes in the same animal, since each occupation uses different physical traits and relies on different aspects of temperament. Kyle thought that this was an amazing insight. Not really, I said. Same thing with sheep—successful breeders wind up emphasizing wool *or* meat, but trying to go for both tends to backfire. Same thing with maple trees: An ideal shape for maximum sap production isn't apt to make a premium sawlog.

"You should write this up," he told me, grinning in a mildly intoxicated way as I brought out the Ben and Jerry's. "This is a publishable nature essay in the making." Diamond in the rough, he said. He even offered me a title: "No Perfect Deal."

Or, I countered, "Perfect Incompatibilities."

And then, putting the farm to bed for the night, we found Caligula was so far back into his game that he jumped out of his pen when he saw me coming with the needle. Without Kyle's help, I'm not sure how I would have managed to give the ram his shot—and Kyle caught on right away about pinching up a fold of skin into a subcutaneous "tent" to hold an injection. He even offered to take over that chore from me, but I told him no—it's too important that I stay right on this, see Cal's illness through. Not let it turn into a sickness unto death.

At the end of the day, when he thanked me for the umpteenth time before heading down to unpack and grab a shower, I thought I was about to have to deal with the whole sex thing rearing its familiar head—at least in innuendo. But, no. He played it perfectly cool. He asked if he could come make coffee in my kitchen, first thing in the morning—he needs caffeine to write, and hasn't been to a grocery store yet. Sure, I said. No problem. Then he said he'd look for me at noon, ready for work. A handshake—actually more formal than affectionate—and he set off jogging down the driveway.

With the upper mountain in a shroud of fog all day, the helicopter runs were canceled—thank God for small blessings. Unless they're all done moving their machinery. Idle, late-night thought: Can the same mountain serve as both spirit-food *and* broadcast central? Incompatible, I think. But then what deal is perfect?

Saturday, September 14

When I came downstairs this morning—6:15, as usual—I found Kyle studying the hiking map tacked to the kitchen wall. The quadrangle takes in the length of the mountain's ridge, plus Smugglers' Notch, most of Underhill and Stowe, and even the northeast boundary of the Ethan Allen Firing Range, a few miles south of here—though that huge tract of land is off limits unless you're a National Guardsman. The thermos Kyle brought along was filled with black coffee, and he nursed a big ceramic mug as his fingers traced the various trails up the mountain. "I'm almost out of here," he said. "Just got hung up checking out this map—you live in one heck of a location. Way strategic."

"My father had an eye for real estate," I told him.

"Place is like a gold mine."

Later—in the afternoon—I went through Winesap with him and made up a list of work. I told him about Dad's dream of agri-tourism, and the reasons I had let the cottages go to seed. He said something that I couldn't really argue with—he said the whole trick was to just bring in the right people, not a bunch of random strangers from the suburbs. He said I have all the right ingredients here to make a really great community come together. People who are thoughtfully aware could take a long-term interest in the place and build a network. There should be a newsletter, a Web site. All these grandiose ideas were unfolding as he swept out cobwebs, pitched dead mice out the back door, cleaned dirty windows.

I'll admit he got me thinking, but I don't believe I am the kind of person who sets out to "build a community." This seems like a bed-rock value in my makeup—I *am* a private sort of person. In fact, given the choice I seem to choose being with animals and plants more than hanging out with my own kind. Was I always this way, or is it just a residue of what happened with Jason? Probably some of each. Thoreau writes of happily hoeing beans from dawn till lunchtime, day after summer day, and I think I can relate. But then at other times he says he likes to sit on his doorstep all day long, just chilling . . . I need to accomplish more than that. Still, Erin wasn't wrong when she said Henry David was the man for me, the writer I should get in touch with. If anyone had urged Thoreau to use his Walden cabin to help "create a thoughtfully aware community," I'm pretty sure he would have told that person where to go.

I'm not trying to make fun of Kyle, here—in fact, I really like the way that guy can express himself. True, his talk is peppered with too many New Age expressions, but it isn't mumbo jumbo. I like his passionate engagement with details, and the respect for all living things implied in each choice that he makes. Like deciding how to rebuild Winesap's flagstone terrace so as not to interfere with an active nest of ants. Where to mount a soap dish on the wall, in a place where people will really use it. When to put aside the task at hand and take a well-earned break.

So I'm optimistic this is going to work out, and that I'll easily adapt to Kyle's presence here. This gentle man. This gifted stranger. This companion.

N.B.: Need to arrange for this year's first slaughter lambs. Grain feeders in the barn were empty again, this morning . . . some of those guys on feed look like little meat wagons.

Sunday, September 15

Kyle keeps asking me about the llamas—how they fit into the overall farm picture, why I raise them, and how they came to be so profitable. Mostly, though, he seems to be obsessed with going hiking with them. He spent time in South America some years ago, where he saw llamas being used on treks high in the Andes. "They can carry just about anything," he told me. "Backbreaking loads, and at impossible altitudes. And they don't complain—you couldn't kill a llama with a blowtorch."

"Yes, well, these are not the Andes," I countered. "We Vermonters may be kinder to our livestock than Bolivian peasants are."

"I'm just thinking . . . people go out hiking on the Long Trail, Appalachian Trail—they may want to carry more supplies than fit into a pack. Think about it: Rent-a-Llama. Could be a whole new sideline."

"There *are* people in that business. But you can't take a llama anywhere you feel like it—most of our trails in Vermont are just for hikers. Fragile terrain, prone to wear and tear. And they're plenty crowded, without llamas adding to the traffic."

"Later in the season, maybe. Once the plants are dormant, and— I'm curious. I'd like to know how it's done."

The upshot was, I took him out and showed him how to catch and halter Abelard, who is far and away my most manageable llama. Then we got the frame saddle down, hung the panniers from it, and loaded them with stones . . . and Kyle had a ball leading the gelding all around the upper pasture and—once he got the hang of it—up and down the long driveway that goes to the pick-your-own. Abelard seemed to be enjoying himself, too . . . I don't think the gelding gets as much attention as he'd like.

It's true that when I started raising llamas, one intention was to set up a business where I'd take people onto the mountain with a packer or two—not all the way to the summit, but as far as Sunset Ridge. I figured we could bring along a nice supper, dine on a ledge where we could watch the evening colors—this would not be just another agritourist boondoggle, but a pleasant way of earning extra bucks. Once I got to know them, though, my own taste in llamas ran more to the guardian side. Packers are too docile, and annoyingly dependent on the sociability of humans. Better, it seemed—both for doing something useful and making my obsession pay—was to breed and background llamas who could live with sheep or cattle, joining their societies and actively protecting them by driving off predators. When I have a proven guard llama three years old, I can get $3,000—they are worth that to a livestock farmer facing coyote losses. They're buying damn good insurance for—with average luck—the next twenty years.

This is another place where I part ways with the others in our writing group—and with Kyle, too, it became apparent as we talked. Everybody seems to have this big romantic thing about the wily coyote. The trickster. *El coyote.* None of those romanticizers ever has to walk into a pasture, though, and see the work that these assassins do. Lambs that look blown apart, limbs and guts and throat-slashed heads scattered in all directions. I don't say I want to see the coyotes made extinct, but I do think people ought to understand why I don't like them. Guard llamas, though, are a way of giving farmers a way to fight back. So I like to think I'm doing something useful in the world, breeding and training these exotic creatures.

But as for the packing thing—I told Kyle he could play around with Abelard all he wants. Won't do the gelding any harm, and Kyle can indulge his Bolivian fantasies. He's doing an amazing job with Winesap, by the way—new paint, whole new deck, and even the casement windows finally operate the way they are supposed to . . . after years of sticking and letting in mosquitoes. I'm impressed. I told him so.

Monday, September 16

Kyle left his writing desk halfway through the morning to help me unload sacks of grain, and as we were backing the pickup to the barn I heard a helicopter buzz in the distance like an angry bee. Monday morning, back to work—we both looked up the mountain to see more pieces of machinery flying toward the Nose. "What's with that?" Kyle asked and I explained about the monster drilling rig, the test holes needed so that engineers could site three new broadcast towers. "Son of a bitch," he said. "Somebody should do something."

"Like what?"

"Whatever it takes to make them quit."

"I was thinking I might write a letter to the editor," I told him.

The look he gave me said he thought I must be off my nut. Naive, idealistic—he didn't have to say a word. And his response made me all the more determined to sit down and really write something impassioned and persuasive. Since I'm like an eyewitness to what's going on here, there's a decent chance that I could get my letter published. Which would be a first for me, and maybe lead to bigger things. Anyway, Kyle excused himself and went back to his cottage till he finished the morning's writing, and I—well, I had to move electric fences to enclose new grass before the sheep broke out. Then I had to brush the llamas, move the water tanks, and go take care of business down at the pick-your-own. And it occurred to me this might be unfair competition, sharing the farm with a real working writer.

Tuesday, September 17

Okay, time to confess that there's a mild flirtation going on. A restrained but obviously sexual tension—an awareness of each other as able to throw sparks. I'll admit, too, that I've been toying with the thought that at some point—and for no good reason—Kyle and I may find ourselves in bed together, acting on a moment's impulse. I can't let that happen, though. That would alter everything. There's a sense in which I wear the pants around this place, and *need* to. That means we have to keep a certain distance from each other.

Reasons why a man can be quite useful on the farm:

1. Good at heavy lifting: sacks of grain, water buckets, hay bales, stones in field.
2. A certain forced alteration of perspective. Such as when I watched him from across the meadow, peeing on the stone wall. And then spitting on it while he zipped up.
3. Better than me at catching/holding Cal for his injections.
4. Useful male obsession over lubricating things that squeak: machines, gate hinges, doorknobs all turning smoothly.
5. Different timbre voice. I like the tonal duets of our conversations—how the sounds of our different voices complement each other.

Okay, this is starting to get cheesy. Time to get some sleep.

Wednesday, September 18

It's been a couple of years, at least, since I've been on top of Mount Mansfield. Hiked there this morning, though, on the Halfway House Trail—the steep one—straight up to Frenchman's Pile. Vasilis came tagging along to afford protection, get a change of scenery. I remembered coming here with Dad as a little girl, thinking I must be in heaven. Now the view's scale is more comprehensible—I look out and see familiar landmarks, places rich with memories. I think, This is where I live.

Traffic on the ridge—and I mean foot traffic—was a bitch, and this was a weekday. I know the four-mile Toll Road run by Stowe Resort has been around forever—since there used to be a Summit House hotel, back in the 1800s—but it seems unfair that anyone with fourteen bucks can drive his air-conditioned car up to a big, busy parking lot a stone's throw from the Nose. That must multiply the ridgeline crowds considerably, since most of those "hikers" lost no sweat in getting up the mountain.

On the other hand, maybe it's good for people who would never actually make the climb to have a glimpse of heaven, anyway. Maybe it will make them want to care for what we have here.

Of course I was on a reconnaissance mission to get a firsthand look at what they're doing on the mountain, so from the summit station I struck out to find the old Triangle Trail that climbs over the Nose's tip . . . until I reached a sign that just blew me away. Triangle Trail has been closed to the public—no more hikers, no more picnics on that rocky outcrop that is every bit as breathtaking as the Chin itself. Ralph Waldo Emerson climbed that trail, for Chrissake, and wrote in his journal about the fantastic view. And get this—according to the "Keep Out" sign, the trail is closed on account of radiation from the transmission towers, which have been determined to pose a human health risk. Those TV stations can't stand the liability of hikers getting cooked.

Stan, down at the general store, showed me a newspaper clipping about the 1859 agreement by which the university acquired 400 acres of the mountain's ridge. There were some interesting deed restrictions: The summit was supposed to be forever open to the public, and there weren't supposed to be any structures built up there, ever . . . except for a possible scientific laboratory. What a joke. Now we have these huge, ugly broadcasting towers—which are technically a violation of the deed—polluting the air to the point where public access has had to be denied. So much for "forever open."

So instead—since the trail is off limits—I followed the service road south along the ridge until it came to where this crappy slum of maintenance buildings and Quonset hut garages and gigantic, bomb-like propane tanks are tucked away beneath the profile of the Nose. Amazing—you don't notice this by looking up from the valley, but they've got this sleazy little village going on up there to service and protect their precious transmitting structures. And not far beyond lay various arms and legs for the monster drilling rig, spread across the bare ledge like a giant's disassembled doll. Nobody working to bolt it all together, no helicopters zipping back and forth today. I made some notes and sketches—what I'll need to tell this story—without anybody coming to bother me.

But then, as I was heading back around to the summit station, one of the Green Mountain Club's official "caretakers" came over to say he wished I hadn't brought an unleashed dog, and to warn me not to let Vasilis step off the trail on account of fragile alpine tundra. Unbelievable—I wanted to clock this guy. How does he keep a straight face when his "walk lightly" rap is being disregarded just around the corner? Not to mention right above our heads—the biggest tower of all went soaring up into the air right above where he was admonishing me. And this colossal steel wand is tethered to the mountain by six thick cables, anchored in fat blobs of concrete. A spider web of steel spreading out across the summit.

Back down the mountain on Sunset Ridge, for nostalgia's sake. Storm clouds were rolling in by early afternoon, and by the time I scrambled off the bare ledge there were bursts of lightning, thunder in the sky over Lake Champlain. Back home before any rain began to fall, though. Kyle says some people from Oregon came by to have a look at Winesap cottage, while I was on the mountain—a married couple who fell in love with the place and asked about a two-week rental. Saw my notice tacked up at the General Store . . . here we go. I have to hand it to Kyle Hess. If this deal comes through, the guy has earned his keep.

Thursday, September 19

Dear Editor:

Something quite alarming is taking place up on the Nose of Mount Mansfield, Vermont's highest and most majestic peak, which lies in direct view of where I live and work—as it does for thousands of other Vermonters. We take it for granted—foolishly, perhaps—that whenever we raise our eyes up to the summit we'll receive a familiar lift, a spiritual reward. Maybe it's a blessing for getting to enjoy this Green Mountain State where it's so easy and satisfying to stay attuned to nature's splendor and its beauty.

For many years now, we have tolerated a ragtag collection of communications towers on the mountain's "Nose," but in recent days an enormous yellow drilling machine has been arriving up there, ferried in piece by piece via helicopter. Once assembled, this machine will crawl around the ridge's delicate ecosystems taking test cores to determine where three new towers should be located—each of them rising over 200 feet into the air above this emblematic mountain that our Abenaki forebears called *Moze-o-de-be-Wadso*. These towers, if built, will make a travesty of our state's professed concern with responsible environmental behavior.

Any fair-minded person who reads the terms under which the University of Vermont acquired the ridgeline real estate in 1859 would have to conclude that the current broadcast towers on the Nose are technically illegal. Even worse, the right of citizens to enjoy the mountaintop—a right that deed restrictions were designed to guarantee—has been violated, on account of radiation from the towers that are already up there. Triangle Trail has been closed to the public because of this pollution, even though the towers themselves should technically not exist. This is an affront to common sense, and to all Vermonters. Do we need to make things worse by building three more towers? And enormous ones, at that?

I ask all who love this state, and who cherish the natural beauty that enriches our lives here, to join me in protesting the ongoing desecration of this proud ridge, which is surely "one of the seven wonders" of our Green Mountain world.

Lauren Blackwood
Underhill

Later—After Writing Group

Sitting in the circle at writing group tonight, I got an inspiration after reading my letter out loud to the others. What did Thoreau do when he came up with the idea of civil disobedience? He wasn't running around destroying things, he just refused to pay a tax he didn't like because it went against his principles . . . and he spent a night in jail on account of his refusal. That's a model for the kind of activism I can get behind. Then I'm thinking, So they want to keep the public off the Nose, in violation of an 1859 agreement? What if people just ignored their "Keep Out" signs, ran the risk of radiation to go hang out where they have a perfect right to be? And if law enforcement types felt they should arrest those people, fine—the trail's liberators could have a field day calling attention to their legal right to be there.

So at the end of our sharing time, I asked the group if anyone would like to meet me at the head of Triangle Trail, Sunday morning—the plan is, we'll take an "illegal" hike to the summit of the Nose, have an "illegal" picnic there, and read some nature writing to each other on the mountaintop. And we'll be protesting the unjust prohibition of access to that promontory.

"Whoa," said Erin. "Great idea. Thing is, I have Bernie's parents coming for the weekend. They're too old for hiking."

"I admire your spunk," said Marianna Finch. "Good luck. But I'm swamped with houses I arranged to show people."

Rachel Katz, the hard-bodied athlete I've come to like, said she was taking a group of kids rock climbing at Smugglers' Notch. Barbara had her sister's children with her, and they hate the outdoors. Even Kyle begged off, said he had a longstanding date to go up with a glider pilot over Stowe. This left two people out of our circle who were ready to join me in an act of civil disobedience: Roger, the retired high school science teacher whose overall frailty—two heart attacks, a mild stroke—makes me wonder about whether he is up to this, and Schuyler, the UVM graduate student who comes to group with Kiki, his blond fiancée . . . those two can't seem to keep their hands off each other. But Kiki was away somewhere this evening, and Schuyler said she wouldn't be back till Monday so he'd love to take part. We're going to meet at Roger's place in Essex Junction, and Schuyler's going to drive us to the summit on the Toll Road.

So despite my disappointment in most of the writing group, we've got a small party of hikers and a plan of action. I'm going to get a copy of that deed restriction guaranteeing public access, so I can wave it at anyone who tries to bust us. I hope someone does—I'll make so much noise that they will hear it in Montpelier.

Nice to find what Kyle calls "a personal comfort level" with a kind of activism that I think can make a difference. Nice, too, having an adventure to look forward to.

Friday, September 20

IN MEMORIAM: CALIGULA OF BLACKWOOD FARM

He was a large and well-hung specimen of ramhood, and he loved his pleasure. Part Border Leicester, part Cheviot, he was born in Keene, New Hampshire, out of purebred English stock. During five years in Vermont he sired, in round numbers, 700 lambs. And his stud quality was proved not just in numbers but also by his exceptional prepotency—the way his sons and daughters expressed the traits for which I prized him. Long, thick saddles; nicely rounded, meaty rumps; exceptional efficiency at transforming grass to meat.

I'm not getting this right, at all. Caligula embodied a spirit and an essence of sheer masculinity, and losing that deserves mourning more than crass commercial traits. He was like a four-footed bundle of testosterone, pure libido on the hoof. I still can't accept that his lusty spirit's gone—or that the seemingly invincible body that housed that spirit lies now buried in the woods beneath a mound of clay. I loved to watch him flare his nostrils at a ewe in heat. I loved his obsession with the physical act of sex, and yet his gentleness with those who stood for him to mount. I loved the way how even I, at times, became the object of his interest—impossible ambition, but why shouldn't creatures dream? I loved watching him that first October day—the same year as my father died—when I turned him in to meet the flock and watched him settle seven ewes in twenty minutes.

He died of a virulent urinary tract infection. For a time antibiotics kept his death at bay, but the end came quickly once he'd finished up a weeklong course of medication. Just this morning he was on his feet, bright-eyed and randy as he wolfed down a pound of grain; at noon he was lying down, breathing hard and looking tired; just before supper he was found expired in his pen. In death, his sheer weight was astonishing to me—he had always been so nimble, so light-footed as he ranged across these fields. Amazing that I could not summon strength enough to move him, and had to seek my tenant's help to drag him from the barn. Then we rolled him onto a stone boat, hitched that to the tractor, and dragged him to an unmarked grave. Wordlessly we set him in his place. Rest in peace, sire.

Saturday, September 21

REST OF THE STORY

After we had buried him, I had an overwhelming urge to take a scalding bath and scrub all traces of death from my aching body. But before doing that I asked Kyle to join me for a stiff drink—Dewar's—because I needed something strong. It was nearly dark when we put away the shovels, but he was agreeable. Two or three shots later, neither one of us felt even tipsy. I excused myself to run the bath, and on the way I thought I heard him say good night.

I am not trying to explain away anything, or to make excuses. I am as responsible as anyone for what we did.

Later, stepping out with my wet hair in a towel, there was Kyle sitting where I'd left him half an hour ago. For one quick moment, I had the urge to cover up . . . and then I decided not to. He said he didn't want to see me spend the night alone, if I needed company. I told him not to go and put this all on me—I made him tell me what *he* wanted. It didn't take long to conclude our negotiations, and the bedroom door swung open . . . and that, as they say, was that.

I am not trying to explain away anything. I take full responsibility for choices made.

Then, at first light, he got up and went back to his cottage . . . so I sit here at the kitchen table, feeling kind of spent and yet alive, alert.

Activated. And insisting no excuses can be made, or need to be. Anxious, too, to get all these impressions down on paper.

Was last night a kind of wake? The stud ram on my farm was dead, yet here was this new male who I'm certain would have been content simply to hold me all night long. To give the sort of comfort arms were made for offering . . . but arms soon started getting tangled up with legs, and then we wound up offering all we had to give each other.

Had we made some kind of pact to grieve together, keen the dead? No. And it was more than that. We were celebrating an attraction whose denial had become simply wrong, dishonest. And as for what comes next—whatever happens will. There will be some difficulties, maybe even sharp regrets. But I will work through them.

I am not trying to explain away anything.

I like to think of Kyle writing right now, too—these are his good, best, early morning hours. And I like it knowing that my scent will be on his rough hands, that I'm bound to be upon his heart and in his words.

Sunday, September 22

Incredible day up on the mountain. I can't think when foliage has come on this strong this early, but beneath clear skies the Champlain Valley stretched beneath us like a spun gold fairyland. Not that many reds yet, but if the weather holds it's going to be a banner year. Crowds of tourists were hiking the ridgeline, taking in the perfect day and top-of-the-world views.

Now I'm sorry about having ragged about the Toll Road. With three of us in Schuyler's car, the $14 ticket was a do-able thing and the ease of getting to the summit meant we all had plenty of energy to climb around, once we got there. Even Roger Morton, who I stopped worrying about once I saw him scramble up a ledge and jump across a crevice. He joked about his pacemaker getting jazzed by the bombardment of radio waves, giving him a burst of superhuman strength.

So our trio liberated Triangle Trail, and nobody came by to read us the riot act or get up in our faces. In fact, we snagged a few more hikers who were passing by, and convinced them to come up and break the law with us. We sang songs, drank wine, and took turns reading to each other—I read the passage from *Walden* about when Thoreau strolled from his cabin into downtown Concord, and got himself arrested for obeying a Higher Law.

Snooping around, we found that the various pieces of the drilling rig have been assembled—this ungainly yellow insect has been crabbing its way along the mountaintop, boring eight-inch test holes. Schuyler said he read they have to get down sixty feet in rock of really high quality to guy these monster towers. And so this matter of finding the right location could take quite a while. Roger said he'd heard they still need permits to erect the structures; all they've been approved to do so far is this site testing. Then we walked over to examine the existing slum of weather stations, maintenance buildings, and Quonset huts scattered near the main group of broadcast towers. What a disgusting pile of rusting, weather-beaten metal. Some of those older towers look ready to blow over—Schuyler said an ordinary socket wrench would be enough to take apart one of them, so cheaply was it put together.

There were sleek gliders overhead, skimming the ridgeline . . . eerily quiet except for the occasional thrum of vibrating wings. I kept thinking how Kyle must be up in one of them, soaring. The airport they tow them from is north of Stowe, near Morrisville. I wondered how Kyle's obsession with bird flight meshed with his other ones: endangered species, forest activism, llama trekking . . . me. But I'm not the kind of person who needs to keep bringing up her lover's name—in fact, I don't think any of us mentioned Kyle Hess all day.

As for Schuyler, though, I get the feeling something's gone pretty sour between him and his fiancée. Kiki. He didn't tell us this in so many words, but he did read a poem that was obviously meant for her, questioning why the arrival of cold nights should turn *her* chilly, rather than seeking the warmth of the man who loved her. It was moving, sad . . . then I talked a little bit about the death of Caligula, how that made me feel the urge to hold somebody tight.

All in all, a good adventure on a nearly perfect day. I needed this, I realize. And despite my nagging reservations about the writing group and whether it is actually doing what I hoped it would, I like the way the three of us could bond together.

Ten-fifteen, and Kyle's still not back . . . I suppose I should have guessed he might respond in this way to the change in our relationship. The run-and-hide syndrome . . . but I'm a bigger person than that. Better than that, too. Good thing there's a lot of room for both of us in Pleasant Valley.

Monday, September 23

Kyle came up to the house this morning with the couple from Oregon—the ones who want to spend a couple of weeks staying at Winesap, which is pretty much fixed up and set to go. Better deal for them than the motel where they've been holed up . . . we agreed to what I think is a fair rent of $500 per week, given that it's foliage season. He's some kind of honcho in the National Guard—Major Kenneth Cooper—and as part of his vacation he's doing some consulting at the Ethan Allen Firing Range a few miles down the road. Some kind of ordnance systems analysis. A large man. But crew cut, clean shaven, hawk eyed . . . all-business kind of guy. His wife, on the other hand—Chloe—seems entirely different. Petite, even shockingly delicate. And an artist type—she's the reason why they want so badly to stay here. She does charcoal sketches, watercolors, oils . . . she kept framing compositions as we walked around. *Loved* that she'll be able to take an easel to the pasture, get close to the animals. They want to start on Wednesday—that'll be a stretch for Kyle, but we think it's do-able. And that's a thousand bucks I didn't have before.

Kyle has told me to hold off on renting Jonathan cottage, though. Mice have done a lot more damage in there than I thought. More than just a job of installing new baseboards—one whole wall needs to be torn out and reconstructed. New insulation, since the old batts of fiberglass are riddled with rodent nests. Several new runs of wiring, on account of places where sharp teeth have bitten through the plastic and exposed bare copper. Don't mice get a jolt that way? Don't they trip a circuit breaker?

Then I asked him whether he'd been trying to avoid me, now that we had let our friendship turn toward the physical. He said he didn't know how we ought to let things stand . . . he's got a lot on his plate right now with his current writing project, and he says the energy it takes to be in a relationship comes right out of the fuel he needs to do his work. He said he had a hard time seeing how we could become "something like a couple." I said that he thought too much—he didn't have to freak out on account of our having sex. And then we managed to fall into bed together—this was down at Winesap, so I guess we can say the mattress there has been field-tested before the Coopers get it.

I have been allowing this nature observation journal to evolve into more like a private diary, and I'm feeling guilty for it. Have to try to rein in this lapsing into self-absorption. Need to bear down firmly on the central purpose, focus on the kinds of observations and reflections that will take my writing to—as Erin always says—the next level.

Tuesday, September 24

This is what they printed on the op ed page of this morning's paper:

Writer Questions Tower Erection

Editor:

In recent days a drilling rig has been arriving on the Nose of Mount Mansfield, via helicopter. Once assembled, this machine will start taking test cores to determine where three new towers should be located. These towers, if built, will make a mockery of our state's professed environmental concern. Do we need to make things worse by building three more towers? I ask all who love this state to join me in protesting.

Lauren Blackwood
Underhill

First I saw my name in print and got pumped, gave a little cheer—then I read the few awkward sentences that some doofus butchered my letter down to, and I'm feeling burned. If I were a reader, this watered-down version of what I wrote would not persuade me of anything . . . except perhaps that someone with my name resides in Underhill.

Took it down to show Kyle at noontime—he was barefoot, shirtless, just putting away his writing—and he wasn't exactly sympathetic. "What did you expect?" he asked me. "Newspapers edit things."

"Don't they have to ask permission?"

"I'll bet there's a word limit, and you overshot it." He finished off the bottle of beer he was working on—a Long Trail Ale—and then started on another . . . before lunch, even. "But let's pretend they had printed the whole thing. What would it accomplish?"

"You think I'm just venting?" I picked up his beer and took a long sip. "Hey—at least I'm doing more than looking at the mountaintop and fuming, every time I see it."

He took the bottle back. "Maybe you could think of ways to actually make a difference."

"Such as?"

"I can't tell you what to do. Think about the struggles out west, though. Where would the movement to save the redwoods be if people hadn't started climbing trees and sitting in them? Don't underestimate the power of direct action."

We moved from the kitchen to the cottage's parlor—I noticed that he'd managed to clutter the place up. He'd also papered over an entire wall with maps of the mountain and vicinity—everything from Geological Survey quadrangles to ski trail maps from Stowe.

"You think there's a way to stop those towers by 'direct action'?"

"Maybe, maybe not. But there are ways to make them more expensive for those assholes to erect. *Much* more expensive. Maybe that alone would—"

"What are you suggesting?"

He opened a drawer in the coffee table and removed the makings of a joint, which he rolled with casual expertise. "Smoke?" he asked, eyes twinkling as he licked the paper shut. "Or did we stop that after college?"

"I don't smoke. But go ahead—I won't call the cops."

He lit up, and the once-familiar smell evoked memories that functioned as a contact high. He held in a lungful of smoke for maybe twenty seconds, then exhaled suddenly. "So they've got this drilling rig poking holes into the mountain. You were up there—anybody guarding it?"

I tried to wave his fumes away, then opened a window with a view up to the ridge. "I don't think so. Been up on the Nose twice this week, and no one's bothered me."

"This is why I love Vermont." He took another vigorous toke, then turned his head so as not to blow the smoke my way. "If it's a machine, it's got to have some lubrication points—probably a lot of them. Look for little grease nipples, like on your tractor. You know what to do with those, right? You've got a grease gun?"

"Yes, of course I do."

"Well, I can hook you up with a special grease cartridge. Climb back up the mountain some dark night, and give that rig a lube job. Wipe the fittings, after. I guarantee you they'll have trouble—big, expensive trouble. I mean, think—that machine came in on a helicopter. What will it cost them to–?"

"Monkey-wrenching," I said. "This is what you mean by 'West Coast activism'? This is what you came to Vermont to accomplish?"

"Where I come from, it's called *night work*. And it goes on all the time."

I walked to where he sat and took the joint away, then stubbed it in a saucer. "That smell is getting to me," I said.

"Sorry. You decide you want that grease cartridge, let me know."

"Why aren't *you* all over this? Why dump it in my lap, if you're such an expert?"

He went to the open window, stared at the mountain. "A certain amount of shit went down in California," he said. "I'd rather not get into why I left, but—the best thing I have going is that no one back there knows I'm here. I want to keep it that way."

"People know who *I* am," I told him. "I am rooted here. Thanks for the suggestion, but I will not be your Edward Abbey. Stupid vandalism, pranks—"

"Whatever." I couldn't tell if he was crestfallen or philosophic. He was stoned, though—I could see that. "Nice mountain," he said with a nod to where the ridge was stabbed with steel bristles. "Don't underestimate what it's going to take to save it. Maybe more than just a token letter to the editor."

So it's later now—it's evening—and I get the feeling that this argument over tactics is going to change the way I interact with Kyle . . . again. I don't want to sound naive—of course I've heard about this radical fringe in the environmental movement, wanna-be Robin Hoods who secretly go out and break the law, damaging property in order to obey what they like to think are Higher Laws . . . Thoreau's expression. Such as the "Higher Law" that says we need to save the planet, or give nature a chance, or respect creation for its own sake. I know all these things—I watch television, I read the newspapers. I have heard of Greenpeace, Earthfirst!, Rainforest Action Coalition. But hearing about them in the abstract is not the same as sitting in a room with someone who wants you to join the cause, sneak a grease gun up to an expensive machine, and "lubricate" it with abrasives.

I'm not sure if any cause is just enough that people should go out and break the law, take matters into their own hands. Once started down that road, where does someone draw the line? What's the difference between terrorism on the Earth's behalf and the kind that flies commercial airplanes into tall buildings? Don't both begin with the notion that the ends a person seeks will justify the means?

And yet I actually do understand the impulse to take action. To make things happen directly, usher in a change. I think back to just a couple of months ago . . . what did I expect when I first started hanging out with nature writers—just a heightened pleasure in making verbal origami? Flower arrangements fashioned out of pretty words? Beyond a certain point, I find words make me want to scream. So precious, and so ultimately useless. I can understand the urge to make a difference in a way that goes beyond language . . . or maybe the goal involves turning words into deeds. But I'm still confused about what's right and what's wrong here. So I'm not ready to become Kyle's grease monkey.

Wednesday, September 25

FIRST FROST

Heavy dew turned, last night, to ice out of the air . . . woke up to find each blade of grass encased in white. Old autumn miracle . . . and now I want to bless the season's first frost—a hard one, killing— that drops plants and insects like so many fallen soldiers, heralding the end of yet another growing season. Now the frost-hardy forage species—clover, trefoil, vetch—can have their day and come on strong, since most of their competition has been neatly toppled. Now the maples can bring on their fiery reds before unleafing. Now the last ripe tomatoes can be plowed into the ground, the pick-your-own put down for winter.

I think a four-season climate is the greatest blessing . . . how do people live in places where this yearly massacre is never on the menu? I love the healing force of death, the cleansing power of ice.

Ken and Chloe Cooper moved in today at Winesap, and I'm finding that I like that tiny woman quite a lot. I watched her painting in the orchard for a while—delicate hands, attached to wrists so slender you could break them off like twigs. There's a gentleness about her when she moves among the animals . . . I've never found a way to teach that, some people have it and others just don't. Even Vasilis was remarkably calm, unconcerned with drawing lines and barking to enforce his turf.

Ken seems quite the geologist, a real rock hound. I set him off on the trail up Maple Ridge to check out the formations there. As a married couple, though, I find this duo hard to fathom . . . so very different from each other. And a riot to imagine them in bed together—this imposing giant of a man, and this frail damsel. But no one ever knows what brings two souls together, what two lovers find and nourish in each other.

Not sure what to do about the chill between me and Kyle since our disagreement over tactics, yesterday. So we have some different values— I don't see why philosophic differences should keep us from exploring an attraction that exists on its own terms, has its own validity. That is, in a fundamental way, deeply physical. But I think it's hard for men to take criticism well. Or anyone, for that matter.

Carmen has a sore leg—a patch of skin is missing from her left front knee, and she's reluctant to put weight on it. How does that happen to a llama in an open field? Maybe something bit her, or she gnawed herself to scratch an itch. . . . I can't get over the toughness of these animals, their refusal to complain. They love adversity. Still, I led her into the barn and slathered pine tar on the wound to keep flies away. Thank God the flies will be fewer now, with autumn here.

Thursday, September 26

Mounting the mower to my tractor first thing today, I saw its dozen grease fittings in a new light and wondered how I'd feel if some stranger—for whatever reason—pumped abrasives into the joints of *my* machine. I'd be goddamn furious, no matter what the person's "cause" or how just he thought it was. Maybe I am wary of all true believers.

Unrelated question: Why are a machine's lubrication points and fuel lines, hydraulic hoses, and drain plugs all out in the open? Hanging right out there, exposed in places where anyone can reach them? Right where, in five quick minutes, anyone with bad intent could ruin the machine? Because *people trust each other,* that's why things are built this way. Nearly everything we do as humans runs on basic trust. Which makes our societies vulnerable, for sure. And yet the web of trust connects us, fostering a strength that goes beyond ourselves. And to go against that may give temporary power to the radicals, the activists, but the price may be too high. The price may be a fatal separation from the human project.

Still thinking, Kyle. But I think we really disagree, here.

Later–After Writing Group

Glad I wrote that earlier, because now I have some ground to stand on as we reconcile. Sitting there in writing group tonight, I couldn't keep myself from making a list of Kyle's finer qualities. What a good listener he can be, and how his thoughtful questions make a person feel cared for, truly special. Rachel read this incredible piece she wrote about soloing on a rock wall—how to do it well you need to give yourself over to the cliff, merge with it rather than acting prideful, showing off. She talked about a time she nearly fell by "over-thinking," focusing too hard on each next maneuver rather than forgetting herself and going with the flow. And then when we talked about it, Kyle showed her just a few places where a different touch with the language would make a huge difference—take the reader right inside the moment, rather than being held at arm's length. Well, anybody might have offered that suggestion, but Kyle did it in a way that was so self-deprecating, so thoughtfully concerned with the writing's best interests, that it was a model for me of wise criticism.

Then he read us all a section from his current project—maybe it's a book, although he doesn't know for sure yet—about some things he thinks that humans need to learn from animals. *Unnaming the Beasts,* he called it, based on the concept that according to the Bible— and according to experience—people name the animals and not the other way around . . . and the animals aren't naming *us,* so far as we can tell. And how to get beyond the arrogance implied by that basic inequality . . . well, this capsule summary is not doing justice to the genius of Kyle's work. But it was written so beautifully that certain people were in tears. Marianna, Kiki . . . and then *I* was in tears, because I realized that living on the farm has come to mean so much to him—some of the experiences Kyle's putting down in words are things I've had the privilege of showing him, and sharing with him.

Then he read this passage on the death of Caligula, and that just blew everybody away. I sat there with my own little epitaph in hand— the piece of writing I had brought to share, when it was my turn— but after hearing Kyle I just closed my notebook shut. Afterward I wanted to go kiss him, right in public, but he ducked out of the room before the workshop ended . . . had to go meet someone, and now it's past midnight but he hasn't come home yet. *Note: I need to stop obsessing about where he is and what he's doing.* But his shyness in receiving everybody's praise proves that he's a person of real humility. I should be proud—I *am* proud—to have him as a friend.

Friday, September 27

Stopped in at Golden Delicious this morning—the name of that cottage has begun to make me smile—but Kyle was still away. Only after entering and finding the cottage empty did I see his van was gone. *Still* gone, since last night. Well, I'm not a snoop so I turned right around to leave. But then some new additions to his map collection on the wall caught my attention. There was a series of photographs— eight-by-ten inch, black-and-white glossies taken from the air above Mount Mansfield. I am sure they're from that glider trip he took last Sunday—well, that was obvious because one of the photos showed Schuyler and Roger and me sitting on the Nose. Most of them, though, were of the huge construction project for Stowe Resort's expansion. A fleet of bulldozers is totally reshaping the terrain to build a condo village and a golf course.

Then I heard Kyle's van come up the drive—I ran out to greet him, and in the time it took us to walk back in we managed to strip away most of each other's clothes. God, I love that stage in a relationship where there's still some magic from the newness, but you've got a pretty good idea what is going to happen. And how it will feel. That man and I just fit.

"So, have we made up?" he asked me after we had finished.

"Let's just agree to disagree about certain things."

"Deal."

Then I asked him what the photographs were for, and he explained that he was doing research for Defenders of the Earth, an activist group that had taken an interest in the Stowe Resort expansion.

Something about diverting mountain streams and destroying bear habitat. I asked him what kinds of things these Defenders do, and got a short course on how to screw with ski resorts. Methods to sabotage buildings while they're going up, but in ways that won't become apparent till they're occupied—when having to go back and fix things will be way expensive. Strategies for aggravating bulldozer operators, loggers, and surveyors. It all sounded like it might amuse somebody with a *bandito* complex, but I had a hard time seeing how such pranks would really make a difference. And I asked Kyle whether *he* was going to do these things. No, he said looking right at me . . . and I believed him. I believe his eyes. He's just gathering intelligence for this Defenders group, and they have their own process for deciding what, if anything, to do about specific projects. What he's come to realize, Kyle told me, is that he's a long way from California. Attitudes are different here. Then he kicked me out of bed in a playful/friendly way and said he had to do his writing.

That's why I've done mine.

Saturday, September 28

Erin Furlong called me up out of the blue this morning, asking if I could possibly meet her for lunch in town. Impossible, I told her, what with weighing and sorting lambs to go out on a truck Monday. Plus I have to get a dozen cutting lists in order—who wants their ribs in chops, who wants a crown roast—and do the weekly books down at the pick-your-own. "Why don't you come here?" I asked her. "That way, I can make the time."

"I was hoping we could talk someplace where Kyle's not around."

"Kyle's gone to Stowe." I double-checked the driveway—yes, his van was gone. "Why don't you meet me at the pick-your-own, around twelve thirty? We can make a salad there, or—"

"Good call. What can I bring?"

"Feta. Olives. And some high-end oil."

"See you in a bit, then."

Let me just set down a couple of things about Erin that seem relevant to understanding where she's coming from. For starters, she's a completely responsible and dedicated teacher. I've never seen a person work so hard on behalf of her students. When she gives our manuscripts back with her notes and comments, sometimes it looks as if she's spent more time responding to our work than we spent writing it.

Behind all that hard work, though, is a calculating side to Erin that I have a hard time getting behind. She's come right out and said she wants to write her next book about our little group—a guide to teaching nature writing to a mixed bag of ordinary grown-ups who happen to be all different ages, have different levels of ambition and ability—as a model for increasing environmental consciousness in a community like Burlington. So the pieces that we write are fair game for her to use in her book. We all signed a piece of paper saying she could do this. But the fact that we're all working for her, in a loose sense, has not poisoned the atmosphere in our weekly meetings . . . and that's a testament to Erin's finer qualities. As well as our own.

I should mention, too, that Erin wrote one much admired book in the nature writing genre—*Peas in a Pod*, about the dangers of experiments in bioengineering. It's creatively accomplished . . . the narrative moves back and forth between these beautiful, essaylike descriptions of how healthy plants grow, and a fictional story about graduate students who subvert their university's research on genetically altered vegetables. But this book came out seven years ago, already—way out ahead of the curve of interest in this issue—and Erin would be the first to admit that nothing she has written since has really panned out for her. Sometimes I can see a shaken confidence behind her eyes. I can see her wondering if she's already a has-been.

One more thing I ought to set down about Erin Furlong—and I came on this by sheer chance, because it's not the kind of thing she would ever come right out and say. Erin was Miss Oregon back in the early eighties . . . third runner-up to be the reigning Miss America.

Today you'd never guess that—oh, her posture is terrific and she's got a certain poise, but the perfect curves and drop-dead features of a beauty queen have pretty much slipped down the tubes of middle age.

Her husband is in finance—makes a bundle, treats her fine. The writing thing for Erin is about identity, not trying to find a way to pay monthly bills.

So I'm waiting at the pick-your-own, and around 1:00 I see Erin's blue Prius—pretty little eco-car—zipping up Pleasant Valley Road. She comes striding into the wooden booth where people write down what they took and stuff their money in the box; she's wearing a spectacular sundress, low-heeled sandals, and a broad straw hat. I'm slicing overripe tomatoes into fresh lettuce, and after adding what she's brought we take our Greek salads to a picnic table underneath the maple tree. She comments on the astounding beauty of the farm, its undulating contours, its wonderful "sense of place" . . . and after several more polite remarks, she asks me how the situation has been working out with Kyle. I can tell she feels responsible for his being here—she admits the way she helped negotiate his moving in was not exactly straight-up.

"But it's fine," I tell her. "Water under the bridge. Kyle's a real asset. Fast worker, too." I felt a sudden blush. "*Hard* worker."

She nodded. "Good with his hands."

"That, too."

"This is awkward, Lauren, but—I think Kyle needs looking out for. I've been talking to some people on the West Coast, and—you know, when Kyle came here it was sudden. In a big hurry."

"He did mention that."

"In my book—you've read it, right? *Peas in a Pod?*"

"I've read it several times."

"Well, one of the fictional characters—the one who goes by Top Soil—was actually modeled on Kyle Hess. I was a lab technician at the university—this was back home, in Eugene—and he was one of those radical grad students who would break into the greenhouse and rip out plants."

"Why is this not surprising me?" I asked. "I know Kyle used to dabble in the 'outlaw' branch of environmental action. That's in the past, though. If the law is after him—"

"It's not the law I'm worried about," she told me. "They don't have enough on Kyle to make a case, and in the overall scheme of things he's just a small fish. A minnow." She pulled out a pack of cigarettes, which threw me for a loop. I watched her light up. "The thing is, there are people in the movement who are angry at him. Actually, *angry* is not the right word."

"Why? What did he do?"

"There was a campaign last year at Tahoe, to disrupt expansion of a California ski resort. And seven good people ended up in jail for it. They think Kyle made mistakes that got them all arrested."

"Mistakes . . . ?"

"What I gather, he was sharing information with the wrong sort of people. Amateurs—wanna-be radicals, but people who had no real discipline or deep commitment. You know that old saying about loose lips sinking ships?"

"Right."

"Well, that's what happened. And really, if this hadn't come out Kyle would still be in California. Fighting for the redwoods. Anyway, what I'm saying is that if you sense anything suspicious going on— unexpected visitors, cars with California plates, anything that feels slightly out of the ordinary—I want you to call me. This could really be important."

"Will do," I promised nervously—I couldn't help glancing around me with suspicion. Then I remembered that I have a large, noisy, highly territorial dog. And a pack of guard llamas. "Actually, this place is protected," I said. "I don't think anyone could show up unannounced."

"Good to know. Well—thanks. For keeping him from harm." She stood. "I know you're busy, working."

"One thing," I added, getting up to walk her to her car. "When you and Kyle were—I mean, back in Oregon. What kind of friendship was it?"

at often, these days. You grow meat the way Picasso paints.

s enough to feed my spirit all day long.

October 1

lk with Kyle last night about my writing . . . and, eventu-
 else. First I showed him several of the entries I've been
out raising sheep, how hard it is to make others under-
t seems like a contradiction: raising these animals lovingly,
king them to slaughter. He said this is certainly the best of
he's read—I should stay focused on this general meditation
syche of a shepherd," and see where it might take me.
book? At any rate, he offered to present what I showed him
itor of *Orion,* after I have polished the writing and put in
text, more narrative background. Wow, I thought. *Orion.*
getting published in a venue like that.
picking up on that idea of contradictions—or seeming con-
s that are actually not—we started talking about Henry
oreau. Amazing to me that Kyle's read the man so carefully—
Thoreau is mainly this cranky old grandpa in the nature
ield, but Kyle takes him as a personal hero. And one thing he
ut Thoreau is his comfort with contradictions. One minute
s to wolf down a woodchuck raw, and the next he's railing
anybody who eats meat. One page has him sounding like
t, and on the next he's become a party animal. People don't
reau credit, Kyle says, for being a really complicated person.
makes him a modern writer—our contemporary—not some
th-century graybeard.
 we went on to what I said was a contradiction between
close attention to the world around us—nature—in order to
own in language that is honest, graceful, *tenderly* written . . .
 that, and Kyle's interest in committing illegal acts to "save

"You mean, were we lovers?"

"Yes, I guess that's what I'm asking."

"How'd you guess?" She laughed. "The thing is, Kyle could say that about a lot of women. There's still something affectionate between us, but I got tired of always playing second fiddle to the current honey." The way she looked at me, I knew we understood each other. "You take care, okay?"

"Will do."

So now it's later, getting on toward the heart of Saturday night. All my chores are done, there's no one else here on the farm but me sitting with this notebook and a glass of chardonnay. And I'm wondering, on several levels, what I've gotten into.

Sunday, September 29

Found Kyle and the Coopers roasting marshmallows and making s'mores down at the fire pit last night, getting on famously. It's amazing how Kyle is able to strike up conversations with all kinds of people—if there really is a "gift of gab," that guy has got it. Then I noticed what he'd gathered for a woodpile, and I swear to God it was a bunch of survey stakes—long, thin pine slats like they use to make snow fencing. I remembered how they once were set up all across the farm, when Dad put in diversion ditches to begin the cottage project—I figured Kyle must have come across them stashed somewhere. He saw me noticing and gave this sheepish look, then said he guessed they ought to be fair game as kindling. No use to anybody now, and wicked good fuel.

I accepted that explanation at the time, but this morning's paper has a story about recent acts of sabotage at Stowe—sand in the crankcase of a bulldozer engine, blueprints stolen right out of the construction office, and the removal of several hundred survey stakes that had been placed to mark the golf course. So I'm more than a little suspicious. Also, I don't see what good these eco-stunts accomplish . . . all that's going to happen is the slowing down of what they're doing. Then I'll bet the contractors will beef up security, and someone's going to wind up busted.

What really upsets me, though, is that Kyle burned these stakes with Ken and Chloe sitting right there. Doesn't he understand who Ken works for? Just looking at that guy, you'd think he was a cop. And I don't know if I should go confront Kyle, have this out, or let it slide.

LAMBS TO SLAUGHTER

I loaded the truck tonight with twelve lambs—everything that weighed in at one hundred pounds or more—and first thing in the morning I will drive them to the funky old slaughterhouse in South Barre. These are the first fruits of the coming harvest season, and they're looking ripe to make their way into people's freezers. I am trying to describe the sense of pride with which I do this, but I doubt that anyone can really understand unless he knows firsthand what it's like to raise meat animals. All the things that can go wrong, and how hard it is to see that everything goes right, sometimes. Some of the women in our writing group—Kiki, Rachel—looked at me as if I were a Nazi when it first came up that I was feeding lambs for slaughter. As if I were Hitler or Goebbels, blood upon my hands. But I just don't see it that way . . . I see, instead, the hypocrisy of people who enjoy a nice piece of meat but don't want to consider where it came from. My meat comes from a good place, a loving household, and my lambs enjoy a good and happy life. I don't feel guilty when it's time to sit down and eat them. What I feel is joyful, glad. Incredibly thankful, too.

When I got them all onto the truck and slammed the tailgate, I wanted to take a picture . . . mentally, I did take one. *Look at those lambs!* I bragged to an imaginary audience. *Aren't they filled out beautifully?* Raised organically, which isn't exactly easy. Look at that depth of loin, the blocky shoulders, rounded legs. Think of the feasts to come, when families and friends will gather over this meat and renew the ties that bind them, celebrate enduring friendships. Good eating. Memorable meals. We're alive, aren't we?

But I still expect to be misunde[...] of those women in the writing gr[...] not a vegetarian.

Monday, September 30

New month tomorrow! And my[...] when autumn sweeps in, dresses eve[...] helps disrobe them, leaf by leaf, to g[...]

CUSTOM CUTTER

I love the slaughterhouse south of[...] used to be a barn—well, it *is* a barn–[...] and inviting to the animals arriving[...] jump off the truck, run into their hold[...] the calves and pigs waiting for their t[...] love the gentleness of Ben, the former[...] tion. Not that he's a saint, but he is tru[...] the livestock so as not to spook then[...] looking lambs," he told me. "How old?'[...]

"Seven months."

He nodded. "Want the pelts back?"

I told him he could keep those, tak[...] shook hands, agreed on when the meat[...] that. By now—a couple of hours later[...] hanging in the cooler. Ben will age their[...] meat can cure; then they'll be chopped[...] Then the cuts get wrapped and labeled,[...] deliver those lambs to my customers and[...] Not wages of sin, but fair compensation[...] done. Done with loving care about those[...]

Ken Cooper knows where I'm coming[...] sell him a package of loin chops out of[...] night. "Damn fine meat," he let me kno[...]

don't get th[...] Or Chloe."[...] That wa[...]

Tuesday, [...]

Early A.M.[...]

Long t[...] ally, much[...] making a[...] stand wh[...] and yet t[...] my work[...] on the "[...] Possibly[...] to the e[...] more co[...] Imagine[...]

Then,[...] traditio[...] David Th[...] to me, [...] writing[...] loves ab[...] he want[...] against[...] a herm[...] give Th[...] Which[...] ninetee[...]

The[...] paying[...] set it d[...] betwee[...]

the planet" or whatever. How we shared a common obsession with the first objective, but didn't see eye to eye about the second. Kyle quoted my own writing back to me—if people never get directly involved, he said, they'll never come to see there's no real contradiction. He said I shouldn't knock activism till I tried it.

I brought up the matter of the survey stakes, and he freely admitted where they came from: the golf course going in as part of Stowe's expansion. But he swore he hadn't pulled a single one of them himself—he was just making them disappear on behalf of those who did the deed. The thing is, Kyle confessed, at this stage in his life he's really scared of getting busted. It's like one more strike and he'll be out. So he's working on the fringes of this quiet campaign to make life difficult for the developers at Stowe—gathering intelligence and offering advice and even helping out the way he did the other day, by getting rid of what might otherwise be used as evidence. Just a modest effort on his part to serve the greater cause. And the time would come when I myself would want lend a hand.

"Why?" I asked him. "How can you be sure?"

"Because we're in love, now—there, okay, I said it." He stroked my cheek, staring so hard into my eyes that I felt naked. "And when people love each other, they support each other's projects."

By that point we were making out pretty hot and heavily . . . and then we went to bed. And somewhere on the way to an incredible orgasm, I told him that I wanted him to use me—somehow—on the mountain. Nothing really dangerous or scary, but I was prepared to see how it would feel to step outside the law. "Use me," I whispered. "So that I can see things your way. See the world through your eyes."

He said he would think of something worthy of my special gifts, my unique passion. And I'm thinking: Whoa, now. Have I ever been in love before?

2:30 P.M.

So maybe I'm a little slow at doping stuff out, but it finally occurred to me that Ken and Chloe Cooper might not be exactly who they say they are. It was recalling that they came out here from Oregon that got me suspicious—that, coupled with Erin's warning to be on the lookout for people from the West Coast who might be tracking down Kyle. I don't want to come off as a paranoid, a worrywart, but the more I thought, the more it seemed plausible that there was some connection. Major Ken Cooper—but I've never actually seen him in a uniform, and everything he's said about his project at the Firing Range has been extremely vague. Never anything specific. As for Chloe, how could I be sure she wasn't more than just a plein air artist? I remembered how it was Kyle who had brought them to me. But if there was some connection, were the Coopers really allies? Or were they perhaps Kyle's surreptitious enemies, come to get some payback for what happened out in California?

After lunch, when Ken was safely gone to work and Chloe had just set off to hike up Sunset Ridge, I stopped by Winesap with an armful of clean linen and enough time to look around. There was a laptop running on the bedside table; on a hunch, I opened the word processor and called up several files . . . nothing out of the ordinary. Then I hear a noise outside and look out the window to see Chloe's coming back—I start freaking out because she's going to catch me red-handed. I get the word processor closed, then see the closet door and figure I can just duck in there, hide until she leaves. I can hear her footsteps on the deck now. So—this is incredible—I open the closet and this avalanche of balls comes tumbling out. Basketballs, volley-balls, great big beach balls rolling all across the floor. And just then I hear the cottage door swing open.

"Chloe?" I call out, and a moment later she comes in. "I wanted to change your sheets," I tell her.

"What are you doing in my closet?"

"I just—"

"Don't bother trying to explain." She gave me a disgusted wave. "I suppose you'd like to know what I'm doing with these." She picks up a volleyball and sits down on the unmade bed, gives me an appraising stare. "Kyle says you want to join us—truth?"

"I said I'd help," I told her. "With this Stowe thing."

"I need to know you're really on our side. No bullshit."

"Whose side are *you* on?" I fired back. My heart was pounding. "The thing is, I care about Kyle . . . deeply. I know he has enemies, people in the movement who—"

"You mean the Tahoe screw up. Ken and I know all about that. We came here to help him recoup, after what happened."

"Well, that's a relief," I told her. I think I grabbed a pillow off the bed and fluffed it . . . something to look busy. "Yes, I want to join you. So—why the balls?"

She gave me a final can-I-trust-you look, then apparently decided to. "At some point," Chloe says, "we'll be taking out the Toll Road."

"With *these*?"

"That's right. And that's all you need to know. Not knowing things can help—believe me—when the shit comes down."

"But—"

"And I can change my own sheets." She took the linen from me. "You may be the landlord, but don't let me catch you here again. Do we understand each other?"

"Sure. We do." I nodded. "Something I don't get, though—what's your husband doing at the Ethan Allen Firing Range?"

"Didn't I just say not to . . ." But she relented. "Lauren, think . . . is it so hard?"

I thought, and then it came to me: "Explosives," I said. "That's where the explosives are."

"Bingo." She laughed. "Like Willie Sutton and the banks."

"But if—"

"Ken is covered, no worries."

"How many people—?"

"No more questions," she says, shaking out a clean sheet. "I've said too much already. You have second thoughts, you wimp out—"

"You don't have to worry about me."

"I won't," she says. "Because I'll have an eye on you." She pointed to the door. "Get out of my house, now."

So I'm back home at the writing table, furiously trying to get this conversation down . . . I seem to have joined up with an eco-terror cell! I must be their junior commando, or something. And my Pleasant

Valley farm is *home base* for their current project . . . pretty damn scary. I wish Kyle were here to hold me and explain my role . . . what are they doing that is going to take explosives? I wish I knew that I am following my head's urgings, as well as my heart's.

I can see that Mister Rogers has jumped the fence, and that he's in danger of breeding half a dozen ewes. Down, you bad boy. I need to catch that llama, pen him in the barn. Thank God I have farm chores to attend to, while I process things.

Wednesday, October 2

Claudia had a late-term abortion this afternoon—I found her in the three-sided shed, keening over this stillborn *cria* that she'd just delivered. Fourteen pounds . . . I weighed the bloody fetus, then took it from her. Checking last fall's breeding records, I see Claudia wasn't due for five more weeks. Imagine, carrying a baby ten months only to lose it in the home stretch. Claudia was going crazy—pacing, whining, shivering. Major financial blow for the farm, too—a whole year's work for that breeding dam has gone to waste.

Jackie stopped by to examine poor Claudia, to make sure the afterbirth was fully expelled and to check for uterine infection. No vets around here have extensive knowledge of these creatures—we're all flying blind, when a llama gets in trouble. But Jackie did remind me of the obvious—that underfeeding or overexertion late in pregnancy can cause a mammal to abort. I showed her the *cria,* and she said it almost surely died a few days ago. She showed me telltale signs of fetal resorption that had been underway, before the dam's internal system made the call to ditch that baby.

Well, I can think of years when the pasture has held up better, but I can't believe there hasn't been enough nutrition to let a llama in her prime carry a *cria* to term. The waste of it all—the waste of precious life, and time.

Llamas are such incredible animals. As soon as a dam becomes open, the male is apt to go ahead and breed her. I mean immediately.

It's a complicated system . . . females don't ovulate on their own, they do it in response to the male having sex with them. And Claudia, poor thing, is one of those overly submissive females who will *kush* as soon as an interested sire puts a move on her. So we had to catch Mister Rogers, throw a halter on him, and confine him in the barn. Thank goodness Kyle was around to help me out, because Mr. R. had that glint in his eye . . . he came to sniff at Claudia and get her hot and bothered even while we were still cleaning up the mess. Kyle was astounded when I told him dams are generally rebred within two weeks of giving birth . . . and that they go through their sex act lying down— for half an hour—like no other creature on the planet, except humans. He wanted to see the stillborn *cria,* but I had buried it.

Kyle was really moved. He was almost crying.

Funny how Caligula's death was the catalyst that brought Kyle and me together, but with this comparable tragedy I felt aloof—for some reason I didn't want to let him touch me. But he understood . . . he was quite gentle with my complicated feelings, my fragility. We took a long evening walk, after doing chores. A cold front blew through, dropped a miniscule amount of rain and then gave us the blessing of a double rainbow . . . flabbergasting. Radiant, iridescent—my heart was in my mouth. We held hands, then, and stared in wonder while the arch of colors swelled brighter, brighter—such an eerie glow, as if to strike us blind . . . and then it faded, fast as it had emerged. I felt as if the sky would never look the same again.

"So, I've talked with Chloe," he said when the light was normal. "I hear you found her sports equipment."

"Give me some credit, would you? No one needs that many balls."

"She said you were snooping."

"Not really. But I gather you and Chloe and her husband—"

"Let me come clean about that. Ken and Chloe are not married."

"Well, for—that's the least of my concerns."

"You're right, though. The three of us go way back. And we're all involved in the Mansfield project."

"That's what we're calling it?"

He nodded.

"So, the balls . . . what for?"

"This is a place that I've been thinking we could use you, Lauren. If you're up to it." He opened his wallet, pulled out the map Stowe gives you when you buy a ticket for the Toll Road. There were numbered circles drawn at several places on the route, and some feminine hand—Chloe's?—had made a neat table:

.6 mi. at hairpin curve	basketball
1.1 mi., major runoff	beach ball
1.5 mi.	beach ball
1.7 mi.	basketball
2.1 mi.	volleyball
2.5 mi., critical	volleyball
3.2 mi., at hairpin	major beach ball!
4.1 mi., base of steep ascent	basketball

Shopping List: 3 basketballs, 2 volleyballs, 3 beachballs

"Well," I said, "I still don't get it."

"A gravel road up a mountain is a cinch to take out," he said. "Because it shouldn't be there in the first place. It takes a lot of ditching to keep water off the surface, and they use culverts to run the water underneath the road. Culverts come in standard diameters—so do balls. Push the right sized ball into a culvert before a storm, pump it up to seal it tight . . . and you can walk away. After a good hard rain, the road's a washout."

"Gee . . . I never thought of that."

"Even a tiny gal like Chloe can take out a road. I was thinking *you* could."

"Why, though?"

"I can't tell you."

"When?"

"When the time comes. You're still with us, right?"

"I said you could use me, and I—yes. Of course I'm with you."

"Good." He tucked the map into the pocket of my jeans. "Don't lose this—and don't leave it lying around. Think of it as like . . . your passport."

That's where I've stashed it—in the desk drawer where I keep my *real* passport and important papers. Interesting days, for sure.

High wind coming up—I hear shingles banging on the roof. Lights in the house have flickered on and off as I've been writing . . . need to get some candles close at hand, in case—

Thursday, October 3

Strange high wind last night, and terribly destructive.

Today I want to write about the violence in nature. Funny how I used to think that "nature" was essentially benign, an attractive beauty, worthy of quiet contemplation in a mood open to learning, to *receiving* transcendental knowledge. Which struck me as incompatible with the get-angry attitude of people who—

Whoops, off on a tangent that's becoming too familiar. Back to square one.

I want to write about the instinct to violence that causes animals in rut to go berserk, that caused Mister Rogers to destroy the wooden hurdles of his pen last night, charge through the barn door and go find the female who was open on account of having just aborted. How I found her *kush*ed for him first thing in the morning. No way could I tear those two apart, not until he'd finished dribbling his seed into her. Then, when they stood, she attacked the male violently—spitting in his face again and again . . . until he retaliated by trying to butt her into the electric fence. That piece of business carries 4,000 volts, and to save Claudia I ran to turn the charger off. I'm thinking, Is this any way for creatures to get bred? Why is sexuality in nature such an S&M show?

The odds are, Claudia's pregnant again already . . . one day after losing her baby.

I want to write about the violence of winds that rip off leaves before they reach full color. After last night's gale, we're picking up the pieces of what might have been the best autumn foliage in years. And—forget the leaf-peepers up here from New Jersey—those of us who live in this landscape year-round are diminished, dependent as we are on the spiritual lift that October is supposed to bring. Storing up visions of fiery leaves against the winter.

I want to write about the maple tree uprooted at the edge of the pick-your-own, seventy years in the making and suddenly—overnight—a corpse, thanks to one ill wind. How its roots tore a mound of earth out of the ground, refusing to let go of the soft stuff they were dug into. No more summer picnics underneath that canopy, no more sap buckets hung in March to welcome spring. Did it groan, toppling? Did it scream against its fate?

Wastes of pleasure, wastes of pain.

I want to write about the violence aroused in me, long buried underneath the sweet facade of being a good shepherdess, a patient farmer. Now I want to cultivate an anger that's explosive, mindless— I want to lash out at things that are repugnant, wrong. Violence is everywhere in nature, so why not in me?

Why not in me?

Later—After Writing Group

Weird vibe tonight. Kyle didn't show up at all, and Erin went off on this riff about consistency of metaphoric purpose, the ways in which a piece of writing's full range of imagery needs to feel connected. Maybe . . . but it came off as textbook stuff—a canned lecture—not attached to any of the actual work at hand. And Erin has a way, sometimes, of telling people more than they can sit there and listen to.

Something else. Rachel Katz read this piece about night climbing on a mountain laced with winding ski runs, coming in the dark upon the head of a chairlift and using the structure as a giant jungle gym— hauling herself to the top of the bull wheel, finding the cable and working her way along it, looking for a weak point. How this was a different way of utilizing climbing skills, showing her mastery over what was, on its face, an insult to the mountain.

So I'm thinking Rachel's maybe caught up in our project, too. The Mansfield project. Wondering how many others there are out there, and when we'll have a powwow.

Friday, October 4

Kyle told me I should go with Chloe this afternoon over to the Stowe side, and we took her car loaded up with lots of "art supplies." Down through Smugglers' Notch to the base of Spruce Peak, which is like ground zero for the huge new development. Acres of poured foundations, tons of gravel being placed around a maze of plumbing lines and wiring conduits. "Four hundred condos, plus a hotel," Chloe told me. "They call that a *hamlet.*"

"Bigger than a lot of Vermont towns," I admitted. "And a lot less quaint."

We hadn't come to make drawings of the project, though; we had come to pose as visiting landscape painters. Chloe set up easels for herself and for me, scarcely fifty yards from the tall cyclone fence surrounding the construction site . . . the fence itself, Chloe said, was proof that the developers had started getting serious about their security. Which, of course, was going to cost them bucks they hadn't planned on spending. We turned our backs to the noise and dust of earthmoving, and instead framed the sweep of Mansfield before us— riddled though this side of the mountain has become with ski trails, lifts, a top-to-bottom gondola, and assorted lodges, parking lots, and restaurants. Still, the mountain's spine from this side looks a lot more like a human face than from Pleasant Valley. And it's a familiar—even famous—landscape subject.

It's been a long time since I've fooled around with paints and brushes, and at first my strokes were rusty, obviously uncontrolled. Amateurish. Chloe's very good, though, and she said if anybody came over to watch us work we could pretend to be teacher and pupil. That was her way of saying, I suppose, that the canvas I was working on wouldn't fool anybody into thinking I could paint.

"Why are we *really* here?" I asked her eventually.

"Kyle has a task for you. Sort of a dry run, so we'll know if you can do this stuff."

"Like a test?"

"You could call it that. It's getting on toward four thirty, which is when those bulldozers quit for the day. At twenty past, you're going to walk into the job site and use a Porta-Potty—anybody hassles you, you tell them that you are just a painter looking for a place to pee. But you stay in there until they close the site and lock the gate. You might even want to stay till dark . . . that's around six thirty."

"You want me to spend two hours holed up in a Porta-Potty?"

"So far as we know, there's no night watchman yet. But dark is best."

"Then what do I do?"

"Open my handbag," she said. I picked it up—*heavy*—and pawed through a bunch of mushy brown blobs the size of croquet balls, each wrapped in cellophane. "Plastic clay," said Chloe. "Very effective. Sticks like cement inside the walls of a four-inch pipe. And when water gets to it—sooner or later—it swells up and seals tight. So you drop those clay balls into waste lines, then get out of there. Next summer, people will get a surprise when they flush their toilets."

"No thanks." I shook my head. "This is just the sort of thing that—"

"You made a promise. Now it's time to keep your word."

"I don't see why I should have to—"

"Are you in, or out?"

I thought it over for a minute, realizing that if this was Kyle's way for me to prove myself, I should deliver. "Okay," I told Chloe. "How do I get out, after?"

"There are ways. Be resourceful. And don't leave a trace of where you've been . . . keep the handbag with you. Anytime past seven, you'll find Kyle waiting at the Matterhorn. Two miles down the road."

"But—"

"Time to scoot." She pointed to her watch. "Now go out there and impress us."

So I strolled through the open gate of the job site, wearing the heavy bag slung across my shoulder. There were three Porta-Potties lined up inside the fence, and when some hardhat hollered to me I just pointed and he nodded. In like Flynn. And not long after, I could hear the earthmoving machines start shutting down; pickups revved to take the operators home.

I suppose a real nature writer would find lots to say about two hours spent standing in a plastic outhouse, bathed in stomach-turning vapors wafting up from piles of shit soaked in blue-green chemicals . . . but enough about that part of my initiation. Long before dark came on, the site seemed deserted so I snuck out to do what Chloe had dared me to—I know enough about construction that I found the major waste lines draining the entire complex, and I stuffed them in places that will soon be buried out of sight and out of mind . . . for several long months, at least. Then they will be very much on somebody's mind—a big, expensive headache. And, yes, I want to say I got a buzz from doing this—a thrilling satisfaction about saying no to progress in a way that was active and risky . . . and nonverbal. It didn't seem that immature, once I started doing it. No adolescent prank—it was deadly serious. Not that I could dupe myself into thinking I was really "saving planet Earth," or anything so grandiose . . . but I *was* punishing a bunch of heartless fat cats who seem to feel they can have their way with Mount Mansfield forever. That felt good—punishing developers in a way that's going to cost them.

Getting out wasn't that difficult, either—in a bunch of places they had piled building materials close enough to the fence that an agile person could easily scale it. *I* am an agile person. Their fancy security fence only worked, that is to say, in one direction. I walked half an hour in the dark down the Mountain Road to the Matterhorn—après-ski establishment in winter, mere bar in autumn—and, sure enough, there was Kyle sitting in a booth facing the door. With another man, distinguished-looking. Tall. In his fifties. Steel-gray hair, dark eyes. A penetrating stare—not unfriendly, though. The two of them were drinking beers, and Kyle waved to get me one.

"So . . . ," said Kyle. "Did you manage to lose your cherry?"

"Don't let's joke about this. I did what Chloe said to."

"Lauren, this is Jerry. As in Jerry Rigg. From Earth Defenders."

"Nom de guerre," the tall man added.

"You're the one in charge? The planner?"

"I'm the one who gets to coordinate the total picture. But as for a plan . . ."—he tapped his forehead—"it's evolving. As we get our team together. Good to know that you're on board, though. That now we can trust you."

I nodded. "What if I'd been picked up and questioned?"

"This is a well-run project. Anybody you might name would clear out overnight."

I looked at Kyle, shocked to hear my lover was prepared to vanish on a moment's notice. But he nodded, then added: "Let's make sure that doesn't happen."

"I'm going to stay at your place for the next few nights," said Jerry—as if he thought he had a perfect right. "Kyle's got that third cabin—Jonathan?—all fixed up."

"It's not a cabin, it's a cottage," I said. "And it rents for one fifty a night, during foliage season."

"I'll be happy to pay that."

My beer came and I gulped it down, suddenly realizing that Kyle had accomplished just what he once told me he thought I should do—turn my farm into an intimate community of eco-conscious activists. With a shared concern, commitment. And he'd done it in three weeks. Fast worker, all right. And he had managed to bring me in the movement with him.

Kyle called for the check, and we were out of there in Jerry's BMW—the nicest car I've had a ride in since I can remember. There is money in the movement, evidently. And Jerry insisted Kyle sit in the back with me, chauffeuring us back to my side of the mountain while we held each other, snuggled. On the way home, as we zipped past the construction site, I peered out a tinted window toward the grid of gray foundations looming in the moonlight. A maze of waste plumbing that will have to be torn up, next year. Dug out and re-placed, at great expense. Thanks to me. Yes, I thought, I certainly have lost my cherry.

Home way late for chores, but no farm catastrophes seem to have taken place while I was striking my blow against the empire. Cannot wait to wake up to the new me.

Saturday, October 5

Big, high-energy meeting this afternoon about evolving tactics in the Mansfield project . . . down in newly renovated Jonathan cottage, where this ringleader, Jerry Rigg, is staying for the weekend. I wasn't in on it at first, but then Kyle came to find me in the barn and said I ought to come join them. I had been worming every ewe in the flock— an annual prelude to the breeding season—so I was a mess, but he said no matter. He wanted to give me a taste of how decisions get made in the movement—this branch of it, anyway—and thereby deepen my commitment to the cause.

Jerry says the Mansfield project has been following a too-familiar pattern: A few early actions—such as pulling out the survey stakes, stealing the blueprints—get picked up by the media and consequently people were beginning to take notice, but then the target corporation goes into blackout mode to keep the situation out of the headlines. The flacks at Stowe, for instance, seem to have decided they'd be smart to put a lid on things. To preserve their public image, and keep copy-cats from getting in the act. That's okay for now, says Jerry, so long as we keep the game up—keep putting pressure on the contractors and making them look stupid. Ultimately, though, we need to work toward something big. Dramatic. Something that the media can't help getting wind of and turning into a story that will wake people up, call attention to what Stowe is doing to the mountain. His idea is to somehow sabotage the dams they're building to contain mountain streams . . . that involves serious habitat alteration, just so they can make more snow. And this pond construction is going on halfway up the mountain, in places that are difficult to get to . . . that's a plus for us, because security will not be tight. And Ken apparently has a line on some explosives from the Ethan Allen Firing Range—mines that could be buried in the dams and detonated later, once the ponds start holding water. Doing that, Jerry feels certain, would make the news.

Ken says no—the damage to the mountain will be worse, if we blow up those dams, than what is going on there anyway. Which is like defeating our own purpose. Chloe says the risk of hurting by-standers is just too great . . . like the people downstream when a wall of water comes their way. There's a strict ethic in eco-defense circles: Nothing that we ever do can risk harming innocent lives. We are not murderers. We care about our fellow humans, even when they're doing bad things to the planet.

Kyle's on the fence about the dams . . . after looking at some topo maps and aerial photographs, he thinks the risks are tolerable but the chance of *negative* publicity is way high. Like when someone fire-bombed a restaurant at Vail, a few years back. The way the press spun out that story, people didn't understand what the real issues were. Consequently, the entire movement got a bad rap.

Hey, I said, I'm new to this—you can't place a lot of stock in my opinion—but they said they wanted me to share my thoughts, to go on record as we talked about our options. As Jerry put it, if we all could get behind this action in a strong, collective way, we could pull it off by Halloween . . . but if we were indecisive, or internally divided, we'd be better off just to pass on the idea.

I said I didn't want anything to do with dynamite, or high explo-sives, or anything that might blow up in someone's face. Including my own. That maybe I wasn't cut out for that kind of action. Good to know, they said . . . but we still need something that will screw with Stowe in a way that cannot be ignored. So if I come up with a better plan, I need to tell them.

Then back to the barn to give the rest of the sheep their wormer, knocking out assorted internal parasites—stomach worms—so that the ewes get a metabolic boost before they meet the rams. I suppose this trick amounts to faking out their systems, but the payoff ought to be a lot more twins next spring.

I have to say I like the way my local, on-site Bader-Meinhof gang is letting me take part in their policy discussions . . . and I like, too, that they can make me feel comfortable enough to share my feelings. I even told them flat out that I didn't want to see explosives coming on this farm, for any reason . . . and after batting it around, they accepted that. Kind of a consensual decision-making process—like the Quakers use—where failing to reach consensus does in itself result in a deci-sion. Like Dylan's song about those who live outside the law: If you do, you've got to be honest. Or like honor among thieves.

Kyle invited me to come down later on, hoping I could spend the night . . . so I'm going to put some effort into getting gussied up, give him something to remember. Then I'm going to tell him that I'm ready for his grease cartridge, in the right frame of mind to put it to good use. Stand back, everybody—Lauren's on the prowl.

Sunday, October 6

ON BEING BORNE

Kyle took me soaring on this crisp, clear afternoon . . . incredible experience of light and lift and liberation. Everybody seems to know him at the little airport north of Stowe, on Route 100—there's a par-ticular glider that he likes to rent, a two-seater Starburst. The tow plane was a stumpy workhorse, loud and smelly; but as soon as Kyle signaled he was ready to cut loose, the droning engine fell away and we started floating upward—slowly, but with a thrilling sense of buoyancy.

I was thinking how even on commercial flights, there's this moment of hesitation (for me, it comes right on the runway) when you realize how totally you've placed your life into someone else's hands—a person you don't even know, who is going to be your pilot. This was so much richer an extension of that trust, though—the way lovers give themselves over in the act of sex is a pale metaphor. Sitting behind Kyle—this pilot whom I knew and loved—I could reach for-ward anytime and squeeze his shoulders, stroke his neck. Then, when we were over Smugglers' Notch, he handed me a camera and told me to start taking shots of the construction site. Banking and turning so I'd get the photographs he wanted, I was amazed at the delicate control—the incredible grace—with which he flew that sleek ma-chine. Flying in total silence, borne aloft on waves of air.

Once I had taken all the pictures Kyle wanted, he asked me where

I'd like to go and I said that I'd never seen the farm from right overhead. We were on the Stowe side and we'd lost a lot of altitude, but he found a thermal and we spiraled up inside it for the next twenty minutes, eventually rising well above the mountain's Chin. Even now, sitting here at this familiar table, I can shut my eyes and see exactly how it looked when Pleasant Valley loomed into view ... then we made a beeline to the west, and minutes later I was looking down *directly* on these pastures and meadows that I've put so much time and effort into. Rocks in the field do not show up from a height like that. Weeds are indiscernible. All that shows up is a larger pattern of intention—mine—to work with the landscape for our mutual benefit, trying to discover a creative harmony with the resources nature has bestowed here.

It was a holy moment . . . it might as well have been an eternity. And the whole time beneath our fiberglass wings lay a sea of liquid air—invisible, but bearing us.

To be in love, too, is a way of being borne.

Skimmed around the Nose of the mountain on the way back, and the big depressing news is that the drill rig has been disassembled— which can only mean they've found a site for their three new broadcast towers. Probably a helicopter will take the pieces away in the morning ... I have missed my golden chance at greasing that machine. And yet ultimately nothing could have brought me down from the high of this fall day. Nothing *can*. "Thank you," I leaned forward to whisper in Kyle's ear as he touched us down out of the blue sky, a perfect landing. And then it became a question: "How can I thank you?"

"You don't have to," he told me. "You already have."

Monday, October 7

I've been worrying about Vasilis lately. Thing about these big, galumphing dogs is that they just will not complain . . . they can be hurting big-time, but they refuse to let you know about it. As if to bark or whimper would be a betrayal of their Stoic's code. Like the day last spring when I found the dog with porcupine quills jabbed into his tongue, his cheeks. Any Border Collie would be going crazy over that, but not a Pyrenees. Not one peep out of Vasilis—in fact, it wasn't till noon, when I went out to feed him, that I saw what he had gotten into.

At night, though, a guard dog is supposed to assert an overwhelming presence. Barking in basso profundo, marking territory. Letting would-be predators know he's on the job, ready to rumble. But lately Vasilis—I don't want to say that he's out of it, but he's not projecting himself all that aggressively. I heard coyotes howling in the distance last night, somewhere up the mountain, and he didn't even answer. Found him in the sheep pasture first thing this morning, right where he belonged but kind of depressed-looking. Heavy-lidded. Fagged. And it took the lure of a treat to get him to his feet.

Well, a dog this tried and proven is allowed to have his moods. Makes me realize, though, how dependent I've become on this tricky mix of animals to look out for one another, keep each other safe from harm. I should ask Jackie about supplemental vitamins, or if something's missing in Vasilis's diet. When I lie in bed at night and hear a coyote howl his lungs out, I can't keep from tossing till the Pyr barks back. Telling the world he's on duty, like he's meant to be. I won't sleep well till I hear that sound again.

Later—Nighttime on the Mountain

This is reckless, crazy, but I want to stay right in the moment and record my feelings even if it's by a failing penlight, crouched beneath this murdered tree that cradles my back and holds me, even in its state of death. All around me, rape and pillage of these ancient trees— our elders, formerly proud and true—to cut another ski run down the sportif slopes of Stowe Inc., where yuppies dressed in Gucci will soon schuss and wedel. I saw this gash in the forest from the air on Sunday, and couldn't believe my eyes. To be really here, though—up close—makes me want to cry. Or scream—but I know better than to give myself away.

What is it that people think they're doing, on this verdant planet? Sometimes I'm ashamed to be a member of the human race. Better to be a moose, or an eagle . . . or a tree, who at least knows its place in the world and stands there patiently, no larger ambition than to be allowed to sway and grow.

Well, there are machines in a clearing down the mountain that have played their part in this destruction. And tomorrow they aren't going to work nearly as well . . . if they even work at all. Thanks to my having been brought to my senses. Made to want to do something serious to stop the madness.

Penlight's slowly dying, now . . . sap is dripping on my hair. I see that this fallen tree is weeping, too.

Tuesday, October 8

ON NOT-SO-CASUAL SEX

Turned in Briggs and Stratton this afternoon, callow young bucks with big aspirations and a whole lot of heart, to get to work breeding my ninety-seven ewes. First I mixed dry tempera with a cup of cooking oil—red for one young ram, blue for the other—and I swabbed that slurry on their briskets so I'd have a way of checking on their prowess, and of keeping score. Six hours later, nine woolly fannies have been marked by Briggs (that would be the blue paint), and seven by Stratton (the red), but six of those ladies are wearing varied shades of purple, meaning that they've had at least one turn with each of them. Those bad boys seem to understand teamwork, too . . . most of the time. An occasional head butt if Stratton moves in on Briggs half-way through his foreplay, but no serious fighting. Genetic concerns aside, I think this is going to work.

I want to set down recent thoughts I've been having about sex and sexuality. First, the obvious: Humans do it mainly from an urge to take pleasure—pleasure for ourselves, for our partners—but the chemistry required to have a truly satisfying encounter is incredibly complicated, infinitely hard to fathom. Sheep—like other creatures?—do it for a reason that has nothing to do with pleasure . . . not as we humans understand the word, at any rate. They do it because they want to procreate, or "need" to procreate; they have this basic instinct, without which they would not be a viable species. Or even a surviving one. So. End of story.

Yet for humans, who have learned to set the sex act free of any procreative baggage, the phenomenally difficult key to good sex is finding the right partner. Choosing, and then somehow contriving to be chosen by that person in return. Even though there's no intention to make a baby . . . even though elaborate precautions have been taken to make sure no baby can be made. But sheep—well, a ewe will *only* have sex if she wants a baby. And when she is in that head, any sex is good sex. Any ram will do.

Or, that is to say, the ram or rams she thinks will do are those a shepherd chooses for her—this year, in this flock, that would be Briggs or Stratton. Or some combination of the two. Fact is, if these ewes have twins there's a fair chance that each lamb will have a different father. And they just don't care. *None* of them cares about this. Shouldn't this work in the opposite direction, though? Shouldn't the animals who only have sex as an act of procreation be exceptionally choosy about who they do the deed with?

Maybe that's why in nature males have to fight to earn the right to breed a dam. I'm not sure I like that, though—or that it amounts to *real* choosing. Not on the female's part, at any rate. And I'll bet a lot of males in nature may win their fight to breed a lady, but then wind up too exhausted—or too wounded—to do a good job in the sack. So to speak.

I was going off on human beings last night, caught up in my fit of rage up there on the mountain. But I do approve of what humanity has done for sex. Hard to get it right, for sure . . . but thrilling when we finally manage to. The richest of union of bodies, minds, souls.

Wednesday, October 9

Coyotes in the distance again last night, and I got out of bed to walk the pasture till I found Vasilis. Gonzo, flat-out snoring, dead to the world. I've only seen him this way one time before, and that was at the vet's office when Jackie tranquilized him. Then it hit me: tranquilizers. I put myself in the position of these California hotheads who Erin said might be closing in on Kyle . . . if they've tracked him down to my place, what would they have to do to get onto the premises?

No, I said on second thought. That is just too out-there. I will not be paranoid. Around that time, the dog began to shake himself out of it—Vasilis got up and charged off, a moment later, to challenge the distant coyotes with a barrage of howling.

I am getting too, too jumpy. Too suspicious, too. I know this is true, because around noon today when the cottages were empty— people gone up on the mountain or into town, off doing this and that to save the environment—I took the risk of searching Ken and Chloe's car. What did I come up with? U.S. Marine Corps Publication FM 21-16 FMFM 13-8-1, "Unexploded Ordnance (UXO) Procedures," a booklet on identifying and safely handling live bombs, mortars, hand grenades, et cetera, that might be found lying around at a place like the Ethan Allen Firing Range. No smoking gun, though. Nothing to justify my level of mistrust, concern.

Evening scoreboard: Fifteen marks for Stratton, twelve for Briggs. All of Briggs's ladies have also been marked by Stratton. That little man has real staying power, too, keeping right with a ewe as long as she is interested. You go, guy. Make lambs, not war. Find yourself a dance partner, put the moves on. Party down.

Thursday, October 10

So there I was, shopping down at Stan's store today, and what pulls in but a classic Volkswagen microbus, vintage 1970 with California plates. And I watch these people get out—dreds and tie-dyes, hemp sandals—and come up onto the porch of the store, check the bulletin board, and then walk in to ask Stan if there isn't a llama farm around here, somewhere. "Not really," Stan says. "But there's someone standing by the milk case who can maybe help you."

That would be me, of course. I play it cool, since being forewarned is forearmed. I walk outside with these retro hippies—Tyler, Gabriel, Mariah—and go over their road map with them, tell them that the only real llama farm I know is in Montgomery, forty miles away. Off Route 118.

"We're looking for this friend of ours, supposed to be working on a llama farm," says Gabriel—the tall one, with the kind of blue eyes that look perpetually stoned. "Good bud of ours, from California."

"Can't help you." I looked at him blankly.

"Goes by the name of Top Soil," said Mariah.

"That means nothing to me."

"How many of these llama farms are there, in Vermont?"

"Don't know," I said. "But you might try asking at the state university. Their Extension Service has a directory." I gave myself silent points for that one, since I know for certain I'm not on that list.

"Yeah, right." Tyler took the map and turned it over, puzzled. "In Burlington?"

"The University of Vermont. Someone there can help you."

"What do *you* know about llamas?" asked Mariah coolly.

"Not that much."

"The man inside there said he thought you did."

I don't think I managed to betray my panic. "I have raised a llama or two. But now I'm into sheep. Organic lambs—that, and pesticide-free veggies."

"Nice," said Gabriel. "I could be down with that."

"So, no llamas around here?"

I shook my head. "Try the university."

"Will do," Tyler told me. "Peace."

They got in their microbus and I got in my pickup—I raced home and herded every llama on the premises into the barn. Seems like now I'm going to have to keep them under wraps. Then I called up Erin Furlong and went through exactly what had just happened. "Shit," she said. "Where's Kyle now?"

"I think he's in Stowe, somewhere. Doing something."

"Working, you mean?"

"I think you know what I mean. And while we're on the subject, what about these other people he's got hanging around—Ken Cooper? Jerry Rigg? Chloe . . . I don't know her last name?"

"Never heard of any of them."

"What the hell is going on?"

"Keep calm," she tells me. "Kyle said he plans to come to writing group tonight . . . between now and then I'll make some phone calls, try to learn what's up."

"I sent those hippies on a wild goose chase, but if they're after Kyle they'll come back. And when they do, I don't know what to tell them."

"One thing you might do—try to give Kyle a head start with his packing. Take some boxes to his cabin, get his stuff together. He may have to get out in a hurry. Can you do that for him?"

"I don't know. Maybe."

"Don't panic, Lauren. Give me till tonight."

Damn, damn, damn. I don't have a lot of empty boxes, but I took some burlap wool sacks down to the living room of Golden Delicious—they'll fill quickly, and they're easy to move around. Didn't have the courage to start going through Kyle's stuff, though, easing his packing chore if he's got to run away. Not sure whether this was out of my respect for him, or out of personal denial that he has to go. And I'm thinking, This is my farm, but I gave it over to a bunch of eco-terrorists and now they're all off doing things to "save" Mount Mansfield and I have no goddamn clue what's going on.

Friday, October 11

5:00 A.M.

Can't sleep. Totally ridiculous even to try.

So there we are at writing group—Kyle's late as usual, and Kiki reads this piece about the "Radicalization of a So-Called Nature Writer." She's not even sitting with Schuyler, and he's got this pained expression but he's hanging in there, carrying the torch. And this mini-essay Kiki reads is, I swear to God, about pulling out survey stakes. She didn't have to say where. She's got herself posed as an avid bird-watcher, got her field guide and her Japanese binoculars, crack of dawn on a Sunday as she skirts the edge of some forest where developers have been surveying . . . not a bird in sight. A silent autumn. Something snaps inside her—wham, before it's time for breakfast she's yanked eighty stakes out of the ground and tossed them in the bushes.

People in our group have no idea how to handle this, so there's not much conversation till Kiki says it's just a fantasy, a work of fiction. Even then, the other workshop members keep their peace—they don't seem to know where she's coming from. But I ask her, "Isn't there someone in the background—some third party—who is actually behind your taking action?"

No, she says. In principle there could be, but for the essay's sake she feels her gesture ought to seem spontaneous.

Yeah. I'll bet.

She really is a fox, Kiki, in a sort of northern German/Scandinavian way. I mean I'm sure I'd look twice, if I were a guy. But I've seen what happens to her type a few years down the road—I can see her face and body morphing into nothing special.

Kyle does show up, at last, and we all slog our way through the balance of the evening. Afterward, Erin tells him we three have to talk, so we sit out in her Prius as the night turns chilly. Kyle and Erin sitting in the front seat, me crouched in the back. I explain what happened at Stan's store, and Erin says she's made some calls to people on the Coast . . . this may not be payback time, but Kyle is in trouble and it's best for him to leave.

"No can do," he says. "Not yet. I need a few more days."

"You fool," Erin fairly yells at him. "You don't think these creeps mean business?"

He says he needs to double-check the weather, and then—unbelievable—we sit there in the car surfing the radio till he gets a forecast. "What I thought," he tells us when the weatherman is finished. Something about a front coming in tomorrow, 80 percent chance of lingering showers. "Give me till Saturday," he tells her. "That's all I need."

"I am not your mother," Erin says. "But for God's sake, Kyle. Get packed up, so you can take off when this thing is over."

I had to watch them kiss, then, and it was more than friendly. They got quite tender, quite—what I mean is, they were virtually making out. Then Erin had to go. I got out along with Kyle, and I pleaded with him to come back to the farm with me. I felt so ashamed for having to beg like that, and he looked embarrassed, too. He said I had to understand he had a lot to do, but he'd be home by 11:00.

And he was. Not that it was good—I can think of only one other time when I burst out crying in the act of making love, certain that the person I was with would not be there tomorrow. Kyle tried to calm me down, reassure my hurt feelings but it wasn't working. Then he said I had to do something important for him. In a canvas sack were all the balls I came across at Winesap, each one thoroughly deflated and neatly stacked. An air pump was in there, too. Chloe, he said, is going to run me up the Toll Road tomorrow afternoon, and my job will be to walk down it after hours, using my "passport" map to stuff each ball into its culvert and pump it tight. Do that without getting caught. "Showtime," he told me.

"Why? Why now?"

"Because the Toll Road is the way they're going to bring in what they need to build those towers. If the road's washed out—"

"They can't get their gear in."

He nodded. "And with winter coming, they'll be out of luck till June. Buying us a lot of time. This is your moment, honey. You're the main event."

"This is not the way I ever thought we'd say good-bye," I told him.

"For the last time," he answered, "this is not good-bye."

"Right. You think about that. Think about what you just said."

"Will you do this?"

"Yes," I said. "I promised—I'll keep my word. Now go play with Kiki, or whoever."

"*Kiki?*" He shook his blond curls, made his eyes go big. Such innocence. "You don't understand at all. I wish I could stay and talk this through—and make love again. But there are too many things that have to get done tonight. Lauren, this is not the end. I'll find you—believe me—later."

Then I was alone, and I raged around the house for a while before finding some old pills and taking one to get a bit of sleep. No more of that, though. This is the day when I am taking out the Toll Road. This is the day when I do something that will make the news.

10:00 P.M.

Did it. Back home, safe and sound but soaking wet—it started raining when I was still halfway down the mountain, and soon it was pouring at the rate of like an inch per hour. Felt like the tail end of a hurricane. I don't know the physics of this ball-in-culvert strategy, but if it works at all it ought to work tonight.

When Chloe left me at the top of the Toll Road, I could tell it *was* good-bye between the two of us. She apologized for not getting to know me better . . . and for not allowing our relationship to grow more trusting. By that time I was fighting tears—not because of her, but from the inference that Kyle would probably be leaving, too. Then I put those thoughts away and got into the task—pacing off the legs of the road between specific culverts, crawling inside them to inflate the right ball. Nothing happened that could have aroused anyone's suspicion—a couple of hours after dark I stepped out of the woods with an empty pack, and climbed into my pickup.

I've stopped crying because down at Kyle's cottage not a thing has changed. No frantic packing, no signs of getting set to flee. I need to get a grip on fear, become a true believer. I need to trust the special vision that love confers.

Major league storm up on the mountain, but I'm home and dry.

Saturday, October 12

7:00 A.M.

Woke in the gray of dawn to hear a huge explosion coming from . . . I think the mountaintop. Sounded like a plane crash up there. Hard to see a thing with all the clouds gathered on the ridge after last night's deluge. Went to turn on the news, but the television is dead and so is the radio. Anyway, it's time for chores.

8:15 A.M.

This is no joke, three of my llamas have gone missing. Abelard, Claudia, and Carmen all disappeared. Must have broken out of the pasture during last night's storm. . . . Hope they're not in trouble.

8:40 A.M.

Wait a minute, lots of *tack* is missing, too. Frame saddles, panniers, and halters taken from the milk house. Now I don't believe those llamas took off on their own accord. . . . Something else is going on.

9:00 A.M.

Just back from ransacking Golden Delicious, and before me on the table are several balls of ground beef, each with a white pill tucked inside. So now I see who has been doping up Vasilis. Though I'd like to know why.

I would like an explanation.

9:25 A.M.

Helicopters have been flying up Mount Mansfield, disappearing into the clouds around the Nose. Something's going on, all right, and it makes me laugh to think I thought I was the main event.

Laughing? Not really.

Now I'm hearing sirens whining up Pleasant Valley Road, and of course they all slow down to turn into my driveway. One, two, three cruisers—state troopers climbing out. No way to duck this, not a goddamn thing that I can do. Angry men in uniforms staking out the house, getting set to storm in here and take me into custody. Tell me quite a lot of things that I don't want to—

🌱 Marianna Finch's Notebook

9/10 – 10/12

Crack of dawn, time to crack this brand-new nature notebook. Eighteen dollars for a blank journal. Yikes. But worth it, possibly. Hopefully. *I* hope so. Handmade paper flecked with hemp fibers, bound in birch bark. Pricey, but inspiring. I believe I'm worth that. And these days, I'll take my inspiration where I find it.

Cold, heavy dew washes each varnished fiber of this Adirondack chair where I sit above the faded garden. Still no killing frost, although the thick zucchinis and ripe tomatoes are living on borrowed time. Chorus of birds now tuning up for morning prayers. Clearing their throats before bursting into chant-song. Even since the other day, their numbers seem diminished. And their notes this morning sing of packing up and heading south. Leaving Vermont's summer womb. Seeking someplace warm.

Every single one of us is seeking someplace warm.

In the shallow cleft of sky between the twin oaks at the water's edge, I can see Lake Champlain start to emerge. But it's misty out there, damp. Vague. Uncertain. Blue-gray smudge of Shelburne Bay, same gunmetal color as the first light.

Distant blast of steam whistle. First ferry of the day must be lurching from its dock in Burlington. Plying through the fog to Plattsburgh, across the lake. With the help of navigation tools. Sonar. Radar. There's a jagged rock poking up beyond the breakwater. Rock Dunder. Dangerous. An accident about to happen, for unwary sailors.

Been waiting to happen for a long time, though. Erin says the local Indians think that rock is their petrified god. Oops. I mean the local Native Americans. Abenakis. They believe the world's creator, someone they call Odziozo, turned himself into that stone once his work was finished. Lying in those same waters that I stare at every morning, he admires his most captivating handiwork.

Same view as I look at, day after day. Best view on Earth, as far as Abenakis are concerned. Fit for a king, or for a god. Fit for Odziozo.

Why, then, am I depressed?

And that's just the sort of trite, self-absorbed remark that Erin tells me my nature notebook could do well without.

Maybe Odziozo is depressed this morning, too. Sitting out there all by himself in the foggy lake. I'll bet he can't see a thing.

Always this hour before sunrise makes me think of Tom, because it got to be our favored time for making love. Probably because Tom used to drink too much each evening even to fool around. I don't blame him. He had a lot of issues to work through. A frightening perspective on each day. Every passing moment. Especially once he knew how few of them were left.

How time was rushing on.

How it still is.

Alexa will be up and looking for me, any minute. Focus, honey. Big day ahead. For both of us. Off to boarding school in Putney. With her purebred Morgan, Sir Whisky. One sleek horse. Who means as much to her as I seem to, that's for sure. I need to accept that, though.

Smart kid, finding a prep school with a stable and an indoor ring. Even a dressage instructor. I only wish that I had taught her to ride better. Showed her more of what I know.

What I used to know so well.

By tonight there's going to be an empty bedroom down the hall, empty horse stall in the shed. And I will be alone here. Curse, or opportunity? New way of life, for sure.

I hope in my new life that keeping this notebook won't require stolen moments, snatched from here and there. And that I won't keep jotting down my introspections, rather than observing nature like I said I would. Writing group meets Thursday, and for once I want to bring Erin something truly polished. Last week she criticized the way I only read brief excerpts, not full entries when we go around the circle.

What I like best about writing in a notebook is to fondle every word. Thanks to this old-fashioned fountain pen. An honest tool. Simple. Intimate. I've gotten sick to death of writing on computers. Always held away from language by the length of an electronic arm.

Bill Gates's arm, I guess. Or his friendly paper clip's.

It looks like you're . . . writing an entry in your nature notebook. Would you like help?

No, thanks. Hell, no.

This way, though, my hands get dirty. Feels good. I love to look at my fingertips and see ink stains spreading there. Touched by the tool of the medium. Like working with paints, or clay. I like to feel my left wrist fashion each next word. Every single letter.

Erin has encouraged me to try to write like Emerson. *Waldo,* I call him when I want to cut him down to size. For each person in the circle, she's proposed a classic model. I understand that there's a fit in our biographies. He lost a child-bride. I lost a young husband.

Young in years, I mean. Although before the end came, Tom was quite advanced in age.

Like Emerson, I've turned to nature as a way of comprehending. Trying to move on. Or at least pick up the pieces. Thing is, almost every time I try to read Waldo I fall right to sleep. Especially when he's being seriously cheerful. Upbeat. Optimistic about the human prospect. The strength of self-reliance. The power of intelligence. The promise of America. This insipid good news seems to be his basic message.

Waldo ought to walk into a Wal-Mart, have a look around. See what has become of the American prospect.

Who's Waldo kidding? He was a tragic figure. And maybe I am one, too.

Writing in tight aphorisms—that's something that Erin says I ought to learn from Waldo. Hitch your wagon to a star. Build a better mousetrap. A foolish consistency is the hobgoblin of . . . small minds. Stripped down, pithy sayings.

Just a few well-chosen words.

Dense phrases. Packed with meaning.

Or like when he writes that "Nature always wears the colors of the spirit." That's what I'm trying to say this morning. In my own unpithy way. I sit staring at a line I cannot even see, out where sky meets water. And it's all the same.

One indistinguishable hue.

Nature's blue-gray morning wears my spirit's blue-gray colors. And the fit is perfect.

Weds. 9/11

So my teenage daughter is off to boarding school. I am embarked on my new life as an empty-nester.

Alexa was so excited. Eager to embrace the future.

Funny how I see today's date and want to turn the clock back. Find a way to somehow regress to a different era. Back before the towers fell.

Not Alexa, though. This is her time, her moment. Not an easy world to grow up in, but she's down with it. She says bring it on.

I really love that kid, but I wish I'd gotten to know her a little better. I wish I had spent more time.

Only one life, though. If you spend time doing one thing, it means that you can't do something else.

Big nest. Well feathered. Fabulous location.

Empty.

PLENITUDE OF AUTUMN

Still no frost in sight, and I am struck this morning by the sheer quantity of life that burgeons forth in the scant few months we call a growing season in New England. Bushels of lawn clippings. Oodles of mosquitoes, ants, houseflies, and assorted beetles. Riot of vegetables somehow produced out of this poorly tended plot of soil. Scads of eager weeds, too. Late season flowers blooming, each turgid petal held erect and wallowing in color. An enormous swelling, before winter's chilly fingers probe the gaudy bubble.

Then prick it.

This is nature's basic rhythm. Not mere wax and wane, but pumping up this vast excess. This fat balloon that then must suddenly explode. Inevitably. Irrevocably. Spreading seed in all directions. Then it shrinks back down to something limp and spent. The drab of winter.

This is nature's way.

And we are idiots, I think, to try to live in ways that modulate these all-or-nothing currents. These boom-bust cycles. These inherent rhythms. Why try to keep things holding steady, on an even keel?

As if we could.

I see I've been writing about sex again. What's up with that?

Staring hard enough at this blue chicory, I want to cry.

Thurs. 9/12

I don't know how much longer I can work in real estate. Seemed like a perfectly good idea at the time. A plausible career. Something to keep me busy after the bad fall. Once my shattered pelvis healed. And a way to force myself out of the house, assume responsibilities. Give me a way to stay involved with other people.

At first it was primarily a contest. Chasing fat commissions, competing for sales awards at the agency. Then, after Tom died, having a source of current income came to matter. Not that he had left us strapped. Far from. But I stopped looking at the money I brought home as a way of keeping score.

And yet there are other scores to keep, to pay attention to. I read in the paper that the state is down to something less than 1,400 dairy farms. Incredible. A lost Vermont. New England's fabled milk shed. Picture-postcard dairy state. Thousands have quit the business in just the last few years. Most of the farmers left are barely making money. Hanging on until their fields can be sold for suburbs.

And I know some of that blood is on my hands. More than I would like to see.

Hard to scrub it off when you are working in the business.

With each passing year, it's getting rather obvious that real estate development is ruining Vermont. I showed somebody the faux chateaus off Spear Street last week. One of those houses was so huge it blocked the view of Shelburne Bay from the park behind it. "Overlook Park," they call it. Used to be a breathtaking panorama. Magical. Now what does it overlook? The roof of someone's monster house.

And in just a couple years, someone's going to build a trophy home that blocks *that* house's view. I had to admit it, when this client asked about restrictions. None whatsoever, I said. Just a big land grab going on here. And a sky grab, too.

I can remember when that hillside used to be a pasture. Now it's a development of 10,000-square-foot houses, each one sitting on a quarter-acre lot. Cheek by jowl. An upscale development, we call that. And it's unbecoming. Tragic loss of what was once a spirit-lifting landscape. Thanks to folks like me, it has turned hideously ugly.

Noon

I've drained the bird bath, and I'm going to use it as an altar to hold each day's object of contemplation. Just stare and stare until the right words come to me. Today I have this maple leaf turned prematurely gold, blown from its mooring on the tree overhead before it got to ripen. Turn bloodred. Look at its extended palm, each of five fingers fed by five separate arteries emerging from the withered stem. Each of these lifelines tapers, subtly, as it reaches out to feed its finger's far extent. Its fingertip. Then the incredible mesh of tiny capillaries. Branching out like roads in some overbuilt, congested suburb.

Levittown on a leaf.

Every household, each last cell ultimately served. This is like the most amazing highway system ever.

I see the remains of several mishaps, too. Scars from tearings, lacerations. Warts. Pockmarks. Bumpy galls. Perforations and abrasions where some bug or growth has dined. These are carried proudly, though. Unflinchingly, as if—

Must take this phone call.

9:00 P.M.

Something upsetting happened tonight at the nature writing group. Erin brought "a friend" along. This tall, skinny, rather intense-looking guy named Kyle Hess. An old acquaintance, she said. But there's always been a rule that we're supposed to be a closed circle. Strangers aren't allowed to come in off the street. We've built a sense of trust, we've worked through each person's fears about sharing work. Moved past our feelings of shyness with each other. Our vulnerabilities. And for her just to . . .

So this Kyle character. Early thirties, I would say. Dirty blond curls like frayed dreads. Darting eyes like green marbles. He starts laying in to some of the entries that we're reading to each other. Rachel's, especially. And Kiki's. He starts going off on how their writing sounds too precious. Not sufficiently engaged in true experience. A grab bag of perceptions that amount to self-congratulation for being sensitive.

And we haven't even come to my stuff, yet.

Schuyler closed his notebook, midway through. He's not about to let this stranger rag on his fiancée. He stares at Erin as if to say, *What the hell?* And Erin tells us that she thinks it's time to shake things up. Our workshop has become too safe. Too comfortable. Too predictably supportive. But, says Schuyler, affirmation is our chosen style. It's our group dynamic. We have reached this place together. Erin says that sometimes as the leader of a writing group, she has to take a risk to address some underlying needs. Asking Kyle to sit in was just that gamble.

Then Erin asks us, Don't you know—doesn't *any* of you know—who Kyle Hess is? The California forest activist? The author of *Leaves from Mendocino*?

This rings a bell with Lauren, who asks if he isn't the guy who wrote an essay in *Orion* about the foundations of environmental consciousness. Yes. That was him, all right. Erin tells us this is a man who has spent years immersed in Green causes on the West Coast. In the *movement*. We just sort of sat there, dumb. You may not agree with everything he says, she tells us, but it is a privilege to have Kyle

Hess with us, sharing. When he discusses writing, he speaks with a passion and commitment we can learn from.

At that point I excused myself and said I had to run an errand. Get to the copy shop before they closed. Contracts. It must have been obvious, though, that I would have done anything to leave that room. Sort through my feelings about staying in the writing workshop, now that its agenda was about to get perverted.

I mean, I paid $800. I want more than an eco-conscious mind fuck.

I thought the purpose was to make us into better writers. Better observers and recorders of the world around us.

So now I'm sitting by the telephone, fuming. Jotting down my thoughts—my specific grievances—before calling Erin. I'm going to tell her we should meet to discuss what happened. This breach of good faith. She may be a published writer, she may have a string of credits and a sheaf of rave reviews praising her distinctive voice, her angle of vision and her blah blah blah, but the fact is that I'm feeling ... violated.

Violated. By her betrayal of some ground rules that we all agreed to.

Fri. 9/13

Damnedest thing, this morning. I go to meet Erin for coffee on the Church Street pedestrian mall, and first she's like ten minutes late, then Kyle Hess shows up in her place. And he's nicely dressed, he's got his hair combed back, and he's wearing real shoes today. Not the ratty sneakers from last night. And he makes this lame, pathetic effort to apologize to me. I'm really bummed that you're upset, he starts. But I tell him that this doesn't have that much to do with him. Basically he's like an innocent bystander. He could have been anyone that Erin chose to bring along to undermine the sense of trust our group has worked so hard to build. He says something like he knows the way it feels to be vulnerable as a writer. Exposed to strangers on account of words on a page. He knows how when writers share their work, they stand naked. Yearning for acceptance and yet feeling nervous. Self-conscious. Maybe even scared to death.

Then why did you slam those people? I demanded. What have Kiki and Rachel ever done to you?

He launched into a long, impassioned monologue. It sounded like a tape cassette, things I'll bet he's said at least a dozen times before. He said that our era's tragic flaw is an obsession with *appreciating* nature, dilettantelike. At the same time as the ecosystem's going down the tubes. How a smug, bourgeois approach to nature—based on precious observations—can be actually harmful to the planet's health. Because its easy satisfactions blind thoughtful people to the damage going on around us. Every day. Ongoing rape of nature. While we pride ourselves on how well we can describe a flower. Or how flowers make us *feel*. He said we should get up off our asses, take a stand—

Sorry, I said. But we can't all be activists. And there are other ways for people to make a difference. Look at Erin, for example.

I have known Erin for nine years, he tells me. And in that time he has watched what used to be the fire in her flicker out. He says I should have seen her back at Eugene, in grad school. Before she wrote her book and got her little dose of fame. When he met her, she was battling Oregon's research labs single-handedly. Setting free the lab rats. Demanding humane care for experimental animals. He says that it's sad, what's happened. Erin's sweet, satisfied life. The lakeside condo, the two kids. The husband, Bernie—working at a bank, for God's sake. No wonder Erin hopes to keep herself alive through writing. Makes sense. But she has replaced a life of action with a life of words.

Some of those words have been very persuasive, I said. Hasn't he read her book *Peas in a Pod*?

Yes, he says. Of course he's read that. And he says that, granted, Erin's made a real difference. But he is allowed to knock her. She and he go way back.

Tell me why she sent you here this morning, I say. In her place.

He sips his cappuccino, takes a deep breath. Then he gives me what I think must be his trademark look of deep, profound sincerity. Erin just hopes you'll keep on coming to the workshop, he says. Give the group a chance, now that I'm going to be a part of it. Why don't you see if I can bring a new dimension?

Bring a new dimension. Oh, for sure. I'll bet he can. If I stay, I said, you'd better learn a few manners. You can't just go trashing people.

People, no. But their writing, if—

I tell him I don't see the difference.

He gives me this patient smile. Anyway, he tells me, fair is fair. Erin's going to make me share my own work, like the rest of you. Let you have a crack at how I put together words. Actually—

At this point he made a nervous gesture. By some sleight of hand, a folded page from *his* notebook lay sitting on the table. Right in front of me. I wanted to give you this, he says.

I unfold it slowly. And this is?

A sort of poem I wrote. Last night. About you.

I stared at a stanza of his chicken-scrawl handwriting arranged in centered lines. *Wary eyes, yet wide . . .* , it started. I felt a hot color rising in my cheeks. You wrote this about me?

You made a strong impression, he says. Heck, you still do.

I got to my feet, refolded his missive, and stood there for several moments. Awkwardly, I'm sure. Too long. Then I grabbed my bag, because what more was there to say? This Kyle Hess had found a way to get to me, a little. And I could see he knew it. I tossed his poem into my handbag, fished some money out and left it on the table.

Two blocks down the pedestrian mall, I ducked into Borders and went straight to the Nature/Ecology section. Poked around till I found his book of essays. *Leaves from Mendocino.* On the back I saw his photo, sitting high atop some redwood. Bright sunlight filtered down, dappling his expression of intensity and rectitude. And his zest for living—I could see that, too. That rare quality. Like Tom had, before we knew his diagnosis. "This astounding book," the flap copy read, "is a moving testament to the power of a single person's taking determined action in the fight to save our forests."

You'd better order more of these, I told the clerk. There's going to be a run.

Evening

So now I'm glowing. I'm going to copy down the poem Kyle wrote for me. So I'll have it here in legible form, since his handwriting is so terrible. And to have it right where I can turn to it, when I need a lift.

> Wary eyes yet wide, she
> runs two slender fingers through a chestnut mane.
> Winter hair, long and silky. With amazing high-
> lights of mahogany, of kohl. Confident, she
> rearranges her tight body, crosses
> one sleek leg my way.
> Scent of sandalwood, patchouli . . .
> I can't tear my eyes away.
> I think I know all about her. Wanting, though,
> to learn some more. I can see this woman
> has been hurt, but found a way to heal.
> Was once saddened, but then found
> a path to deeper joy. If I had
> another life, I'd start it
> this very minute.
> Sitting here &
> watching
> her.

I don't know how somebody can be that bold. That brazen. Take such risks with exposing his private thoughts. Leaves me feeling really unsure how I should respond.

Except for all the involuntary stuff. The quickened pulse. Shallow breathing. Feeling like the top of my head is coming off.

I'll say this, though: I accused Kyle Hess of hurting people's feelings, last night. But now he's placed himself where I could hurt his. Easily. Totally honest, and utterly exposed. That takes a kind of courage I can't help admiring.

That takes real guts.

And next Thursday kind of seems a long way off.

Sat. 9/14

So here I am, wrapping my shawl around me for another chilly dawn. Discipline of nature writing. Look, observe. Find something special. Then try to put my observations into words.

This morning I am sitting on a branch of the maple tree that towers over my back yard. Not way up in the crown, like Kyle must have climbed to for his book photo. But a good ten or twelve feet off the ground.

Okay, I don't mind admitting that I used a ladder.

I want to sample what this sitting in trees is like. My back wedged against the trunk, I prop the notebook open on my bare knees. *Brrr.* Not a painful way to sit, but not much of a writing posture.

I blow on my hands to warm them. I think I prefer the ground, my comfy Adirondack chair.

All around me, maple leaves are gradually peaking . . . how to set this down in fresh language, yet with accuracy? Dancing tongues of flame surround me when even the slightest wind-puff riffles through this leafy world. Ruffling its fiery feathers. All around, a sense of immolation in slow motion. Gradual, unquenchable internal combustion. Even now, I watch a few leaves cast off from their ancient moorings. Severing the ties that bind them. After all these months of waiting. Finally letting go.

Then dropping lazily toward the ground. Calm.

At ease.

No big rush. No hurry.

Drawn, of course, by gravity. Inevitable, unseen force.

Just like time is.

Tan whirlygig of seedpod breaks away now, falling, too. Helicopters to the lawn.

I think I love everything that falls, tearing loose from what it once seemed fastened to. Bound tight. Attached. Torn away from what it fed. And was, in turn, fed by.

I love watching the instant of separation. Love the rush that comes from watching each leaf's taste of freedom.

Most of my mistakes, I think, have come from hanging on too long. Clinging to one crooked, gnarled branch or another until after the season changed. When the altered length of days should have been obvious. If I just had paid attention.

One twin pair of *leaves* just landed on this *leaf* of my notebook. Joined at the hip. I'm going to *leave* them there. Three-way pun? Or perhaps the suggestion of a deeper connection. Something quite profound. Like Waldo says. Moral facts embedded in the structure of our language.

And I'm going to keep this leaf-pair. Pressed among these thoughts, these hopes and fears that I keep jotting down.

If I were a leaf, I could do worse than falling into Marianna's nature notebook. Then getting pressed shut. Held against its birch bark spine.

Nice place to spend the winter.

Hundreds of thousands of leaves, for sure, on this one maple. I'll bet I can check that number. Maybe there are millions of them. Countless tongues of fire, each one shaking in the chilly dawn.

Shivering.

Flagging the summer's destined end.

Who says that a tree can't speak? We only need to learn to listen.

Sun. 9/15

Maybe I shouldn't have, but I phoned Erin this morning to see if Kyle Hess was still with her. First I apologized for flying off the handle, Thursday. Understood, she said. No biggie. Then I said I wanted to play the real estate card. Maybe hook her friend up with a short-term rental. House-sitting, possibly. Something in the woods, or with a lake view. Someplace worthy of a California nature writer seeking local inspiration.

Kyle's found a housing deal, Erin told me. Lauren Blackwood's going to let him stay with her. On her farm.

So I'm wondering, What's up with that? Lauren always writes with pride about her independent life. Her decisions to be self-employed, self-sufficient, single. I get the feeling that there's nothing any man could do for that woman that her sheep and llamas aren't doing already. All those furry creatures with the comical and kinky names. And that slobber-mouth dog she always writes about.

As if no one else in our group is allowed to write about animals. As if years of training champion horses amounts to nothing worth writing about. Not to mention my shelf of dressage trophies. Trumped by a flock of mangy sheep and half a dozen llamas.

That's unkind, though. Nasty, nasty.

I should be more generous.

Anyway, says Erin, I will let Kyle know you called.

Which is why he phoned me up, later in the day. Just about an hour ago. I got a little nervous when I first heard his voice, but I managed not to show it. He said he was kicking himself to have forgotten that I mentioned working in real estate. That I knew the area. Not that he is flush with cash, but he would have loved to go around with me and see places. Get an idea of what properties are going for.

That made it possible for me to say how touched I was by his poem.

Oh, that, he said shyly. I was afraid you might take it the wrong way.

Not at all. I took it as a beautiful compliment.

This is maybe out of your territory, he says, but he's interested in the new development at Stowe. The one going in near the base of Mount Mansfield. Big condo "hamlet" that the ski resort is putting in. Hundreds of high-end units in a planned village. Being in the business, could I get him certain information? Straight dope, he wants. The skinny. Stuff that only realtors would know.

I said I would try to help, but what exactly did he mean?

How to get invited to promotions, he explained to me. Where he comes from, they have freebies when a big resort hawks condos. Like free dinner if you listen to a presentation. Take a tour of the site. That sort of thing.

I said I could check, for sure. Matter of a phone call. I said I could tell him Thursday night what I turned up.

Too long to wait, he told me. Can't we get together sooner? He gave me his number, said to call him right back if I find out anything. Maybe we could do lunch, he said. Let him pick my brains.

I said I'd get back to him. Then I told him that I thought his book about the redwoods was a special piece of writing. That I had it by my bedside. That I planned to read a couple pages every night, before falling asleep.

Good news for me, he said. I hope you're going to love that book.

7:30 P.M.

Something quite distinctive in the air, tonight. No mistaking. First frost of the season seems certain to arrive. Old familiar chill has been creeping in all afternoon. Bell-clear skies, with fluky breezes dropping off to calm.

It's coming. First night of freezing weather.

Ice.

The end to yet another summer.

Time. The inexorable passing of.

My old obsession.

I should be hustling in the garden right now. Picking the last zucchinis. Covering green tomatoes. But this year my inclination is to let things slide. Even if we get off easy with the night ahead, harder frosts are right around the corner. Bring it on, I'm thinking.

And a long chevron of snow geese on the wing, now. They aren't stupid. They know it's time to ditch this place. Bursts of noisy chatter as they flap their way south.

I light a yellow candle, stab it into loose earth where the snow peas used to flourish. And now I sit here holding solemn, private vigil for the garden's end.

Time to tighten up the house. Clean the woodstove. Dig out sweaters. Time to start remembering how to deal with snow again.

Time . . .

Summers here are short. And yet long enough to just about forget what it means to go through winter.

Candle burning low, now. And the air's completely still.

Each plant like a tiny sailboat, becalmed. Before the winds start shifting.

I do love having long winter hair. A chestnut mane. Highlights of mahogany, of kohl.

I'm ready to welcome an exceptional new season.

Mon. 9/16

6:00 A.M.

Somehow the freezing air held off. Fog rolled in during the night, and everything in this morning's garden is unchanged. Exactly like yesterday. Still green. Still ripe. Still trying to grow.

Thirty-four degrees, we got to. Two degrees of difference between death and this reprieve.

OBJECT OF CONTEMPLATION: GIANT HEAD OF SUNFLOWER

Anyone would have to smile, staring at this long enough. Bobbing like a human head atop its eight-foot stalk. Beaming eye. Or perhaps absurd happy face. Like Emerson writes, you nod to it and it nods back. Proving "an occult relation between man and the vegetable."

Well, it *was* bobbing but I cut it off to place on the birdbath for contemplation. I'm not going to feel guilty—I have fifty more just like it. And the flower that I axed is going to get famous, now. In the pages of my notebook.

Yellow fringe of bright, wispy petals, nearly weightless as compared to the density and heft of the bed of seeds. Thick broad pincushion. Spiraling tan whorls, cunningly arranged in an intricate pattern. Complex geometry. The goal must be for all these seeds to utilize the real estate. Every square inch of it.

Gaudy excess. But I suppose that's what it takes for a barely scented flower to attract attention. Turn a few insect heads. Get some passing bugs to stop in and do their thing. Their inadvertent work. Their gift of fertilizing.

Do the insects know what they are doing? Know, in any sense?

Easy to forget that every flower is a sex machine.

Unbelievable that such a plant grows from a single seed.

Jack and the Beanstalk.

Backside like an artichoke, layer after layer of spiky green petals.

Van Gogh.

Wizard of Oz.

Walt Disney.

Every flower always saying *Choose me! Choose me!* to whatever's flying by. Opportunists. Egotists.

They know something vital about beauty, though. A basic truth. Flowers know that beauty is designed for just one thing.

Tues. 9/17

Rainy morning. Feeling guilty, but I'm going to bag the daily round of nature contemplation.

Not in the mood. Sorry.

Major case of *mal de tête*.

4:00 P.M.

So I got the word from Stowe, and tomorrow Kyle Hess is going to break away from Pleasant Valley to come here for lunch. What the resort has to offer is—well, it's a free overnight at their slopeside inn. But only for reasonably serious prospects. Dinner and breakfast are included. Plus a pass to ride the gondola, and another for the Alpine Slide. All you have to do is agree to sit through a ninety-minute sales pitch, then go on a site tour.

They seem to have high hopes for this development. Whole new village being built from the ground up. Shopping, restaurants, fitness center. Eighteen holes of golf. Anyway, they're going to zap me a brochure. Spec list. Floor plans. Preconstruction prices.

I don't see how I can get Kyle invited, though. This free-night promotion is for married couples only. And both husband and wife have to attend.

Can't see someone like him fitting in there, anyway. Not in Stowe. I mean, nothing about that guy is chic. But at least I'll have the info he requested.

Weds. 9/18

OBJECT OF CONTEMPLATION: TENT CATERPILLAR NEST

Gossamer love shack, custom built for insect orgies. Brothels. Brown naked bodies crawling all across each other. Undulating. Twitching. Shacked up. Come into my tent.

Hairy legs. Striped backs. Moving in their shared, steady rhythm. To a silent beat.

This blighted oak branch has become a caterpillar red-light district. Dive after dive slapped together. Thrown up overnight. Teetering from denuded twigs and nibbled leaves. Peering through the flimsy layers of gauze, I see the same fleshy story being acted out in tent after tent.

As a child, I was paid to spray gasoline on nests like these. Different era. Different values. Probably safer than DDT, though. More environmentally friendly.

I wonder if it worked. That burning sensation, in the midst of pleasure.

But I doubt that caterpillars think of themselves as sexual creatures. Or that they even think of themselves at all. Or that they seek pleasure, in any conscious way.

I mean, "seek."

I mean, "pleasure."

Imagine, extruding a continuous strand of sticky fiber from your derriere. And then discovering you know how to weave with it. That must be a big surprise, the day a caterpillar finds that endless cable reeling out. Then getting down with a bunch of your own kind, all performing this instinctive dance.

They know the steps already. Know each move by heart. How to knit a tent together. Like an old-time barn raising. Hanging out like social insects.

And then to live there, eating leaves and partying till it's time to metamorphose. Change from a brown creeping thing into a pale moth. Time to grow some wings and fly.

Wondering whether these tents are exclusive. Each one just for the use of its own members. Or can anyone who looks the part crawl in?

4:00 P.M.

Maybe I made a big mistake, inviting Kyle here. Putting out the wrong signals. Making it seem as if I'd hop into bed with him just because he wrote a poem.

This modern house Tom built always impresses. So much light and air, but with quiet alcoves tucked along the edges of its hangerlike atrium. Intimate spaces. Lairs. And I could see Kyle approved when I explained about the Green Lumber policy. The energy efficient glass.

Usually when someone finds out that I'm a widow, there's a terrible awkwardness. This black hole opens up in what had been a viable conversation. Or people offer these false, superficial expressions of their sympathy. Not Kyle Hess, though. He wanted to know all about Tom's condition. I wound up telling him more than I like to recall. How my husband suffered from extremely premature aging. Rare and unaccountable syndrome. Like a day of living for anybody else meant two for him. And, toward the end, three. Ironic, because part of my initial attraction to Tom had been his maturity. His seeming maturity. Well, I was seventeen and he was twenty. Though he could have passed for five years older, even then. That became a bad joke when his hair started turning white at twenty-six. When, at thirty-two, his skin was blotched with what looked just like age spots.

What *were* age spots.

Nothing to be done about it. Tom's internal clock was simply running on a different schedule. Double-time. Or faster.

That's something everybody knows how to relate to, though. No two people ever age at the same pace. But Tom's rate of aging was out of the ballpark. Off the bell curve. Way beyond the range of expectation.

Perfectly healthy in other respects. Just that every year he grew much older than the rest of us. Until I was married to an elderly man.

Then, one day, he couldn't bear that. Came home from work early and emptied the medicine chest into his stomach.

I don't blame him. I don't think Alexa blames him, either. Though it left a gap that neither one of us has filled.

Two years ago. Two "years."

This is something I have firsthand knowledge of, and need to keep bringing to my nature writing. If you are a mayfly, you have one day to do your thing. Moths are good for several weeks. A month, perhaps. Songbirds, if they're lucky, may have years to build their nests. Oak trees are allowed to sway a century. Or longer. But all any life really boils down to is the present moment. Each one lived right after the last one. And before the next. Finding ways to seize those moments is the key to well-lived lives. *Inhabiting* the moment. Using each one wisely. Age, time, all our ways to calculate chronology mean nothing if a person's moments are not fully lived.

I think Tom was learning how to do that, toward the end. But then he gave up trying.

I don't judge him, though. Tom's life was far from easy.

Kyle talked about spending a whole month in a tree, once. Thirty-four consecutive days. And nights, of course. Ever since that vigil, he says his sense of time has felt distorted. Off-kilter. But if he had come down sooner, loggers would have moved right in. He said a single day spent in a tree can seem like an eternity. But then so can just a morning. Or an hour.

Or ten minutes.

It all depends on a person's state of mind.

We ate on the patio. Nothing special, soup and salad. I gave him the information Stowe had faxed over to me. He said that I had to understand he wasn't really in the market for a condo. Not anywhere, and least of all at Stowe. In fact, he's quite angry about ski resorts expanding into delicate terrain. Reshaping mountains to suit their profit-driven whims. He thinks what they're doing to Mount Mansfield is a crime.

I said I was more or less inclined to agree. That I have increasing misgivings about large-scale real estate development. Especially in a rural state like Vermont. The long-term price of overly ambitious projects. So why, I asked him, had he wanted all this information?

There's an emerging plan to do something, he told me. Try to stop the madness. At Stowe, and at some other places. There's a West Coast group of environmental activists—Back Off!, they call themselves— that is turning their attention to some projects in New England. He's not a member, but he told them since he's staying here he'd do a bit of research. Basic reconnaissance. That's why he wants to get a tour of this construction site. This new condo hamlet. Even if it means having to sit through a sales pitch.

Thing of it is, I said, this promo is designed specifically for married couples.

He didn't skip a beat. He said we could *say* we're married. I doubt they'll be asking to see licenses, he says to me.

Wait a second, I said. Did you think–?

Just a thought I had. Why couldn't you do this with me?

Wait, I said again. Slowly. Have some respect.

No disrespect intended.

I found a way to back out of where this now seemed headed. If you can't resist making a pass, I told him, that's too bad. That's a sad commentary. But I was thinking professionally. I'm a licensed realtor. I don't do business based on false representations.

I could do the representing, he said. I could wear a gold band. Make us look legit. He nodded at *my* ring, which of course I'm still wearing. For both personal and business reasons. Though more than once I've thought it's time to take off that diamond.

I said, But I hardly know you.

Separate beds? he offered.

I told him this conversation had gone far enough. And that he should go.

Think it over, Marianna. One night of telling a fib isn't going to hurt you. And it might result in something good for the mountain.

That's not much of a pickup line, I told him. Not for a writer.

He said he could only be the person who he really was. I would have to take that or leave it.

And he also said he couldn't wait until tomorrow night. The writing workshop. He wants to see me sitting across the circle.

8:00 P.M.

Later, I sat down to read some more of Kyle's book. I suppose I'm feeling both flattered and frustrated by his coming on so strong. Anyway, I found this passage where he's grieving over some woman that he loved a couple years ago in the "movement." Before her car was run off the road by a log truck. Okay, in his own words:

> *Christy isn't coming back,* I realized with heart-knowledge even before I got the news of what had happened to her. *Christy is a woman that I'm never going to see again.* And all our nights together started melting in my mind into a single night, a single voyage into each other's wide-open eyes. Before us lay the struggle and around us were our foes, but in that perfect night we learned to touch each other for all time. And now everything I do—each tree I manage to save, each forest kept from harm—I do in honor of that woman and our night together. I do it in remembrance of the way our souls made love.

I confess my eyes got moist just now, copying that out. But I don't know if I could stand to love a person that aggressively romantic. Not this time around. Not after all I've been through.

Kyle's perception seems completely on the mark, though. When I think back on Tom, our years together just collapse into a few special moments. And they're not even *real* moments, not like actual events that really happened. Not the kind of moments that a photo album might record. No, it's more like something all compressed together. Made generic. Like a set of icons painted on the inside of my head. Dusted off from time to time. Buffed. And yet never altered.

It's like all the nights *were* one night. I understand that.

I can relate.

Obviously, both of us know too much about grieving.

There is nothing like the feeling of being pursued.

Thurs. 9/19

OBJECT OF CONTEMPLATION: MY (WHITE) BREATH

I'm going to admit that I'm excited for tonight's workshop. I'm starting to grow aware of nature all around me with an energy I don't think I ever had before. It's the difference between looking at things and *seeing* things.

Take this plume of moist air that I've just exhaled, sitting outdoors. White breath. The heat within me suddenly made visible. Manifested. An unspoken word made flesh. And then dissipating (or is it dispersing?) into the surrounding air.

Breathing in something invisible, but all around me. Then breathing it out in a way so that it can be seen. For a while, anyway.

For a while is long enough. *For a while* will do.

I think this is how I want to live my life, from now on. Breathe in. Breathe out.

There.

Who's to say that I'm not getting the hang of this?

Later

Long conversation on the phone with Kiki Johnson. The gist of what she said is that she wasn't that upset by Kyle's critical remarks last week. Not the way I thought she was. Of course, Schuyler volunteered to punch the guy, right after. But she managed to smooth out her fiancé.

Yes, she found Kyle kind of rough around the edges. Lacking in tact, finesse. And perhaps too honest for his own damn good. But she thinks that while he's passing through, we ought to take advantage. Kyle is, after all, an up and coming nature writer. She thinks he's the real deal. We need to be big enough to tolerate his brash remarks. Take them with a grain of salt. And even though we're mostly on the bird-watching end of the spectrum, we can still learn from what this person has to say. This engaged activist. Somebody really committed to changing things.

And I told her I agree. My feelings about Kyle Hess are going through a lot of changes. I look at some things that I wrote about him last week and I shake my head. But it's a familiar pattern. Often someone that I wind up getting really close to is a person who I couldn't stand, the first time that we met.

Stayed up late, and now I'm halfway through his book about the struggles in Mendocino. It's so beautifully and passionately written. Even if the politics were stripped away and tossed, I'd say the man who wrote this is a gifted verbal artist. Highly talented in the field of nature writing.

Maybe not Mister Right, though. That's a whole different matter. But the whiff of proposition isn't so unwelcome, either. Given that Kyle will be joining our writing circle. If he wants to score with *this* up and coming nature writer, Mister Big Critic better cut my words some slack.

And After Workshop—Late

There is something really spooky about how Kyle looks right at you. Something almost spiritual. As if there were not a trace of guile in his searching eyes. And his voice is soft and steady. Kind of like a spoken gaze that lulls you into thinking you have never met a person of such openness. Such honesty.

As if he had nothing to hide.

As if every word he said were true, and came straight from the heart.

I want to write about the tear-shaped dimple that emerges when he grins. A crease appearing right beneath the faint scar that gives his cheek an air of desperate urgency. The clear and unaffected joy when he bursts out laughing. How his rangy frame fills up a chair, even slouching at uncomfortable angles. Something really practical about the way he dresses, too. Blue flannel shirt, tonight. Worn Levis. Hiking boots. Callused, strong hands that are tanned from doing outdoor work. Dirty Band-Aid on one thumb, nicotine stains on the adjacent fingers. Who's still smoking, these days? Who in the environmental movement lights up cigarettes?

I want to put down how a full-blown smile wreaths his face. Stretching its seams until each pore is caught up in the act. Do I sound intoxicated? Then I need to add that Kyle Hess can be an arrogant, insensitive bastard. Someone who takes pleasure in pointing out the faults of others, rather than supporting them. Like what he said about my piece about a maple leaf. *Roads in some overbuilt, congested suburb?* he repeated dryly. Deadpan. *Levittown on a leaf?*

You know, I said. Like when you look down from an airplane.

Why describe nature, he asked, by comparing it to the dreck of human culture? Right in front of the entire group, he asks me this.

And maybe he was right.

I suppose he *is* right. Others in the circle started nodding. They got his point. But I don't see why his offering this insight had to come at my expense. Roger Morton, the courtly older man in our group—a retired science teacher—said he thought I was really describing a circulatory system. Which exist in many natural forms. Like within the human body. Blood vessels. Liver. Kidneys.

Fine idea, Erin comments. That would forge a stronger connection between human observer and the thing observed. Between animal and plant.

Sure, I heard myself agreeing. Like Waldo says. I mean, Emerson.

You've been reading your author? Erin asks me with a trace of surprise. Good for you, Marianna.

Really, it's not that I can't stomach criticism. But there are tactful ways to offer a suggestion, and there are ways that make it grate. Till you just stop listening. Till you'd really like to scream.

Afterward, he wanted to go out somewhere with me. Maybe grab a beer and pizza. I told him he was punching too many buttons. I didn't know whether to like him or to bite his head off. *Love me,* he said. And accept that honest criticism is a kind of flattery. If he didn't care about me, he wouldn't have bothered saying what he thought.

We wound up at the wine bar on St. Paul Street. Very nice. Nearly empty, so we got to sit on leather sofas. And over quite a few glasses of Sancerre, we struck a deal that I'm going to hold him to. I will accompany Kyle—yes, I said I would!—to Stowe. We're going to book a night for that real estate promotion. I'll pose as his wife so he can get his site tour, make notes to pass along to his environmental group.

Nothing of a sexual nature has either been promised or implied.

And for Kyle's part, in the future he is going to let me know *in private* what he thinks about my writing. Not to blab his criticisms out before the whole workshop. He is going to treat me with respect, not make impolitic remarks that hurt my feelings. Even if it means being a little bit dishonest, sometimes. After all, I agreed to tell a fib to help him.

Now I understand the reason he wound up on Lauren's farm. Free rent in exchange for doing work around the place. I didn't realize a published author could be living hand to mouth like he is, virtually destitute. But I guess it's possible. That made me feel kind of sorry for him. Sympathetic. Made me want to help him out. Funny how money, or the lack of it, affects people.

And affects transactions between two people.

When the check came, Kyle tried to grab it. But I said no way. What we drank would probably have set him back a week's book royalties. Not to mention the brie. And the bread, pâté . . .

So I guess we're moving forward with this relationship that came out of the blue. I don't hope for much, but I think it's time for me to make some changes in my life. I owe myself a dose of positive excitement. Soft, heady buzzings of romantic possibility. And at least our hanging out will help me take my writing efforts much more seriously. I might even learn a lot.

Whoa, imagine: *Kyle and Marianna Hess* on a hotel register.

That would be me, I gather. I can see it now.

Fri. 9/20

Kyle told me something about Ralph Waldo Emerson last night. And it rings true by the light of day. When the man writes about "commodity," he really does mean *commodity*. As in stuff. Worldly possessions. People forget that Waldo was well-off, once he got his hands on his child bride's inheritance. That frail waif who died at age nineteen. From T.B. Poor Ellen Tucker just happened to be worth a bundle. Daddy was *très riche*.

Kyle says that Waldo had to sue her family to collect. Eventually, though, the great man made out like a bandit. No financial worries for a long, long time.

And I can relate, of course.

I'm coming to realize why Erin hooked me up with Waldo.

Emerson got used to living really well, says Kyle. Bought the biggest house in Concord. Put on fancy dinner parties. Dressed in fashionable clothes. Year-long trips to Europe. He was a transcendentalist, sure, but he wasn't ashamed of indulging in "commodity." Of learning to enjoy material pleasures.

Material *goods*.

This came up, I think, because the wine was so expensive.

But Waldo's being well-off is no reason to condemn the man, Kyle said. Or was he maybe saying something about me? Because Emerson made it his practice to *transcend* the physical surfaces of life. The *commodity* aspect of existence. He enjoyed that aspect for the pleasures it could bring, but he kept going past it to get in touch with something deeper. Underneath the physical. Or behind it. Or beyond it. Something at the level where each soul encounters Soul.

The question—Kyle's question—is: If Emerson were still alive today, would he be a part of the environmental movement? Or just taking walks in the woods to do his transcendental thing? Getting into his "transparent eyeball" head? Looking at the trees and feeling groovy? Like a nineteenth century acid head, or a raver? Would that be enough for Waldo, if he were alive today? Or would he be actively working to *save* the forests?

I said that Waldo doesn't strike me as an activist. Not, at least, based on what I've managed to plough through. Kyle disagreed. He said the man was a flat-out nonconformist, for his time. A rebel, determined to live his life by principle. Thing of it is, there was no serious environmental struggle in Waldo's time. Nobody fighting to preserve the wilderness, no one digging in on behalf of nature. But Kyle feels sure if Waldo were alive today, he'd be in the vanguard. An impassioned leader in the movement. Crying out to save endangered species. Stop the global warming. Maybe even doing tree-sits and harassing whaling vessels. Getting his hands dirty in the global struggle.

I think Waldo's bank account might get in the way, though. Especially after a century of compound interest. All that exposure to the pleasures of commodity.

And there *is* a contradiction. I can see it in my own life, so I figure Waldo must have noticed it, too. I wouldn't mind seeing the trees preserved, the rain forests. But I also like the Sunday paper, thick with advertising. And I love paper towels when I need to clean a spill. I enjoy having a redwood deck. A cedar sauna. Not that I am trying to be wasteful. But being able to afford the forest products I desire— well, I guess that makes me a part of the problem. All good intentions aside. And it makes a lot of Greener-than-thou types want to run their guilt trips on me.

I'm glad Kyle didn't do that, though. He was sweet, and understanding. Totally sympathetic.

I'm glad, too, that he is showing me how to make sense out of Emerson. If I'm going to read Waldo, it helps to have the kind of insight Kyle brings to him. A way to place him in the modern world. Make him one of us.

OBJECT OF CONTEMPLATION: MILKWEED POD

Mother load of pale white seeds packed like fish scales. Wound around each other fifteen, twenty layers deep. Fertilized bounty just about to burst the seams of this sticky green shell. Candelabrum hook of stem attaching pod to parent plant. Outside rough with tiny spike-lets. Nature's coarse sandpaper. Inside smooth like Neoprene, or patent leather. Waxy.

And the smell is . . . unappealing. Maybe downright poisonous?

Taste is . . . bitter!

Not to a monarch, though. Those guys are on the move, now. Migrating to that mountain they like, down in Mexico. Chiapas. Province of bad hombres. Spend their winters talking Spanish. Hanging out with Zapatistas.

Stay with the milkweed, honey.

Sticky white liquid gently oozing from the woody stem where I ripped this pod away. Murdering, as usual, in order to dissect.

Saturday 9/21

OBJECT OF CONTEMPLATION: MONARCH BUTTERFLY

Okay, so I've caught this flyboy in an empty Mason jar and set it down inverted on the empty birdbath. Monarch under glass. Quick stop for inspection on the long flight south.

What I'm picking up on is the burden it must be to have to carry such enormous wings. Huge. All that powdered surface. Dwarfing the tiny body slung down underneath. Nerve center. Fuselage. One stiff wind-puff and you're out of control, bud.

Intricate pattern of orange cells, rimmed in black. Eyes tipped with black mascara. Kohl. Hundreds of white dots speckling the outer edge. Who devised this painting? Why?

Not at all like the design of a sunflower, trying to pack in the next row of oval seeds. That pattern had a function. This one, on the other hand, seems a pure aesthetic. Something by Miro, or Pollock.

Flexing his bright wings back and forth. Eager. Revving up. So I'm going to let him go.

There. Bye, now.

Safe journey.

Miles to go before you sleep.

After Lunch

Kyle called me up this morning, apologized straight off for the short notice. Then he asked me if I knew how to operate a camera. Not just a point-and-shoot, but something bigger. Something fairly complicated. And if I did, would I be willing to fly over Stowe with him tomorrow? Not in an airplane, but a lightweight glider.

Soaring.

He has a license. He has done this quite a lot, out west. Thought he had a partner lined up, but the person bailed. He wants to photograph what Stowe is doing to the mountain.

I said it sounded like fun, but I had three appointments. Two of them are typical "just-looking" clients, never really satisfied. But not the kind of people you can ask to go away. Much time in my line of work gets wasted this way. Situation where you put in way too many hours. Too much hand-holding. So that the commission, if you ever close a deal, works out to what you might have made by pumping gas. But number three is quite an interesting prospect. IBMer and his wife. Brought up here from Fishkill. Been renting, but now they want to own a home. Three kids, a German shepherd—they need lots of space. And there's a good chance I can show them what they're looking for.

Work with me, Kyle pleads over the telephone. Aren't there other agents who could take that off your hands?

I am trying to manage a career, I told him. Which means showing up, when I say I'll show a house. But . . .

I like that word, he tells me. Keep going.

But I owe a colleague a favor, and I'll make a call. Maybe Sally Hutchins will be able to fill in.

And Sally said she could. She's only had a so-so year, needs some luck to rebound. If she lands this, *she* will owe *me*. I'll get a chunk of the commission, anyway.

Kyle says to be at the airport south of Morrisville by 10:00 A.M. Right off Route 100. He likes the weather forecast. And this far into foliage season, he says the mountain ought to look terrific from the air.

Great day for flying, he says.

All right, so, I guess I know I'm taking quite a chance here. No doubt. Admitted. I am not unwary. But I like how we have started walking this way together. I think this could turn out fine.

Sun. 9/22

Ohmigod. Whoopee. Hooray. What a perfect day for flying.
And what a perfect flight.

There's a silence when you're soaring that is truly . . . transcendental. No engine noises to disrupt your thoughts and make you too aware of why you're held aloft. Eerie quiet. Silence. Pure float. And, every now and then, the sweetest hum of throbbing wings. Like a ruffling of the feathers.

Makes you think that airplanes are a failure when it comes to giving humans what we envied birds for, all those years before we flew. All those millennia, trying to get off the ground.

Soaring. I mean, wasn't that the point?

And to swoop, to glide. To corkscrew in a warm updraft, rising just a few more feet with each twisting turn. Each revolution. Climbing an invisible ladder in the sky.

That flight took my breath away. And I have only just now started to catch it.

Kyle was right about Stowe. They've made a real mess around the base of Mount Mansfield. Never seen such a fleet of earthmoving machinery. I made a photographic record, which may help environmentalists call attention to what's going on. The price of all this "progress." That was a footnote, though, to the day's unstoppable momentum. Its ecstatic lift. The sheer excitement of our bright and positive adventure, cruising high above a landscape filled with trees that seemed on fire. Giant red flowers. Decked out with zillions of quaking petals. Ripened leaves.

And we metamorphosed into raptors as we soared, I told him. Hawks, or eagles. Peregrine falcons. We became, the two of us, a keen-eyed bird of prey.

Funniest thing was to see some of the workshop members picnicking on the mountain's Nose. Lauren, Roger, Schuyler. I got a picture of them. Hope it turns out well.

Afterward, I told Kyle if we're going to masquerade as man and wife at Stowe, I don't want that night to be the first we spend together. I want to know how to be with him. What to expect.

He tried to tease me, then. He reminded me that I had dumped on him, a week ago, for coming on too strong. For being forward.

Times have changed, I told him. I am ready to take this to the next level. Say, tonight?

Nice invitation, he said. Tantalizing offer. But he had to get these rolls of film to someone's darkroom. He needs prints for the people who paid to rent the glider. There was a timetable. What we had been doing was important to a larger cause.

What about tomorrow night? I asked him. Or on Tuesday? I cannot believe how out-there I can be with him. How upfront. He makes me feel like just asking him for what I want.

Let's go with tomorrow, he said. Your place?

I said 8:00. And I told him to come hungry.

I felt him embrace me, then. And I still can feel it now. How he squeezed his arms around my waist, gave a sudden lift . . .

Amazing updraft.

I went soaring.

I haven't forgotten who I am, or what I'm doing here. What kind of journey made my life-path intersect with his. When I take a deep breath, things are well under control. I can manage this, as I have managed so much else before. I know this. I really do.

But I'm still not ready for these feet to touch the ground.

Mon. 9/23

OBJECT OF CONTEMPLATION: WILD TOBACCO (MULLEIN)

This astounding phallus only rises where the ground is rough. Or rocky. Packed with hidden pitfalls. Where things are, by any fair standard, less than fertile. Even in a drought year, though, it heaves this five-foot stalk out of the ground as though it loved the soil. And the last twenty inches look like just one thing.

Pornography of botany. Some days, I see this adult content everywhere.

Nature is the ultimate peepshow. Free admission, too. All you have to do is show up, keep your eyes wide open.

Tobacco in what sense? Does anybody smoke this? Indians, maybe? Native Americans?

In a pipe, or cigarettes? Cigars?

And which parts?

I should maybe try that, sometime. Smoking on this giant penis. Find out what it does to me. See what it can do.

Evening

Okay, for the present Stowe is running these previews just on weekends. So their prospects won't have to breathe diesel fumes. They had a space open for this coming Friday, and I nabbed it for Kyle and Anna Hess. Makes sense to disguise my name to some extent, since I am also in the real estate business. You never know who you might run into, later.

Husband in this couple is an up-and-coming writer, I told the person taking information on the phone. And the wife comes out of money, princess from a horsy Philadelphia family. Main Line. Devon. None of this, of course, was specifically untrue. Except the married part.

I said if this couple really goes for what they're pitching, it's a lock. Instant closing. Signed on the dotted line. No lengthy follow-up, no weeks of phone calls before getting to yes.

Now I'm feeling . . . well, flirtatious. What I'm planning for this evening is a little dress-up party. Just the two of us. Testing what we'll have to wear to get our "married" look together. Learning how to pose as a credible man and wife.

And in Stowe, no less. Which may take a bit of doing.

Been going through a closet of Tom's sports clothes, throwing all these wardrobe choices out across the bed. No guilty feelings. Fact is, Tom would almost certainly approve. And be glad to see me finally getting out. Moving ahead with things. Moving toward the future.

If I believed in heaven, I could see Tom sitting up there watching me. And smiling. That outrageous smile that he used to have.

He'd like me for this.

Tom always loved a good time. Practical joker, too. Nothing was more fun for him than pulling the wool over somebody's eyes.

Fabulous chateaubriand on the kitchen counter, soaking up the marinade. All thanks be to Howie Cofer at the Chopping Block. Three bottles of a terrific Umbrian merlot.

This will be an interesting evening.

I say bring it on.

Tues. 9/24

Ouch, what a hangover. Morning object of contemplation . . . *not!*
Moments distilled from the long night:

1. Kyle is a vegetarian—yikes, why didn't I think of that?! I must be a knucklehead. Why didn't the likelihood even cross my mind? But he was so gracious. He said it was his personal conviction, but not a totally restrictive philosophy. He could make exceptions. And for this occasion, in view of what I'd cooked for him, he wouldn't feel bad about tasting some cow. Then he took one teensy portion of some of the best meat I have ever grilled.

2. The way he wanted to join hands with me before we ate. Share a silent blessing. Grace. A moment of thoughtfulness in honor of the creature who had died so we could feed ourselves. Nourish our bodies. It was a little much, but touching just the same.

3. His amazement when he learned I used to teach dressage, had even trained a few champions. Before a pelvis-cracking spill made me hang it up. His unabashed respect when I took him in the den and let him see my trophies. This, he said, is something I would never have guessed about you. I didn't see it, somehow. And yet it makes perfect sense.

4. His panicky concern that I had altered *my* name for the Stowe

junket, but that he would be down in their books as Kyle Hess. Anything else you told them? he asked. About me?

Yes, I said. I told them you're an up-and-coming writer.

He let out a mournful and self-deprecating groan. You had to?

Well, I said, they do ask questions. About people's occupations. Income levels. Assets. Put yourself in their position. Wouldn't you want to know?

No problem with the date. In fact, Friday is extremely timely in view of Kyle's overall purpose. Plans being made by the environmental group that he is doing this research for. But he's worried that at some point Stowe could trace his name back to his book *Leaves from Mendocino*. Then they'd wonder what a West Coast forest activist had been doing hanging out at Stowe. Sucking up the good life on their corporate nickel.

I told him one of us had better be able to prove who he really is. And if he was so concerned, he should have told me sooner. Anyway, given how I pitched us as a couple, I'd be surprised if what he fears becomes an issue.

5. How funny he looked in an Izod shirt, L.L. Bean khakis, Orvis loafers. Not that Tom's clothes fit him all that well. We agreed to go shopping tomorrow night. Filene's. What can he do about his hair, though? I asked gently. Short of breaking down and going to a barber. Maybe he can find a conditioner to rein it in, make those curls manageable.

By around midnight, though, we had ourselves looking like a plausible couple. Standing side by side before the bedroom mirror. Not perhaps the most compatible of marriages, but, hey. The kind of marriage where each partner sets the other free. To do some personal exploring, midlife reinvention.

6. All right, the sexual dimension of the evening: Seemed to be heading in a plausible direction, until Alexa phoned—late—to get a vet referral for Sir Whisky. The Morgan doesn't like some plant that's growing in the prep school's pasture. Starting to get colicky. But this call came at a really bad time, given that I was partially undressed. Taking a breather between wardrobe changes.

Maybe kind of tipsy, too.

I worry about you, Mom, Alexa told me in her shy voice. Was I slurring? She said, I'm afraid you'll get too lonely by yourself.

Doing fine, I told her. But it's late. I need to get some sleep.

Kyle sat across the bed, listening to the whole thing. That put a damper on the physical exploration. Things went far enough, though, that I'm feeling comfortable with him. At ease. I like the way he smells, and how his skin feels. Still, we agreed to chill our hormones for the time being. Bank that fire. What's the rush?

I could see him thinking, Whoa. This lady's not some average chick. There are other people in her life. Responsibilities. This woman has commitments.

Terribly ironic, getting busted by your own kid on the verge of doing something frisky. Isn't that supposed to work the other way around?

7. Sleeping and/or not sleeping with him for a few hours. Not that long, though. Warm. Friendly. Side by side.

8. Kyle's taking leave at five in the morning. An hour before I get up to keep my journal, even. But he's got this complicated writing project underway. He's vowed to feed it daily.

He has discipline. He has self-control.

Lauren, I gather, cracks the whip at noon to make him do the chores he's taken on. Make him pay the rent.

So that was that. Oh, and Kyle told me this hysterical story about getting a llama to pack for him. On the trail running from the state park in Underhill right up the mountainside. Up Mount Mansfield. Late at night he tried this, when he felt sure Lauren wouldn't wake up and bust him. How these precious llamas that she writes about are actually dumb, obnoxious animals. Stupid. Mean. Recalcitrant. Hard to make one stay on course, even with a lead and halter. How this llama spat right in his face, when he urged it on. That's what he calls direct communication.

Nothing like what he saw in Chile, trekking in the Andes. Something about Vermont—or is it just Lauren Blackwood?—has made those llamas stubborn.

I'm turning stubborn, too, the more I get to know this guy. I think I've seen something that I want. And I am going to get it.

Weds. 9/25

FIRST FROST—THIS NEEDS TO BE REALLY GOOD, FOR SHARING
TOMORROW NIGHT

I can't say this tragedy of cold was unexpected. Still, it's chilling to see every shred of vegetation cased in white. Every blade of grass. Each whisker on the fringe of every leaf. Each flower petal.

Frozen solid. Iced.

Twenty-eight degrees, at dawn.

Then the warmth of gradually emerging daylight, as if the sun were peeking out in shame at what had happened. What it had allowed to happen.

Shamed. After treating us to such a lengthy summer.

Just a few degrees of warmth would have stopped this tragedy.

Where were you, I ask the sun, *when these leafy legions fell? Affirming life's fragility even as they lie here prostrate. Blackening. Decked.*

I know the answer, though. The days are growing shorter. Several fewer minutes of light each passing day. One right after the next.

These things add up.

Darkness has usurped the light.

Now the ice is slowly melting, every place that's not in shade. But it's not as though these flattened stems are going to rise again. Limp. Buckled. Cell walls shattered by the force of freezing water. Punched out. Devastation everywhere. Beyond reviving.

Bow down to ice, then. Cruel master, stepping in to lord it over half the year. His half. The cold one.

Each of us is now required to kneel and kiss the whip of winter.

9:00 P.M.

Took Kyle shopping tonight, and got together the basics of a plausible wardrobe for Stowe. Casual, sporty clothes with halfway decent labels. Credible enough.

He did manage to do something with his hair. Got the kinks out, and even combed a ragged line that parts it down the middle. More or less on center.

Not yet ready for a spread in *Town and Country*, but we make an interesting couple.

Something less than dashing.

He put on a gold band that looks kind of official, too.

Mother's going to go a little nuts when she sees I passed us off as living at her old address. Deal with that later. Whole adventure has a sense of craziness about it. Manic. What a clever way to serve environmentalism.

I'm not going to let Kyle drive his junker van anywhere near Stowe. Will pick him up in Waterbury, Friday. Leave it parked right there.

I suppose the ultimate joke would be if we wound up with a condo.

Thurs. 9/26

OBJECT OF CONTEMPLATION: BARN SWALLOW (DECEASED)

He crashed into the sliding glass door sometime yesterday, and I found him lying on the deck when I got home. Crazy little kamikaze. These birds usually zip about with reckless joy, skimming ground contours at Mach 1 speeds. Showing off their hair-trigger responses. Each a top gun. Not just a matter of running down the bugs, either. Scooping up the next meal. No, they seem to take professional delight in wild aerobatics.

How awkward, then, for the one who made this fatal boo-boo.

Terrible miscalculation.

Not a credit to his race.

Imagining how the point of impact must have felt. Sharp tapered beak slamming into plate glass. Full speed ahead—ouch. Yellow bill stove in. If he lived, he would have had one heck of a headache.

Maybe it was death by migraine.

Impact knocked the crap out of him, too.

Licorice velvet feathers. Dark beady eyes, staring. Curled twig-claws, clutching nothing.

One less pilot to fly circles in the sky.

Late—After Workshop

Well, I didn't do too badly with my impassioned little weather report. Glad I didn't try to read the dead bird passage, though. Because everything that people shared tonight got swept away by Kyle's taut description of a dying sheep. This happened on Lauren's farm, I guess the other day. I mean, it was a flabbergasting piece of writing. Such amazing empathy. What a heart that guy has. Astonishing mind, too. Completely original responses to the world around him.

And I let him know I found his requiem remarkable. Totally moving. Actually, every one of us said the same. But I still don't think we did his piece sufficient justice. He smiled shyly, thanked us in a soft voice. Then, a minute later, he got up and left the room. Before the workshop was even close to finishing.

Felt like we were only half a group, once he shut the door. Diminished by his having gone. And, for me, a sense of feeling suddenly lonely.

Not for long, though. Off to Stowe with Kyle Hess tomorrow.

Fri. 9/27

OBJECT OF CONTEMPLATION: RING FINGER (MINE)

What bizarre cultural debate wound up choosing *this* digit for commemorating, advertising marriage? Broadcasting who might be available, and who is not? Index finger, baby finger, "fuck finger," thumb . . . all these candidates got dissed. Every one of them.

Left hand . . . oh, I get that. Closer to the heart.

The body's general symmetry. And its odd *a*symmetries.

After thirty-seven years, this nail's still in decent shape. Long, but gently rounded. Tapered, but no talon.

Clear lacquer polish. What you see with me is what you get.

I remember how Tom used to rub his penis on this finger, after we'd have sex. Polishing the ring, he'd tell me. With this compound we had made. This special juice. Epoxy.

Dying, he said a time would come when I should take it off. Not sure that I can, though. The knuckle has grown thicker. Stiffened. All these signs of middle age.

Bet I can still crack this knuckle . . . *ouch.*

Lucky to have found a guy who wants to make believe we're married. Might just be the best of possible worlds. Maximized pleasure. Minimized chance of pain.

I love the way this finger tells the world I'm not looking. And I love how that didn't slow Kyle down one bit.

So I think tonight's the night.

One thing Kyle advised me when we shopped for clothes the other night was to bust out of this early morning journal habit. My excessively anal approach to nature writing. You should have that notebook with you everywhere you go, he says. Carry it around all day, tucked inside your handbag. Pull it out whenever something hits you. Be spontaneous. He says I am apt to make a lot more progress going at it that way, than by what I have been doing.

So I'm going to toss you in the suitcase with the skirts and sweaters, dear nature notebook of mine. Slide you in beside a little black dress. High heels. You're about to turn into my constant companion.

Sat. 9/28

Crack of Dawn at Stowe Hotel—After Having Done the Deed

WHY SEX IS A VIABLE MODEL FOR HUMAN PLEASURE . . .
>   Thoroughly convivial activity. Nurtures creative interaction
>   with another person.
>   Simultaneous focus on external and internal versions of reality.
>   (Waldo would approve.)

Classical plotline. Rising action, etc. (Less said here, the better.)

Reinforcement of our creaturely origins. And how as humans we have managed to go beyond them.

Reminder that all life is life in the body. Got to wake up, face the music—this is where we live. So be kind to this amazing home, capable of giving so much pleasure.

AND WHY IT IS NOT . . .

Pangs of introspection in the midst of what needs to pass for focused sociability.

Perception of vast distances between external and internal realities. Actually, more like a chasm.

Classical plotline as curse. A constricting mold. Discouraging creative spontaneity, invention.

Reinforcement of our creaturely origins. And how poorly we've succeeded in transcending them.

Reminder that all life is life in the body. This is all we have. And when we fail to take pleasure there, we fail badly.

Just a few early morning musings, sitting out on the balcony of this hotel room. Kyle couldn't sleep, so I gave him the car keys and he's off driving somewhere. Maybe going to see if he can walk around the "hamlet" site. Check it out by dawn's early light. I watched him pin his name badge on, in case somebody stops him. That way he can prove he has a good reason to be there.

Really, this is working out as well as it could from my perspective. Not from that of Stowe Resort's sales team, however. Last night after supper, they brought the dozen couples who are here for this promotion into an alcove off the inn's main dining room. Coffee and dessert. Liqueurs. Then they turn the lights down and Vice President Pinstripe turns on a computer. He launches into a PowerPoint presentation: "What Makes a World-Class Four-Season Resort?" But the damnedest thing happened. Kyle went to the buffet, and no sooner had he come back with herbal tea than this odor began to sweep across the room. A truly vile smell. Disgusting. Like warmed-over death.

I think they eventually tracked it to the coffee urn. The one filled with decaf. But by then the innkeeper had ordered us to clear the room. Well, that's not exactly true. The room pretty much cleared out by itself when that stench started wafting toward us. Growing stronger by the second.

One woman at the table next to ours got really sick. All over her silk blouse.

Maybe something in the water? That's what the couple with whom we had supper were speculating. Software developers from Houston. Marge and Larry Frost.

Ten minutes later, they cleared the entire restaurant.

So there was chagrin on the faces of the sales team. Trying to recoup, they broke us up into groups of four and took us out to various pubs along the Mountain Road. We went to Mr. Pickwick's. Ron Horton, the rep assigned to work with the Hesses and the Frosts, laid out the fine print about the quarter-share concept they're pushing here. Allows people to get in for low six figures, but they only get to use their condo thirteen weeks a year. Or about one week per month, spread out across four seasons.

That would be enough for us—wouldn't it, honey? Kyle asked. He reached for my hand and stroked it tenderly. I could see Ron salivating.

Then we started talking about summer activities. Fly fishing, biking, horses. Horses were of interest to me. Ron insisted that I let him make some phone calls in the morning. Get someone to give me a tour of the Topnotch stables. Maybe Edson Hill, too.

Later on, back at the inn, they had a new agenda. We're all going to ride the gondola this morning to the Cliff House restaurant, just below the mountain's ridge. Fancy brunch up there with a panoramic view. That's where they'll give us the presentation that they had to cancel after dinner. Then the promised site tour, and we're out of here by noon.

Before hanging it up for the evening, I told Ron I couldn't help feeling sorry for him. All that enthusiasm, all that buildup. Then to be defeated by a bad pot of coffee. He agreed, though, that the smell was atrocious. Kyle said he hoped there was no metaphoric implication, nothing of symbolic import. Ron grinned and nodded. I don't think literary terms are big in his vocabulary.

Then Kyle turned to me. Honey, he said. Isn't it time we went to bed?

That was last night . . . sweet dreams. Now on to the day ahead.

Sat. Evening—Back Home

Comedy of errors continued throughout the day. First they get us all up in the Cliff House restaurant. Then their gondola somehow breaks, and we're stuck there. Stranded. Sales presentation goes on and on, but everyone can look out the window and see why they're stalling. Only other way off the mountain is a long hike down. And none of us is dressed for it.

So much for going to see the nearby stables.

Finally they figured out what had caused the breakdown. With some trepidation, we got back in the gondola cars and rode down the mountain. By now, most of the customers wanted to get on the road. There were only six of us to tour the "hamlet" site, which is what we came for in the first place. The whole point of our charade.

That was okay, though. Kyle took lots of photos, asked a bunch of questions. Midafternoon, we're in the car and set to go. Ron said he'd be in touch, but I could see he had no serious expectations. Can't imagine a promotion going more pathetically.

They need to tune up their act if they want to move some units.

This really ticked me off, though. Dropping Kyle at his van, I pop the trunk lid and find this sheaf of blueprints. Underneath our luggage. I was incredulous. Did you take these? I demanded. When? What for?

Took my own site tour early in the day, he told me. There was no one in that trailer they use for an office.

But that's stealing.

He didn't argue with this. Call the cops, he told me. Deadpan. Then he said, Come on, Anna. They have more than one set of blueprints, don't you think? And these will really help the people who want to make a case against what Stowe is doing. Show the full extent of what they're planning to build.

My name is not Anna, I said. And if you'd been caught—

But I wasn't. Was I?

No.

So forget about it. He grabbed the blueprints, tossed them in his van. Okay, I'm a bad boy. Sorry. You weren't bad, though. In fact, you were great.

Are you coming on to me?

He put his arms around me. I just want to thank you. This was fun, yes? Good time?

Good enough. I squeezed him back, though I felt more petulant than playful. So when will I see you?

Any day now. Any night.

Pick one.

I can't now, he says. I'll have to call you. Busy.

See what you can do, I told him. I'm kind of busy, too. But I'll make the time.

He twisted off his ring and put it in his pocket. He climbed into his van and fired up the engine. Blue smoke. Rattling valves. Then, with a blown kiss, he was on his way.

So, that's it. The story of my overnight as Mrs. Hess. Next time I see him, I'll insist on being Marianna. And if we go out together, maybe I should bring a watchdog. Otherwise, one of these days he'll get in real trouble.

Now I'm thinking I could get in real trouble, too.

Sun. 9/29

OBJECT OF CONTEMPLATION: GRASSHOPPER (MALE) FOUND IN
POSTFROST GARDEN

So I saw him going at it with this lady grasshopper. On a dead tomato. I reached down and plucked him off. You are so busted, buddy. You need to learn about coitus interruptus.

Look, we're almost into October. There has been a frost. A hard one. Killing. The lawn party's over. Too late to knock out babies. Think what kind of world they'd be born into. Ice and snow. Cold days and endless nights. Give it a rest, already.

I feel like a vice squad officer.

Oval eyes staring at me from either side of his long, narrow face. Looks as if his cheeks are clad in chain mail. Busy little mandibles chomping at the air. Delicate antennae flexing back and forth. Waving at me. Trying to get a fix.

Since he refused to hold still, I have placed him underneath a glass tumbler on the birdbath. My fingers stained with the tobacco juice he spat on them. Sticky little pads on the end of each toothpick leg. Hanging upside down comes easy, for a bug like this. Even on a surface that affords no purchase.

So brilliantly adapted. But fragile. Now he is my captive, under glass. Imprisoned. Trapped. I've got him where I want him. Mine to observe to my heart's content.

Feeling just perverse enough to keep him here awhile. Horny little critter. Wondering how long till he gets hungry, or has to pee.

I think he'll be good till lunchtime. Hang in, buddy. Maybe after one or two more journal entries I'll release you.

Later—Still Obsessing About Stolen "Hamlet" Blueprints

I'm not getting over Kyle's little crime easily. Really stupid risk to have run. And if he'd gotten caught, it might have blown up in *my* face. Plenty of things I admire about Kyle Hess, but obviously he doesn't know where to draw the line. Know when he should back off, quit.

At one point toward the end of *Leaves from Mendocino*, he writes about the futility of trying to accommodate "the forces of evil." Meaning, specifically, the West Coast lumber interests. No compromise, he says. Even to negotiate with those who would destroy the planet is an unacceptable retreat from principle.

I think that's a little much. I think there are often ways for people on two sides of an issue to find common ground.

And I can't help wondering, now, how far he might go. Any way I slice it, Kyle broke the law the other day. And it was deliberate. With malice aforethought. Idiot, thinking he could cruise that construction site and rip off a set of plans. Does he think they'll fail to notice?

Makes me worry that he's lacking some basic instinct. Caution. Common sense. I mean, this is Vermont. This is not northern California. We are not "out west." Not living in some paradise for hotheads. No, we're not. I'm sorry.

This is a place where people play by the rules. Obey the law. Respect their neighbors.

And caring for Kyle as I do, I need to have this out. I don't want to see him go and make a big mistake.

Mon. 9/30

6:30 A.M.

Damn. Forgot the grasshopper trapped beneath the tumbler. He's still here, though. Waiting for the nature writer. Patient.

What choice does he have?

There.

Free to roam again. Even hump the odd lady grasshopper, if inclined.

Flew away without a care, as though some complicated puzzle had just been solved.

Probably taking credit for that right now. Telling pals about his incredible escape.

I've got to cool it with these anthropomorphic riffs. Insects, these are. Mindless bugs. Programmed by evolution to do this and that.

Hard wired.

So I'm feeling self-reproachful, I might as well confess. No good reason to have tortured that fellow creature. Locked in a glass prison all day, all night long. Wouldn't want to have somebody do that to me.

Wouldn't like it one bit.

He hardly seemed to care, though. Infinitely patient with his fate.

Little masochist.

Insects are simply not operating on our level.

Change of subject: If Kyle doesn't phone by noon, I'm going to call him. We are at a stage where this relationship will stall if we don't keep it moving forward.

Worse than just a stall. We are apt to lose what we've both invested in each other. And though we certainly have our differences, it would be a shame to write this off as a loss.

Tues. 10/1

New month. Month of autumn.

Nothing that I feel moved to contemplate, this morning. Just to sit in this familiar chair and feel the world turning. Earth cocked on its axis. Gearing up to shove a change of seasons down our throats. Ready or not.

Whether we like it or not.

Okay, he didn't call me and I didn't call him. Standoff. Was that one night it?

No. What's going on between us *has* to mean more than that.

7:00 P.M.

Here comes another bizarre romantic escapade. Kyle phones me up, completely *begs* me to meet him at the state park in Underhill. Eleven p.m. tonight. If the clouds hold off, he says there ought to be enough moonlight.

For what? I asked him. Can't you just come here?

No. He can't. He's doing some kind of complicated project, and it needs my expertise. A horse trainer's professional knowledge.

Former trainer, I said. I gave up that line of work.

No matter, he says. The question is, what do I know about handling llamas? Getting them to take a halter without putting up a fight. Following a lead without having to be dragged and scolded.

I said it was out of my realm of experience, but that there were principles of horsemanship that might apply.

What I thought, he told me. Score.

But eleven's past my bedtime.

Take a nap, he tells me. I am counting on you, Marianna. Please?

So I told him I would be there. Proving again that I'm a glutton for punishment. Look for the llamas at the gate, he told me. Three of them.

How is he going to sneak three llamas off Lauren's farm?

Need to get some shut-eye before heading out on this adventure.

Weds. 10/2

8:00 A.M.

What I half-suspected: The thing about llamas is, you really have to be gentle with them. Like with a high-strung horse. Can't just throw on a halter and expect them to climb the nearest mountain. First you need to stroke them in all the right places. Building up a physical relationship. A sense of trust. And you have to talk to them softly, in a soothing voice.

Then they'll work their hearts out for you.

So he had these llamas in the back of his van, and the tack was with these friends of his in their little Subaru. Big man, tiny woman. They wanted to learn about llama packing, too. I told Kyle he was apt to get on Lauren's bad side if she ever heard about this. He might even find himself looking for a place to live.

I'm not worried about Lauren, he said to me. I can take care of her.

So we got them harnessed and hung the panniers from the frame saddles. All the while, I'm pointing out where to touch these animals. And how to do it. Curry comb and brush. Then hands. Back, belly, withers. Then around the head. The face. That petite woman got the hang of gentling right away, and once we had the llamas relaxed Kyle and the big guy—Eddie—started picking rocks off the ground and loading them into the saddlebags. The panniers. Until they were bulging out. Then we set off up the trail to Mount Mansfield, each of these three handlers leading his or her own beast of burden.

Still night. Calm air. Nothing stirring in the woods except our little caravan.

Downright chilly, too.

But perfect visibility, thanks to moonlight in Vermont.

Kyle says that when he went to South America, he saw llamas that could carry half their own body weight. High up in the Andes, where the air is thin. He says they can trek all day without the least complaining. But when we hit the first really steep stretch of trail, the lead animal ground to a halt. We tugged and coaxed, but no dice. After that none of the llamas was inclined to move. And nothing I could do would budge them.

Then I realized the frame saddles had slipped backward on account of the trail's pitch. The angle of the mountain. What they needed was some britching, like a breast collar to hold the loads in place. Something else, I realized as we moved the saddles forward. The pannier on each side needs to weigh about the same. Otherwise, the lopsided load can make a llama balk. Like when a backpack rides off center and digs into a hiker's back. Who wouldn't stop to fix that?

By that time, though, this trio of wanna-be Bolivians figured they had had their fun. For one night, anyway. We emptied out the rocks, turned the animals around, and led them back to Kyle's van. They jumped in, no problem. Then this other couple drove away, and I was left with Kyle.

Doing something later? he asked me with this sly grin.

Well, I said, it's late already.

Follow me to Lauren's, he said. Help me put the animals back in the pasture. Then I'll show you where I'm living.

I said I didn't want Lauren to find out about us. Certainly not to suspect that we're a couple. I'm not all that fond of her, and I want my personal life to stay private. Not become a source of gossip.

Park at the pick-your-own, he told me. Walk up the driveway to the second cottage. There'll be a light on. And a sign—Golden Delicious. I'll get you out by sunup.

So I saw this rustic cabin where Kyle's living on the cheap while he finishes his current writing project. All about how human culture intersects with animals. The various ways that we depend on each other. How we've coevolved together, and whether that is really such a good thing. Which shows, pretty clearly, why he's gotten on this llama kick. Gathering experiences so that he can write about them.

Maybe what he's doing is a whole lot smarter than how I try to describe a leaf or flower.

He lit a fire in the fireplace, dragged the mattress from the bedroom, and threw it down where we could watch the sparks. The flames rising. Crackling of dry logs. And later, dying embers falling on their bed of ashes. After we had done what we could to take the chill off.

I gave Kyle my curry comb and brush, so he can work around the llamas anytime he wants. Making him their master. Gaining their affection. Trust.

Sneaked out at the crack of dawn, with Lauren none the wiser . . . ha! Although I don't think I'll risk going back there again. Pulled a few ripe carrots out of her organic plot, hosed them down and then nibbled on them as I drove home. Sweet. Chewy. Earthy tasting.

And ohmigod tomorrow's Thursday. Not one entry from this past week seems fit for sharing. But I'll take another crack at it tomorrow morning.

Maybe I should rethink my priorities, or give this up.

No. I have a writing tutor who may be in love with me. I mean, he did say as much. I just need to settle down and work with my new teacher.

9:00 P.M.

Big wind beating up whitecaps on the bay tonight. Tearing limbs from shoreline trees and whipping them across the yard. Good thing the llama expedition went down last night.

Wind to shake the world . . .

Now a sudden cloudburst, too. Huge fat raindrops pelting the glass.

And hail. *Rat-tat-tat.* Icy pebbles strafe the roof.

Where do insects go when nature turns and bites them this way?

What do the butterflies and grasshoppers do? The caterpillars writhing in their gossamer tents?

Tomorrow they will be the walking wounded, I suppose.

Crawling wounded, that is.

But wounds heal. Most of them.

If I were courageous, I would write for tomorrow night something about gentling a llama. Read that out loud in front of the writing group. Put it right in Lauren's face.

I would never do that, though. Does that make me a coward?

Thurs. 10/3

CARROT VERSUS STICK

A dubious distinction, since in many ways they both look like versions of the same thing. Length. Shape. Tapering. Mild flexibility.

Carrot bristles with fine root hairs, put there to suck food from dirt. How a tuber makes its living.

Stick is longer, obviously. Pebbled with a million pinholes. Insect damage. Half a dozen twig eruptions, too.

Here's a major difference. One you eat, and one you beat with. Or get beaten by. Different kinds of motivators. Whiff of sadomasochism. Fundamental choices here.

Which do I prefer? I think the carrot. Orange, chewy earth-food. Moving toward a positive pleasure. Not just dodging pain.

Love, a carrot. Time, a stick.

Given a choice, I would prefer reward to punishment.

Though it might take both to get a llama up a hill.

4:00 P.M.

Here comes trouble—some guy calls the office this noon, says he's in charge of security at Stowe. Where the resort has experienced a rash of recent incidents, he tells me. Vandalism. Theft. Wasn't I the broker who referred a certain Kyle and Anna Hess to them, recently? For a free night on the evening of the twenty-seventh?

No way of ducking that. Hess . . . you mean the writer? I tried to sound as if my memory was hazy. And that horsey wife of his?

He said they had so many incidents last weekend—dirty pranks that sabotaged their sales promotion—that he was attempting to verify who the guests were. And this writer fellow, Hess, did turn out to be an author. Just like I had said. Thing is, this head of security went down to Bear Pond Books and found something Kyle Hess had written. Did I happen to know what he wrote about?

Sorry, no, I told him. These were just some people that our firm was working with, a while back. Looking for a hideaway in Vermont. They seemed well-off.

It's a book, he said, about monkey wrenching. Out west.

Monkey wrenching? I repeated. I don't understand.

Someone dropped some chemicals into a coffee urn, setting off a smell that made us have to clear a meeting room just as our sales presentation was beginning. Someone found a way to cut the power to the gondola, stranding our people at the Cliff House. Survey stakes were yanked out of the ground at the golf course. Someone broke into the site office and walked off with a set of blueprints. These are all examples of what is known as monkey wrenching. And it started just about the time Kyle Hess arrived.

Whoa, I said. Bad news.

I guess the good news is, this episode is over. But that guy had better keep the hell away from Stowe. Which brings me to my next point. Our efforts to track this couple down have gotten nowhere. Bogus phone, bogus address. E-mails bounce right back. They seem to have vanished.

Very odd, I told him. Since they seemed like such good prospects.

Even called the publisher of this guy's book. They have instructions not to give out his whereabouts.

I wish I could help you, I said. But you're way ahead of me.

I just thought these Hesses might get back to you, at some point. If they do, call me right away. Day or night. You got that?

Yes. Of course. No problem.

And if you have more hot prospects for us, think twice. Would you?

I said I stood chastened, and apologized in case this Kyle Hess turned out to be their culprit. He hung up, and I sat there shaking at my desk.

Idiot. I should have known.

So now what to do?

I need to buttonhole Kyle at tonight's workshop, that's for damn sure. He needs to know the people there at Stowe are on his tail. Stupid, stupid. How could I allow myself to be so used? How could I have witnessed that weekend's chain of screwups and not put two and two together? Even *after* finding stolen blueprints in my trunk?

This is going to cost him something. Kyle may need to get the heck out of town.

I must be an imbecile.

Imbecile or not, I see that this is going to cost me, too.

10:00 P.M. —After Workshop

And he wasn't even there tonight, the stinker. That's my current name for Kyle Hess. Then Rachel Katz—I can't believe this—Rachel reads aloud this piece about climbing up a ski lift in the dark, using all her mountaineering skills to poke around the structure. Hand over hand down the cable, searching for a splice that might indicate a weak point. Clambering over the bullwheel, checking how its tension weights are hung. She wrote as if she had been contemplating sabotage. Trying to discover ways to damage this machine. Break it. Make the whole thing junk. Because it didn't belong on the mountain, she said. Wasn't part of nature. Was a symbol of how nature gets defaced by humans.

I've always liked Rachel. More than once I've thought how it's amazing that our workshop's most no-nonsense, focused member is also the youngest. I mean, she's just twenty-seven. And I admire Rachel's style of writing, too. Crisp and pithy. Energized. Filled with sharp details from her wilderness adventures. And yet now I'm wondering, What is up with her and Kyle? Because the way I figure, he *couldn't* have shut down Stowe's gondola. Not while he was sitting right next to me at the Cliff House, listening to those sales people ramble on and on. Was she in cahoots with him?

Is she in cahoots?

Erin was trying to have a Big Message night, but most of what she said struck me as off the mark. Or off the wall.

Much impassioned writing about last night's windstorm. Although none of us seemed to nail it perfectly.

Lauren was having an emotional evening. This past week, one of her llamas had a stillbirth or abortion. Or something. She was broken up about it. I had to hide a smile, thinking of the fun we had with several members of her herd one night while she was sleeping.

Home to find a message on the phone from the stinker, saying how important it is that he talk to me. A.S.A.P. He's going to wait up late, et cetera.

Uh-uh, mister monkey wrench.

Later for that.

Fri. 10/4

So he came over here at midnight, banging on the door till I broke down and let him in. I know you're suspicious about Rachel, he says to me. I know what she read tonight at writing group. About a ski lift.

How would you know that?

Because I talked to Erin, after. Marianna, listen to me. I know what you're thinking.

Do you? I asked angrily. Do you know I had a call from somebody at Stowe today? They know all about one Kyle Hess, a recent guest precisely when a bunch of shit began to hit the fan. They went out and bought your book. Now my ass is on the line.

All I did was borrow some construction plans. By now, the people that I took them for have sent them back. Every sheet.

After making copies, no doubt.

He didn't dispute this. He said knowing the full extent of what Stowe's doing might prove crucial to saving the mountain. And so documents were needed. Official blueprints.

How did you empty the restaurant? I demanded. How'd you make that stink?

He said he had nothing to do with that. He promised me.

What about the survey stakes yanked from the ground?

He said he didn't know about that, either.

Who broke the gondola?

He said maybe Rachel had some kind of involvement, but he wasn't sure. And he had no knowledge as to how the breakdown had occurred. Look, he said, I'm not the only person who is pissed at Stowe. Plenty of environmental groups would like to take them on. He said he'd done his share of "direct action," out west. He knows how these people work, the ways they orchestrate a full-scale campaign. Only one person ever understands the total picture. People aren't supposed to know who else might be involved. They're supposed to keep their mouths shut. Less risk that way. For everyone concerned.

For all I know, I told him, you could be the one in charge. You could be the ringleader.

No, he says. My only role was getting certain information. And I did that, with your help. For which I'm most grateful. But I have no further involvement. Stowe is not my battle. I have a book to write.

I suppose I wanted to be convinced, but hesitated. How did Rachel know what time to break the gondola? I asked.

He shook his head. Ask her.

Well, I might just do that. So you better watch out.

Rachel is someone who I hardly know, he told me. I've only talked to her a couple times, at writing group. I think she's intelligent, but it wasn't smart for her to read that piece about a ski lift. Not in front of everyone. She needs to learn discretion.

What are you doing here? I asked him. It is after midnight.

I need, he says, to borrow five thousand dollars.

Really? And you thought I'd have that?

Well, he says, I *know* you have it.

And you thought I'd give it to you?

Something really terrible has happened, he said. To one of Lauren's llamas. One that we—

Oh, no. I had a sinking feeling. The one she said aborted a ten-month fetus? You don't mean we took a pregnant llama up the mountain? With a hundred pounds of rocks hanging off her back?

I had no idea she was pregnant, he says. But I did this—I'm responsible. I haven't told Lauren what happened, yet. But when I do, I want to pay her for the damage.

Lauren gets five thousand dollars for a llama?

When they're sold as livestock guards, yes. She told me. Anyway, it's just a loan. Thing is, I'm a stranger here. I don't know where else to turn.

Maybe it shouldn't be just a loan, I pointed out. I might be as responsible as you. Or nearly. I should have noticed if an animal was pregnant.

He tells me the money has to be in cash. Because he doesn't have a bank account on this coast. And he doesn't want Lauren to see a check signed by me, and know where the money came from.

I took a deep breath, then agreed to help him out.

In, like, a couple days?

I told him I could get the money by tomorrow. Drop it off in Pleasant Valley on my way to Putney. This is Fall Parents' Weekend. Couple days I've set aside to spend time with Alexa.

And then we . . . well, this is supposed to be a nature journal. I won't go into everything that happened next. This is what was left, though. Torn bed sheet. Pummeled mattress cantilevered off the frame. Pillows bent all out of shape. And two people wrapped around each other, waiting for the dawn.

The thing is, when the chips are down I trust this man. I *keep on* trusting him. He finds ways to make me do that. And that is the main thing. The fundamental truth. As for my petty rants, my moments of suspicion, my episodes of nearly flying off the handle . . . well, I have forgotten what it's like to fall in love.

11:00 P.M. —in Putney

So I got the money from the bank and ran it over to him. Lauren was gone for the afternoon, Kyle told me. Some important business that she had to do in Stowe. He walked me all around, showed me various fix-it projects he's been doing to pay the rent. In the llama pasture I went over to the dam who had aborted. Claudia, that's her name. I stroked her face gently. Offered my apology.

Kyle is still broken up about what happened. I don't need this money back, I said, until your ship comes in. Which I'm pretty sure it will, when he finishes his book. The one about the animals.

Then it was on the road for the next few hours. Coffee reception in the school's new gymnasium. Two boring speeches before I could take Alexa out for dinner. With her roommate, Celia. Sweet sort of hippie girl from Marin County. Turns out they're both taking a lit course titled "Man and Nature." The reading starts with Emerson and goes up to modern writers. Wendell Berry, Annie Dillard, Rick Bass. I asked them if they'd ever heard of Kyle Hess.

The tree guy, said Celia without a moment's hesitation. The guy who fights to save the redwoods.

Have you read his book? I asked her. *Leaves from Mendocino?*

Not yet, she said. Although her mom sent her a copy.

Well, I said, I think he's quite an interesting writer. Sort of a contemporary Emerson. Philosopher. Idealistic, spiritual. And an activist, of course. But basically he's like a modern transcendentalist.

I think he looks hot, she tells me. You seen his photo on that book? Up in a treetop?

Hot, hot, hot, agrees Alexa. And I sat there, nodding.

Sat. 10/5—Putney

Gorgeous sunrise. Early morning ride with the girls. Bridle path drifted over with a million fallen leaves. Red-orange mosaic. Felt like I was drunk, or something. High. It's been so long since I last got on a horse. I promised not to, after my bad fall. I swore off riding. But God, to feel those gaits between my legs again. To move in time. It got to me.

Sir Whisky is looking mighty fine. Worth every penny. Earlier digestive troubles seem to have settled down. Beautiful leg structure, confident moves. Still more horse than Alexa knows what to do with, but she does seem on the way. Someday, she'll be one with him. I say good for her. I say hoorah.

Nice conversation with the riding instructor here. Different generation, but we had a lot to share. He was familiar with Sir's grandsire, Frigate. Seen quite a few good Morgans from that bloodline.

Nice to be reminded of how breeding will out.

OBJECT OF CONTEMPLATION: FROST ON THE PUMPKIN

Plump orange head with whitened surface dimples, creased . . .

Shit. I really stink at this. And I only brought the journal with me because Kyle said to. Maybe if I'd left it home I wouldn't be so frustrated.

Not going to give up yet, though. There's a writer somewhere in me, and I have to set her free.

9:00 P.M.

Really bad coincidence tonight, at a reception in the headmaster's house. This tipsy-looking man comes up and says I recognize you, weren't you at Stowe last weekend?

Which there's really no denying, so I said I was.

Jack Harmon, he says. And you would be?

Marianna Finch. This is my daughter Alexa.

He just stares at me. And I'm thinking, all right, was he one of the resort's people? Or just another prospect looking for a condo? Now I realize I'm sweating.

Man, was that a comedy of errors or what? he asks me. We try to put our best foot forward, look what happens.

Sales team, I think in rising panic. Then he tells me he's the manager of the inn we stayed at. In fact, he's the one who made the call to clear the restaurant. Well, I tell him, there'll be other weekends. Other customers.

Is your husband here? he asks me.

No, I say. He couldn't make it. He's been awfully busy lately.

Alexa gives me this funny look.

Same thing with my wife, Jack says. Don't you love this school, though? I'm so proud to have Benjamin going here.

And we made more small talk for a few long minutes, then I managed to excuse myself. What was that? Alexa asks me sharply. About Dad?

I don't think just anyone should know that I'm a widow, I said. And I didn't want that creep to start hitting on me.

I've never seen you tell a lie before, she says to me. Just to stand right there and lie to someone. Wow.

But Alexa's feelings are the least of my concerns. If Jack Harmon has a brain, he'll check and find that Marianna Finch was *not* a guest at Stowe. Then he'll maybe find out I'm the person who referred Anna Hess, along with her troublemaking husband. The nature writer. Author of . . .

I figure in the morning I'll take the girls to breakfast, then get the heck out of Putney. Before something else happens.

Kyle needs to be informed they're tightening the noose.

Sun. 10/6

Drove straight to Underhill and didn't even care if Lauren Blackwood might be there. Although it turned out that she wasn't. No sign of Kyle, either. Then that tiny woman who was llama trekking with us came walking down the driveway. Ellie. Said she saw my car pull in. Paint-spattered smock, paint on her hands and smeared across one cheek. She was in the pasture, at an easel. Likes to work in oils. Turns out she is living in another one of those rustic cabins. Mirror image of the one that Kyle rents. Here for the foliage season.

Kyle's gone soaring, she tells me. Over Stowe. With Lauren.

To hell with that! I wanted to shout. But I just said that I would leave him a message. Turned out that his door was locked, so this woman says to give my note to her. She'll see that it gets delivered. I tear a sheet out of this notebook, make a few brief points as strongly as I'm able to. One: that he has got to keep the hell away from Stowe. Two: that we need to get our stories straight, before somebody comes by my office and starts asking questions. Three: that I really need to see him. Soon. For our sake. For the sake of our relationship.

Soaring with Lauren. God.

So I seal this in an envelope, walk out in the pasture, and hand it to this Ellie woman. Now I'm home, it's early afternoon. No news. Nothing on the answering machine. Not much for me to do but sit around and wait. And worry.

10:00 P.M.

Still no word from Kyle.

Reading Waldo's private journals all evening long. Shows a whole different side to the man, which I find amazing. And, at times, horrifying. Well, there's this horrific scene in which he opens Ellen's tomb. After she's been lying in it, dead, for fourteen months. Grief-stricken. Right out of his mind. To the point where he had to see how she was doing. Check how much she had decayed.

I can't imagine ever doing that to Tom.

How come people think of Waldo as an optimist, a booster for the human spirit?

What did Waldo see? What was there left for him to see of Ellen?

Now I am remembering a creepy line from Waldo's *Nature*. How he writes that even corpses have a certain beauty. That was not some abstract thought, I see now. Not mere speculation. Sad, heartsick guy. Waldo knew exactly what he meant.

Mon. 10/7

OBJECT OF CONTEMPLATION: OVERRIPE/ROTTING TOMATO (BIG BOY)

Black on wrinkled red tissue. White fuzz tufting from the black. Mold-floss eating a membrane of dead skin.

Touch it oh so gently. And then watch the pale juice stream out. Bleeding.

Two weeks ago, I would have happily put this same tomato in a salad.

Something to be learned here. But it's not an appetizing lesson.

First you ripen. Then, if left unplucked, you turn overripe.

Better to be plucked on time and eaten. So you nourish something.

But something here *is* being nourished, after all. Something low and spore-producing. Turning red-ripe flesh to goo.

Waldo, Waldo. Fourteen months? You waited too long.

4:00 P.M.

I have called Rachel Katz and said I want to talk to her. Said I have some thoughts I want to share about the writing group. She has to work till 8:00, but then I'm going to meet her in the Old North End. At her place.

I'm going to find out what went on that day, at Stowe.

Still no response from the soaring man. The saboteur. Is this any way to treat a woman who coughed up five grand?

Tues. 10/8

I guess I realized that Rachel was strapped for cash. Still, I wasn't ready for the squalor of her three-room pad on North Winooski Avenue. Low rent district that, if Burlington's city planners had a lick of sense, would have been razed by now. Bring in the wrecking crew. Make way for something halfway decent. Fit for habitation.

But she has expensive toys that clutter up the squalid digs. High-end fiberglass kayak. Fancy mountain bike. Piles of camping gear, top of the line stuff. And a small fortune in climbing equipment.

On the rickety table where she keeps her notebook, I spy a copy of Kyle's *Leaves from Mendocino.* I pick it up, turn it over to expose his picture. Don't you think he looks intense? Rachel asks me.

I tell her he looks like what my daughter would call hot.

Not in an ordinary way, she says. What makes Kyle hot comes from someplace deep within. Commitment.

She hands me a mug of all-organic chai, and I sip at it. Yuck. Kyle's "commitment" may have gotten him in trouble, I say. And I think you might know why.

I don't understand, she tells me.

Listen, I said. Someone broke Stowe's gondola on the morning of the twenty-eighth. Shut it down for over an hour. I was there, stuck at the Cliff House. And so was Kyle. There was a sales promotion. He was posing as somebody who might buy a condo.

Interesting, she says. I had no idea he was there. Were you with him?

No, I said. Coincidence. I *am* in real estate.

How is he in trouble?

Stowe has figured out who Kyle is. They've got his book. They know he's an environmental activist from California. They've got a good idea he was involved in this. They're going to track him down.

She looks at me, unimpressed. She just doesn't get it.

I say, Maybe if the person who actually broke the lift would come forward—

Oh, so you're accusing me?

I know what you read about at workshop, last week. How you spent a night climbing around on a ski lift. Planning different ways to break it.

Considering, Rachel said. Fantasizing. But not planning. Then she stood up and dumped her chai out in the sink. Do you like tequila? she asked, setting out shot glasses. Lime wedges. Salt. And Cuervo.

I say I've been known to drink that. And we proceed to get ourselves intoxicated, while all the time she's talking a blue streak. Shaing secrets. Spilling beans. What is going on at Stowe is bigger than I realize, she says. There are many players. Even the resort knows that no one person could have had a hand in all that has been happening. If they try to nab Kyle, they'll lose. He's a coyote. But this campaign to screw with Stowe's expansion is winding down, anyway. All of this will soon blow over. Because in a way it's been a ruse. Just a big diversion. Series of pranks to throw their people off guard, keep attention misdirected. There is bigger quarry. Something huge, and more important. Something right beneath their nose.

Which is what? I'm wondering. What more could they want to do? Burn down the Cliff House? Tear up the Alpine slide?

You want to know how I stopped the gondola? she asks, and I see her eyes are glazed now. You really want to know?

I just think if someone would come forward with the facts—

I blew the operator. She laughs. A business deal.

Now I can't help laughing, too. That's a whole lot simpler than I thought, I say. And no one caught him?

He said there was trouble with the wiring. A circuit breaker.

Does Stowe know about this?

Sure, they know. Not who turned the power off, or why. But they know there wasn't any damage. And they know it wasn't Kyle's fault, that's for sure. Just a case of operator fuckup. So to speak.

Well, I said, that's good to know.

There might a place for you, she says. Now that we're speaking frankly.

Place for me in what?

The movement. This campaign to save the mountain. I could hook you up with someone who is way involved, if—

Kyle isn't way involved?

Actually, no. He's way off on the fringe of things.

I said that was very helpful knowledge, and I thanked her for it. As for my own involvement, I'm just going to try to keep Kyle out of trouble. Keep him from being punished just because he did some things a while ago in California. And then wrote a book about it.

It was late, and I had gotten more than I had come for. I told Rachel that I'd see her Thursday night.

8:00 P.M.

He called—he told me Ellie made a huge mistake. That painter woman totally forgot to give my note to him. She means well, he says, but Ellie can be a ditz. Single minded. Self-absorbed. A typical artist.

Anyway, he thought I wasn't getting back till last night. Late.
Coming over in an hour, so I've got to straighten things.

Weds. 10/9

OBJECT OF CONTEMPLATION: PENIS (RATHER TIRED/FLACCID)

As it lies curled on this sleeping man's inner thigh. In repose.
Cyclops, spent. Nest of wiry black hair. Pink wrinkled skin of testes.
Fat central artery looping down the central shaft. This is where the
blood courses. Triggering the miracle. All things coming in the fullness of time.

When the time is ripe.

How, even asleep, it wanes and waxes to some inner rhythm. Always in a kind of motion. Never staying just the same from one moment to the next.

Breathe in, breathe out. Blood pumping patiently. Keeping time. A
kind of music.

No wonder it's referred to as a sex *organ*.

Ripe times, swollen like my heart and close to bursting. This is
where I want to be. And who I want to be with.

Afternoon

So this is where things stand: Kyle's going to send Stowe a letter of
apology for borrowing their blueprints, admitting that he loaned
them to an activist outfit that has made themselves a watchdog over
Northeast ski development. He has a way to have this letter sent from
California, so they'll have a bona fide address to work with. But one
where they will not find him. After that, he's pretty sure the whole
thing will blow over. He promised that he wouldn't show his face
again in Stowe.

I am going to get a serious makeover, then stick by my original
story. Made a date for that tomorrow. Hair and change of makeup,
new outfits, everything.

Kyle says the last person he wanted to soar with was Lauren Blackwood. I believe that. Soaring with his landlady, for God's sake. This taskmaster, who'd rather make him fix a leaky roof than let him write his book. But in view of Claudia's abortion and everything, he wanted to smooth Lauren out. Actually, he confessed and made his restitution to her while they were in the air.

But he's had about enough of living on that rundown farm. He's ready to entertain a different situation. Someplace closer to Burlington, and me.

I told Kyle the gist of my long conversation with Rachel Katz. He said he had no idea what this major action was that she kept dropping hints about. How, for that matter, loose talk is dangerous for people in the movement. He really is too far out on the perimeter to know what's coming next. But then he broke down and said the late-night llama trek was not just a way to get some anecdotes for his new book. Actually, he has something else in mind. Something harmless, but a way to make a creative statement.

What would that be? I asked.

And so I got him to lay out his big plan: One of these nights, he wants to pack some huge banners into one of those llamas' panniers. Large, heavy streamers that are readable from miles away. Then lead the animal up that trail—Sunset Ridge—and attach the banners to the broadcast towers on the summit. People will discover them the next morning, at the peak of foliage. Out-of-state tourists everywhere. And the banners will have words on them like SHAME and DISRESPECTFUL. Maybe phrases like NO MORE TOWERS! or TAKE ME DOWN! Slogans that will really call attention to what's going on there. Up on the mountain's Nose.

I said it sounded like he'd talked too much to Lauren Blackwood. Taking on her pet cause. Trying to ride her personal hobbyhorse.

Actually, no, he says. He hasn't told Lauren anything about this. And not just because it means borrowing a llama. She's too much the pacifist. No way would she buy into this in-your-face plan.

I said it sounded like a pretty cool idea, if he could pull it off with no chance of getting caught. Keep to a strict schedule. Get a llama up there some dark night, get the flags attached, then get off the mountain by the crack of dawn. Have the llama home by sunrise, grazing in the pasture.

That's where you come in, he tells me. You can be the llama handler. You understand how to keep a packer moving.

But I already showed you everything I know.

I'd feel much better doing this with you, he told me. And Kyle can be quite persuasive, when he wants to be. I said for sure that I would think about it, let him know. He told me not to think too long. This thing might happen soon. Possibly on short notice.

Well, I said, I'm used to that. The only way you operate.

After this, though, he's just going to work on his book.

Thurs. 10/10 – Really Good, to Read Tonight

THE FULLNESS OF TIME

No need to contemplate a natural object, since nature manifests itself as much in unseen things as in the visible world. Time . . . you cannot see it. And you can't hear it, touch it, taste it. You can't smell it, though this autumn air *is* laden with a potent whiff of memory. Special odor to the shifting planetary gears. Familiar. That's not the same, though, as actually smelling time.

And yet time does keep unfolding. Always. All around us. Time is the precondition for all other sense perception.

Living time. Time spent knowing we're alive.

I used to hate to think of passing time, the clock's ticking. I used to think of time as measuring finitudes. Mine, and those of other people. Days that would not come again. Reproaching me for words unsaid. And for deeds undone.

Time for me was not ripe, then. Time was a painful yardstick. But in the fullness of time, I've learned to give up counting. Stop paying attention to the surface *tick tick tick* and look beyond it. See that transcendental plane beyond the clock face. Where time is the very oxygen we breathe. The pure air that sustains us. Making all things possible.

In time's fullness, there is nothing that we cannot do.

Later–After Workshop

Kyle said he's coming over, but not till later. Late-late.

Funny how tonight people hardly recognized me, with my new look. I can hardly recognize myself, for that matter. Pixie haircut, penciled eyebrows. Whole new me.

New prescription sunglasses on the way, too. Ferraris. I'll bet I could go to Stowe and no one would mistake me for that Anna Hess woman.

And yet—sadly—this is not the face that Kyle wrote me that beautiful poem about. The face that moved him, that first night. That face had to go, though, to lend credence to a fiction that our mutual attraction caused.

A fiction that our love required.

Speaking of works of fiction, Kiki read this piece about making believe she was pulling out survey stakes on one of her bird walks. We just sort of sat there not knowing what to say. Then she confessed to making everything up, but it shows how Kyle's vibe has started galvanizing people. Everybody trying to think like an activist. Finding imaginary ways to strike a blow for nature.

Kiki is a bird-watcher, for God's sake. Kiki hasn't got an activist bone in her pale Nordic body.

Lauren and Erin both in some kind of distress. Worried glances back and forth between them, all evening long.

Is there a signal people send out, when they are in love? Even sitting opposite each other, in a room of people? Everything I've done with Kyle has been totally discreet, yet people seemed to be looking at us differently. Glancing instinctively from one over to the other. Sensing a reality that lies beneath the surface.

Fri. 10/11

Found out that it's on for tonight, the llama-banner caper. I told Kyle that of course I'd come along with him. Wouldn't want to have him make that trek all by himself.

Not much of a weather forecast. Evening showers, maybe a significant rainfall. Followed by a clear, cool morning. But there is no such thing as foul weather. Only people who haven't learned to dress appropriately.

Plastic bag to keep you safe and dry, dear notebook. In the nylon daypack.

So it's almost time. As in the fullness of.

The ripeness.

Saturday's shaping up to be a perfect day, he says. Clear and sunny, once this front goes by. Once the clouds have lifted.

Come tomorrow, all eyes will be turning to the mountain. Just as I'll be crawling into bed with Kyle Hess.

Sat. 10/12

2:45 A.M.—Trapped in Weather Station on the Nose of Mount Mansfield!

All right, let me put some facts down for the record. Didn't plan to make *this* kind of journal entry, but I'm going to get my side of the story down. Before this bad night is over.

Night of horrible betrayal.

Item one: There were *three* llamas again this evening, not just one of them. Three llamas, and four of us. Kyle, myself, that big guy from the other night—Eddie—and that Ellie woman. The petite painter. Not exactly the "date" that had been advertised. And whatever they had stuffed into those saddlebags, it didn't look like banners. Not to worry, Kyle tells me. Wires and rigging to support his streamers in the wind. Bad weather coming, but we move out. And by midnight I have coaxed this pack train all the way up the mountain. An incredibly difficult and tiring feat. Stupid me. And when we reach the top, the others start high-fiving. This guy Eddie lights a joint. And then . . .

Item two: Rachel Katz walks out of this weather station, built into a Quonset hut near where several towers are clustered. I ask, What the hell is she doing here? And she says she's an integral part of the plan. She had a job to do, and she has completed it. No worries about the ski lifts, she tells us. They won't operate tonight, no matter what goes down. We can blow up stuff all night, she says. No way can anyone get up the mountain, short of hoofing it. Not likely, in the rain. Something has been done about the Toll Road, too. So now I'm yelling *What the hell?* and . . .

Item three: They start opening the panniers and pulling out all these explosives! Lots of heavy tools, too. Huge set of socket wrenches, two giant sledge hammers, various drills and chisels. Army flashlights. Flares. They break into the main garage of this Quonset hut, get their gear arranged, and Eddie starts spewing out this demolition lingo. Like we're in Vietnam or something. Rain beating down so hard I think I'm going crazy. I grab Kyle by the shoulders, shake him, ask what's going on. He says, well you didn't think we'd go to all this trouble just to hang a few banners, did you? And then . . .

Item four: When I refused to cooperate, Eddie pushed me into this weather-recording booth and slammed the door. Jammed a steel beam against it. Threw me in a prison cell, with nothing but an old computer sitting on a built-in shelf. Not a scrap of furniture, else I'd heave it through the window that lets me look out and see, from time to time, what they are doing. Those maniacs. What they are doing is blowing up the broadcast towers. One, two, three of them so far. A fourth is set to go.

One of those towers fell a stone's throw from where I'm standing.

Rachel Katz is right in the thick of things. She's in this with them. Lying little bitch.

I must be an idiot. The world's biggest fool. To think I thought this was a man who cared about me. Wanted me. *Loved* me, dammit.

Banners, my ass. I've been assisting eco-terrorists. Monkey wrenchers. Saboteurs.

And someone's going to pay.

6:00 A.M.

All quiet as the sky turns light. We're in a moving cloud, though. Cold, drippy residue of last night's storm.

Four towers toppled over, here on the Nose. I can see each one. But the really big tower next to the summit station still looms through the first-light mist. Erect. Unharmed. That one is anchored by a web of steel cables. I bet they tried their best, but couldn't bring it down.

How long will they keep me here?

Has everybody gone?

6:15 A.M.

Heaved the damn computer through the window, and I'm out of there. Free. No one is in sight, so I'm going to walk over to the Summit Station. Cautiously. Maybe there's a phone I can use there.

Now I realize this written record might just save my neck. Documentation. Proving that I had no part in this.

Not knowingly, at least.

So. Each detail matters.

Time: 6:20. Going to climb the Nose's peak to look *down* at the Summit Station. Make sure that the coast is clear.

6:35 A.M.

Dead llama blown to smithereens along the trail. Looks like it got hit by a bomb, or something. Yuck.

I took my life into my hands, leading those llamas up here.

Somebody is still here on the mountain. I can hear a hammer banging, just beyond the rise. Find a way to check that out without being noticed.

6:38 A.M.

Sitting right on top of the Nose now, looking down. I see Rachel Katz beneath me, working on the anchor point for one of the support cables to the giant tower. She's whacking a sledge hammer where the cable meets its base. Trying to drive a pin out.

Now I see that all the other cables have been disassembled. Driven from their anchor points. And I think that's why she's having trouble with this last one. Each blast of wind makes the whole tower shake and shiver. In between gusts, the cable slacks off just enough to let her budge that pin.

Two llamas not far off, grazing stunted shrubs. I wouldn't want to be anywhere near that tower.

Where are the rest of them? Where is goddamn Kyle Hess?

Rachel's got it—timber! Jumps back, catlike, and I—

7:15 A.M.

Now I've stopped my shaking, sort of. Crouched against the Summit Station door. Waiting for what's next.

For whatever's coming next.

Let it be recorded here that Rachel Katz is dead. I shouted when I saw the tower toppling, and she looked up at me. That's when the slack cable jerked like a living thing. Wrapped around her, lightning-quick, and grabbed her. And would not let go.

Action and reaction. Physics.

Mangled steel scattered now all across the mountaintop. Broken wires. Plastic. Glass. Llamas took off down the mountain, getting the hell away.

Saw it all from up there on the Nose, in slow motion. Heard Rachel's scream, then locked eyes with her as that cable yanked her off her feet. And sent her soaring. And then dashed her back against the mountain.

I came running down the trail, calling out her name. She was gone before I got here. No last words. No explanation. Nothing I could make her tell me.

Helicopter *thwock*ing in the distance, heading right this way. When—

✑ Rachel Katz's Notebook

7 September–12 October

9/7—*Saturday*

Erin hasn't given me much *positive feedback,* to put the matter bluntly. Not about my nature writing efforts, at any rate. But she called me up this morning—I still don't believe this!—to see if I would come to dinner at her place tomorrow with one of my *personal heroes.* Kyle Hess. Author of that book about the redwoods, *Leaves from Mendocino.* Turns out he and Erin go way back, and he's here in town visiting. Erin said she has a feeling that I'm going to *love* this guy.

Which made me suspect, right off the bat, that she has done the same. I could hear it in her voice. The way she told me they were *dear old friends,* I could smell the deal. *Dear old lovers,* she might as well have said.

Never try to fool someone who has a latent psychic gift. She might as well have said, "Kyle's come to look me up. And he's *way horny,* but I'm married. Take him off my hands?"

He's crashing on her sofa for a couple nights, just passing through. Bet her husband *loves* that.

Have to take a climbing group to Smugglers' Notch tomorrow, though. Playing with my motley crew of juvenile delinquents. But I said I'd have us back in time that I could come for supper.

Should I take my copy of his book, get him to autograph it?

No. I may be Kyle Hess's *fan,* but I'm not a *suck-up.*

Just when you least expect it, life gets really interesting.

Going to make believe this isn't Saturday night, and curl up in bed to re-read *Leaves from Mendocino.* I want it fresh in mind before I get to meet the author.

9/8—*Sunday Morning*

There's a certain creativity to what Kyle Hess calls his *forest activism*, and yet after a while it must get as dull as shoveling coal. And as tiring. Take this *tree-spiking business* that he writes about. I don't care whether these people are driving real nails into trunks, or drilling holes to stuff with welding rod or rebar. I *don't care* about the efforts they take to hide their work, gluing chunks of bark in place so foresters won't find their holes. I mean, I do care, in the abstract—I care if people then notify the timber interests, let them know they'd better not cut a certain stand unless they want to break their sawmill. But it's such a *long and drawn-out* way to get things done. Really *boring,* too. How many hours would I want to spend putting spikes in tree after tree? Maybe they are ultimately saving the forests, but not in a way I'd be psyched to spend *my* nighttimes doing. Got to be a better way.

Kyle can write like an angel, though. He writes about the *spiritual force* within those redwoods in a way that made me almost cry, last night. And I've read his book before. Twice. I love the way that he avoids being *prideful,* too. Never pats himself on the back, or puffs his chest out. He just assesses certain dangers and assumes some risks, and finds a way to get the job done. Anyhow, I'm *psyched* about the evening ahead.

Daytime agenda is to go on an outing with my favorite class of kids. Seven young teenagers who got in trouble with the law. *Minor stuff,* like unreturned videos and shoplifting. Now they are required to take a mountaineering course as part of their alternative sentencing. Their parole. I don't know if rock climbing will turn them into law-abiding citizens, but I love to see the *wonder* in their eyes when they do something that seemed impossible, three months ago. Cranking up an easy face or even simple bouldering can get those kids *pumped.* When I showed them crack climbing tricks last week, it was like they'd *sprouted wings* and learned to fly. And to watch each person trust his safety to another, like when they had each other on belay—that one afternoon, I could sense their lives were *changing.*

Their whole attitude. I don't know what genius in Corrections thought up this idea, but the guy deserves a medal.

Time to pick up rental gear from the store, then head for the mountain.

9/9—*Monday Morning*

Wham-o. Pow. Feels like I've just been *punched in the head* all night. Or maybe in the heart. Someplace where I really feel it. *Hurts,* but in a good way. Staring into Kyle Hess's face and seeing . . . what?

Well, seeing something that looks just like *my destiny.* For the fore-seeable future, at any rate. And, in a way, seeing the sibling that I never had. Maybe my *twin brother.*

I knew *things were right* between us when I didn't feel nervous about meeting someone I respect so deeply. No butterflies, *no cottonmouth struggle* to come up with words to say. When Erin led me into her living room, I found him hunched over the issue of *Climb High* with the photos of me halfway up Poke-O-Moonshine, demonstrating heel hooks. My head leaning back, long hair flying in the breeze. Wearing just my climbing bra, black shorts, and nylon harness. Boreal rock shoes. Not a whole lot else.

"Put that away," I told him. "I see Erin's hyping me."

"I love how these climbing magazines are the new *Playboy,*" he said. "Lovely, well-toned women captured in gymnastic poses. Tanned skin, taut muscles—pretty damn erotic."

I laughed, offered him my hand. "Rachel Katz. Don't get up—I know who you are, obviously." Funny how, in the flesh, his face *looked smaller* than what the book jacket had led me to expect. Because his features are so delicate, like *living porcelain.* Surrounded by that shaggy golden halo.

Erin told him I'm the only *activist* member of her nature writing group. That's why she wanted to get the two of us together. I was going, No, you can't compare my stance on chalk to anything that

Kyle's done. But she said it's actually totally relevant. And then I explained to Kyle how I have this issue about climbing walls where every hold is *covered* in white chalk. Which not only kills the challenge of finding routes, but defaces the rock.

We have precious few big walls, here in Vermont. They get overused. Step back from any of them and take a hard look—it's as if *graffiti artists* had been up there with white paint. We need to respect Earth more than that. And respect our sport. So I'm on this kick of getting all the local climbers to *add pigment* to their chalk bags, mixing it until they've got a color close to what they're climbing. At the store—Extreme Outfitters, in Winooski—we now give out a sampler of dark chalk to anyone who's buying gear. Free. Because it just *makes sense.*

"See?" said Erin. "Got a live one, here. I wasn't kidding."

Actually this is an important issue, Kyle said. What with the explosion in the sport's popularity, this could be to our generation of climbers what the battle over pitons was thirty years ago.

Erin's husband—Bernie—and their two kids came in to say hi, get a chance to meet me. Not for long, though. I was *dead-on* about Bernie's attitude toward his wife's old boyfriend. No love lost there. But Dad took the boys out to McDonald's so the three of us could eat in peace, not have to compete with a three year old's tantrums and a four year old's clamoring for everyone's attention. Sat outside on the screened-in patio, with waning sunlight painting pastel brushstrokes over Lake Champlain. *Afterglow.* Good talk. Australian wine. Skewers of shish kebab, with couscous and falafel.

"Kyle likes the vibe here in Vermont," Erin told me as she squeezed his shoulder. "He thinks West Coast activism's ready to take hold here."

"Really?" I asked, skeptical. "Here in Vermont?"

He nodded. "You people have the right obsession with the world around you. Everyone seems bonded to the landscape, the environment. Just a short step from there to making people fight for it."

"But we're way too smug," I told him, teasing just a little. "We've got a good thing going. Most of Vermont's land has *already been* protected. We don't have the *burning issues* that you face, out west. So if you're expecting easy converts to the forest cause, think again. Tough sledding."

He said he was moving toward something like a *zen* approach. That he'd figured out some ways to make people help the movement without even knowing it. Wise use of capital, he said. Conserving human effort. And when you get the average people on the street involved, they do not arouse suspicion. Walk into a forest with a backpack full of *who knows what,* and no one gets arrested. Foresters think they're seeing hikers, campers, tourists. Ordinary people do not call attention to themselves. Which makes them just about impossible to bust.

"So you're planning to *manipulate* Vermonters?" I asked. "Better not count on it. We are independent cusses."

"People get manipulated all the time," he came back at me. "Why not on behalf of something *good,* for once? Think about your writing group—Erin's been telling me about some of the members. If you wanted help teaching climbers about chalk, who would you *not* turn to? Who would be *least likely,* in that group, to come on board?"

I didn't have to think hard. "Kiki Johnson," I said. "First you'd have to smash her binoculars to get her attention. Long as she has birds to watch, she's chill. Working on her life list. She's like, 'Ohmigod, is that a spotted purple warbler?'"

"She's just the person that you want, then," Kyle told me. "Maybe it takes a bit of—yes, all right, manipulation. But I'll bet someone like that could help you to succeed. You just need to find a way to let her serve your interests while she *thinks* she's watching birds. Maybe taking—let me think out loud, here. Maybe taking photographs of peregrine falcon nests hanging off a sport wall, and showing holds all smeared with chalk."

"This is cool," I said. "I like that. Kiki *has* sold photographs to nature magazines."

"So it works. You see how this is possible, right? Same thing with environmental action, right across the board." He turned to Erin. "Who, in your writing workshop, would you say is the least committed?"

"Lauren Blackwood," Erin volunteered. "You know, that llama woman I brought up the other day. She kind of disturbs me, really. Plenty of direct interaction with nature, but not much concern for the world beyond her farm. I mean, she hates *coyotes*—she would like to see them go extinct. She even *shot* one, once. And she would happily sell house lots for development, if she thought the price was right."

That made me think about Marianna Finch. "Picture this," I said to Kyle. "We've got a *real estate agent* in the writing group. Works for RE/MAX. Foxy sort of middle-aged woman, lives along the lake. In Shelburne—that's the local gold coast. She's a widow. Dresses well, lives in this amazing house. And she drives a new Mercedes SUV—no shit. Used to train dressage horses. Husband died young and left her sitting on a wad of dough. You know what she writes about? Leaves and flowers. Vegetables. Bugs. Tight little pieces of description, like these well-formed *turds*. No environmental consciousness whatsoever. How do you get someone like that to help the movement?"

"Maybe I can't," he admitted. "But the goal is just to try to think creatively. Outside the box. We don't have to make these people converts, to get them to help us. I'm about accepting people as they are, and using *that*."

Once Bernie and the kids got back, our conversation flagged. Or it got *derailed*, to be perfectly accurate. Watching the kids fight over Happy Meal toys, run around the back yard screaming. Bedlam. But then Kyle asked me if I'd like to *duck out* with him, grab some cappuccino on the Church Street marketplace. I told him sure—although first I glanced at Erin's face to check her reaction. She just smiled coolly. "Thought you two might hit it off," she told us. "You kids run along."

I said we should take my car, because his rusty van looked filled with all his crap. No argument there. And then in the car, driving, I felt I should *make my move* if I was going to. I told him, "I'm not *fast*, in case you're wondering. If you knew me, you would know I don't go to bed with someone unless there's a good reason. But if you want to skip the coffee and just go to my place, that would be okay."

He placed a hand on my thigh and held it there. "Straight up," he said. "I like that."

"It just feels right to me. Even Erin—obviously, she had a sixth sense. She wanted to fix us up. Why disappoint her?"

Then later, standing by the bed, I got uptight. *Put off* by the way he shut his eyes while kissing me. I said, "These aren't second thoughts. But I don't want to see you close your eyes and think of Christy."

"Christy?"

"Hey—I've read your book, buster. *Three times*, for your information. So I do know all about her. I want you to *be with me*, though. *Stay here*, in the moment. I don't go for men who use sex to play their *private movies*."

He nodded, working at the buttons of my blouse. "Don't have to worry," he said. "Christy was a—actually, Christy's someone I invented. Like in a novel. She's a made-up character I put in, for the story's sake."

"Really?" I reached down and squeezed him. Hard. "Well, you could have fooled me."

"Sounds as if I did." He found my zipper.

"But you won't again," I told him. "This will be the last time."

"I believe you. And I'm going to hold you to that."

By sunrise, we knew we are *incredibly alike*. Putting out the same candid vibe with each other, utterly direct and honest. No holds barred. Balls to the wall. But also he's accustomed to the same kind of *awkwardness* I feel so often in dealing with other people. Feeling like we're *hiding* something, holding something back. Not really being *dis*honest, but . . . what's the word? *Disingenuous*. For sure. And then wishing people could just look at us and see what's there, hear what we're really saying. Trying to say.

He comes from Los Angeles; I was raised in New York City till my parents moved, when I was in high school. Both of us were seemingly well-adjusted urbanites who never really found ourselves until we took a chance on stepping out, risking adventures in the great outdoors. Went into the wilderness and *reveled* there. Where we belonged.

He even thinks that he is something of a psychic, too. Though he doesn't put it out there, doesn't wear it on his sleeve. But when the chips are down he knows he has this hidden power. This other faculty for seeing, understanding things.

Kyle doesn't know how long he's staying in the area, but we've decided that we're going to use the time we have for all that it is worth. Called Chip at the store, and he will let me have the *three days off* I've had coming. Luke O'Connor's just back from the Gunks, and he can cover.

Three days. I'm going to take Kyle canoeing tomorrow—someplace where there's fast, cold water. And he's going to take me *soaring* Wednesday, from an airport that he's heard is north of Stowe. He's a glider pilot. Thursday we'll go climbing, if the weather holds—three *awesome* days. As I write this, he has gone to Erin's to dig through his shit, try to find his rack and harness.

Hope Erin's still inclined to wish us well, not feeling *ticked* because I made off with her boyfriend. Her old boyfriend.

No. I didn't steal a thing. We two just collided.

Whew. Let the games begin.

9/10—*Tuesday Night*

We have decided to refer to what we're doing as our *Three-Day Event*. And when it is over, if either of us wants time off that will be okay. We'll be chill. This is like a *mini-lifetime* we are going to share together. Maybe mini-marriage, even. Three days of *total bonding* in the out-of-doors, in nature.

I'm not going to sandbag the Three-Day Event by getting all obsessive about keeping up this notebook. Just a few *broad strokes* each day, to leave a general outline. Later, there'll be time to think back over things and add details.

So . . .

SO, DAY ONE: WHITE WATER

Chip let me borrow a well-dinged canoe from the store's stash of rental gear. Put it in below the Belden dam on Otter Creek, and then ran it down through the *amazingly steep* gorge. Rush of pounding water where the river slips into a crease. Way narrow, lined with granite walls pocked with holes where chunks of marble have been scoured out. Forty foot cliffs with projecting ledges, overhangs. Standing waves the size of go-carts. *Vroom!*

I knew from Kyle's book that he's seen his share of rapids, but mostly he has seen them from kayaks or rubber rafts. Running the gorge in a canoe is much trickier—you can't afford to get hung up and ship a lot of water. So I made him take the stern for our first run, screaming to him when to do a draw stroke, when to back-paddle. Dancing down this *foamy jungle gym,* this liquid roller coaster. Two-headed water strider sheathed in bright aluminum, using the pounding river as our *private playground.*

Then we took out, carried the canoe back up and came down a second time, so that he could try making decisions in the bow. Hearts thumping, grinning back and forth like happy idiots. Almost caught a hidden snag and capsized in the thick of things, but he *stabbed* a bow rudder at the last moment and we managed to straighten out. Then spilling into the deep, boiling run-out pool where rainbow trout were leaping, gleeful. Paddling ashore and making whoops from sheer adrenaline. Rush of water, rush of blood. Thrilled to be there with each other, *kicking ass* together.

Red wine on the smooth granite slab below the run-out. Talking about John Muir and what Kyle called the great man's *love shack* in Yosemite. Hand-made cabin, built across an estuary of some High Sierra stream that had just plunged over a thousand-foot cliff. Indoor plumbing, sort of. Water right beneath the floor. Vines growing on the windows, wildflowers on the desk. Bed suspended from the rafters by four ropes—a *horizontal swing.* Think about it, Kyle told me. People have this crackpot notion Muir was a celibate, but he built himself this crib where *anybody* could get laid. And he had a series of romantic entanglements, helping foxy San Francisco ladies check out nature's wonders while they toured Yosemite. Muir would show them around, then take them to his shack and *entertain* them. Read between the lines of his letters, Kyle told me. It's pretty obvious that Muir was a stud.

I didn't argue with this—I was laughing much too hard, for one thing. But I said I don't think that's the reason Erin told me I should read this famous nature writer, learn a few tricks from him. It was more about our *shared obsession* with adventuring—having these incredible experiences in the out-of-doors, then getting them down on paper. So that readers could experience them, too.

Kyle told me that was fine, so long as I didn't make Muir into a saint. Don't buy the bogus Sierra Club line, he told me. Muir liked his women—as a man at home in nature should.

You mean as *you* do, I whispered in Kyle's ear . . . because by then the two of us were snuggling down. Bare skin on the rock slab flanking the river's edge, polished from 10,000 years of liquid scrubbing. But I like to think today we polished it a little further. Then dragged our canoe up to the highway, lashed it to the car, and drove home to plan day two.

9/11—*Wednesday Night*

Resolution: All my future boyfriends will be glider pilots. Maybe soaring isn't quite *exactly* as good as sex, but wow is it a close second.

We went up from the tiny airport south of Morrisville, where Kyle showed them his credentials and then rented this *featherweight bird* made of fiberglass and plastic. Two narrow seats, one right behind the other. Cramped—the glider's canopy stood no higher than the button of my jeans. We got settled in, got the tow rope attached, and then a pug-nosed airplane yanked us off the ground, dragged us skyward. Like getting hauled up the first hill on a roller coaster. Moment of suspension, equilibrium—and then *release*. Sudden loss of altitude, at first. Butterflies in stomach, heart in mouth. Followed by a gradual awareness of forward movement, not just plunging like a stone to the ground.

Kyle said this aircraft had a *glide ratio* of eighteen to one. So even if we couldn't find a single warm thermal, we had bought enough altitude to stay aloft for several horizontal miles. Each foot of altitude we lost could push us six yards forward.

But we *did* lose altitude steadily for several minutes, and I started wondering how short this ride might be. Then he found an updraft— a broad wave of rising air that we burrowed into, gradually proving Kyle's mastery over gravity. Higher and higher, topping out above the ridge of Mansfield at a point where we could stare directly into Smugglers' Notch. Then, looking south, I made out Camel's Hump, Mount Abraham. Maybe even Killington. To the west, our view took in most of the Champlain Valley. Then the vast blue lake speckled with islands, and beyond that range on range of towering Adirondacks.

This was a training glider, with dual controls. High above Stowe, Kyle gave me a beginner's lesson and then had me *fly the plane* while he pulled a camera out and started snapping photographs. Aerial shots of the terrain being logged and bulldozed to carve new ski lifts into the mountain, cut new trails, and make way for a golf course. So for maybe fifteen minutes I was *piloting our craft*—incredible sensation. Nothing aerobatic, just carefully holding us so he could get the shots he wanted. He said he was working on a magazine piece about the perils of developing mountains like this one into four-season resorts. If the photos turned out, he would show them to his editor.

Don't give me this *bullshit*, I said. Even sitting where I couldn't see his face, I smelled a lie.

All right, he admitted. Sorry. There's this environmental group that I've agreed to help—Trees, Not Skis—and they want these photographs to—

Liar, I said. Kyle, come on. I can hear it in your voice. Do I seem that gullible?

Okay, he said. Truth. And he put away the camera, turned off my controls and banked us southward, coasting down the ridgeline. He said, "I am thinking about taking action against Stowe. You can see what's going on—whole swaths of mountainside are being clear-cut. Trees are falling. Someone needs to make them pay."

"That sounds more like you," I told him. "That sounds like the person who wrote *Leaves from Mendocino*."

"But if anybody asks, I never said a word about this."

"Absolutely. Understood."

We were well off onto the west side of the ridge now, and he pointed down to where Lauren Blackwood has her farm. We could see the barns, the white house. Even grazing sheep ranging like *fluffy white ants* across a field. "That's the place I wish I had for staging this campaign," he told me. "Give me that as home base and I'd mess with Stowe's head for months. Half a dozen footpaths up the mountain from that Pleasant Valley. I could hike up after dark to where they're cutting timber, do some work on their machines, and be in bed by sunup. Perfect."

"Wouldn't leave a lot of time for me," I said. "I have a day job."

He said we should talk about that after the three days are over.

Gliding down the ridgeline toward that *hideous* arrangement of broadcast towers, both of us began to hear these *Pah-puh-Pah-puh* noises to the west—toward Jericho. Gunfire. And not rifles, but artillery. Violent, explosive rounds. Concussions. Kyle had just begun to ask what the hell was up, when I realized what we were seeing in the distance. "Ethan Allen Firing Range," I told him. "Huge tract of land— big enough for several towns. That's where the National Guard goes for summer camp. They play their *war games* down there, shoot off their fancy weapons. Trying to make Vermont safe for democracy."

"Getting kind of late in the season for them, isn't it?"

I told him I didn't know that much about their schedule. But if it was summer camp, those boys were still going at it—we heard *Pah-puh-Pah-puh* all the way down past the mountain's Forehead, till he swung us eastward and began a slow descent in the direction of the airport. On the way, he turned on my controls for a second time. That's how I got the *amazing experience* of tacking in a gentle updraft, gradually adding eighty feet to our altitude. I loved that feeling—

taking *baby steps upward* in a blanket of warm arm. Gravity, he said, is not our enemy. It's not against us. More like the challenging friend who keeps you on your toes. It's a way to test our ingenuity, build inner strength.

Same thing, I thought, as climbing. Two ways to touch a force that all nature *depends* on, that all nature must *respect*. Two ways to revel in the beauty of creation.

9/12—*Thursday Morning*

Waking in the night to find him staring at me, teary eyed. Why? Because I love you, he said. And because we both know time is moving forward. This can't last.

Evening Before Workshop

Now he's gone back to Erin's, and I think I'd rather get day three recorded than put food into my stomach. So:

I guess you know you've found a *dream partner,* climbing, when there's not a lot of conversation going back and forth. I knew I could trust Kyle's judgment as he led a pitch, and it was perfectly clear he trusted mine. We have this *dual head* when we're with each other. Working, playing, making love—even when we tease each other. Letting our conscious fields open just totally to *embrace* the other's mind. Thinking *with* it, or at least anticipating its next thought.

When we climbed together, that meant knowing where and how each other's body ought to move.

I *love* having this body, I really do. I love having arms and legs and knowing how to use them.

I thought I might talk Kyle into driving to New Hampshire—plenty of big walls in the Whites seem worthy of a guy who cut his teeth at Tuolumne Meadows. But he said he wasn't feeling up for that much challenge, so I took him back to Smuggs and we tackled Elephant Head. Only three pitches, but technical enough for us to get to know each other's style. Learn how each of us *dopes out* a tricky face.

Ninety minutes later we were sitting right above the Notch, over on the east side. Staring *straight down* into the caves, and then across to Stowe. Rush of watching steel-nerved falcons skydive for their lunches, swooping down to dig their talons into unsuspecting prey.

Saw in the distance some amazing crags behind the Cliff House, rising up beyond where Stowe's gondola drops off skiers. Don't know why I never noticed that terrain before, but maybe on account of all the *tacky glitz* that lies beneath it. Artificial madness that comes along with downhill skiing. Still, there's quite a lot of mountain past where skiers get to go. Kyle checked a topo map—700 feet of vertical rise between the Cliff House and the mountain's Chin. Incredible. Mansfield spreads out across so much terrain, Vermont has nothing else *remotely* like it. This was not a monolithic wall, but it looked like decent climbing just the same. And we had our gear—we were all dressed up and looking for a place to go. So we rappelled down off Elephant Head, drove to the base of Stowe's gondola, and went in to price tickets for a one-way ride.

This cracked me up—the guy running the lift was this kid who *went to high school* with me. Had a monster crush, as I recall. In eleventh grade. Jimmy Paquette. At first we didn't recognize each other—then, all at once, *we did.* Spent ten minutes chatting, getting caught up. When I asked about a ticket, Jimmy broke the rules and let us ride the lift for free.

Scaling the last few hundred feet of Mansfield gives this *really weird sensation.* Kind of *schizophrenic.* Keep your eyes focused on the rock, and you almost think you're somewhere off in the boonies. Out in the wilderness. But when you look down or out, you see the huge extent to which the mountain has been fucked with. Coney Island atmosphere. The mountain as amusement park. Everywhere, the fingerprint of *human disrespect.*

Reading back over that, I admit it sounds like Kyle. As if he had brainwashed me into spouting his own views. But I've always had a vague revulsion to the downhill ski crowd and the glitz they stand for. All the fancy clothes, expensive cars, and designer gear. Their *bogus* athleticism—I mean, honestly. They only ski in one direction—

down. How hard is that? Anyway, Kyle helped me shape my sim-
mering misgivings into *words that bite.*

Once on top, we put away our rock shoes and walked the ridgeline
to the colossal broadcast tower that we cursed on Wednesday, when
we saw it from the air. Colossally ugly from the ground up, too. Several more transmission towers poke into the sky beyond it, halfway
up the mountain's Nose. But this tall one next to the Summit Station
is the worst, for sure. Next to where the Toll Road feeds a skyline
parking lot. I told Kyle this *flat-out desecration* puts chalk marks on
climbing routes into laughable perspective. This makes downhill ski
runs look like mountain decorations—daubs of chocolate sauce
swirled on a giant sundae. This tower, though, was a case of *world-class
disrespect* for Earth. If Kyle wanted to do something for the mountain,
why not find a way to take that down?

"Taking down a tower isn't easy," he told me—and it sounded like
he knew what he was talking about. "Difficult, dangerous work."

"Gee," I baited him. "I thought you came from California."

"I'm a *forest* activist. For this, you'd need someone who's an expert
with explosives."

"You said you were in a *movement.*"

"Actually, I am," he said. "And, actually, I do know someone. But
this is not my thing."

I think at one level I was joking with him—just this teasing banter
we had going back and forth. But at the same time I was *voicing a
criticism* that has been emerging in my head over the past few days.
Maybe because the Three-Day Event was ending—virtually over—
and I wanted us to have a *spat* to put some space between us. Anyway,
I found myself really going off on him. "Your kind of thing is putting
spikes in trees, sand in motors," I said—as if work like that were no
big deal. "Oh, and I forgot about your camping out in trees. It's all
right, I suppose. Better than nothing. But aren't there bigger targets?
Better things to do?"

He flashed me a wounded look, and then one of real anger. When
he raised his arm, I almost thought he meant to hit me. I took a quick
step back—but no. He had a different plan. He pointed to a truck-

sized concrete block emerging from the mountain's mantle, fifty yards away. One of the anchor points for the steel cables that are used to guy the broadcast tower. "Go stand over there," he asked me—no, this was *an order*. "And then smile. Say *cheese*."

"What for?"

He pulled the camera from his fanny pack, exposed the lens. "I want to take your picture." Which he did—not once, but *thirty-two times* over the course of the next half hour. We moved all around the tower's base, and he would pose me next to one structural detail or another. Engineering features. *Click*—a photograph that *seemed* to be of me, but wasn't really. Tourists milling all around, not to mention hordes of hikers on the Long Trail. Even a ranger there to answer questions, ask people not to touch the fragile alpine plants. Nobody figured out our surreptitious project, and when we were finished Kyle had a solid roll of film. "I'm going to send these to a friend in Oregon," he told me. "Tower specialist. It's a long shot, but he may find them interesting."

"You'd do that for me?" I kissed him.

"Yes," he said. "I like a challenge."

Then going back down the crags by a different route. Not as steep, but every bit as technical and complicated. Found a narrow cave reaching deep into the mountaintop. Moss-covered opening, protected from the sun and wind. Magical, *beautiful nook* we used for making love. Middle of the afternoon, high above the Stowe valley.

They don't call it *nooky* for no reason, Kyle pointed out. *Nooky* makes perfect sense.

And then, much too soon, the Three-Day Event was over. We hiked off the mountain, drove back to Burlington, and went our separate ways. Kyle said he'd see me at the writing group tonight, though—Erin has *invited him to sit in*. After that, he has to find a way to start the work at Stowe. Which means we won't be together for a while.

And this won't be easy, but he asked me to behave tonight *as if we haven't met*. That's the way it has to be, for Erin's sake as workshop leader. And for the good of the entire workshop. So I said I'd do that for him.

Then the drill will be to find out how long we can go without one of us breaking down and running to the other. How long we can put this relationship on hold. He has a life to live—and I have my own life, too. But if we find we *cannot* be without each other, we will know. A *spirit-message* will go back and forth between us.

No regrets, or expectations. What a great three days it's been.

Okay, got to put my *game face* on. Stiffen my upper lip. Time to be a stranger to my lover at the writing group.

9/13—*Friday*

All right. Last night worked out well enough, and I know it's *going* to work. Why? Because it has to. Only real drawback was when Kyle started *ragging on* the short piece I read aloud—the one about why a simple hexcentric nut is better protection than a fancy, spring-loaded cam. How climbing has become the *victim of technology* in ways that undercut the sport's original joyfulness. John Muir, I pointed out, climbed with hardly any gear—and nobody has reveled in the mountains more than he did. I'll bet Kyle felt he *had* to be critical, just to throw the others off the scent of our amazing closeness. Our *intense connection*—an aroma that, till he attacked me, almost seemed to fill the room.

Erin told the group that Kyle's an expert on John Muir—who is, of course, the writer I'm supposed to read and emulate. Kyle was modest about his expertise, but he mentioned several places where Muir writes about getting really stuck, thinks he's going to fall and has a full-blown *panic attack,* followed by a blinding flash of revelation. Then he climbs his way to safety. On a Yosemite wall, on an Alaskan glacier, halfway up Mount Ritter—even, once, while digging a well in Wisconsin. This was Muir's terrifying psychodrama, Kyle told us. Something that he had to *re-enact* time and again. Not at all what I had called it—"reveling in the mountains." It was a darker and more complicated project—getting into trouble, nearly dying, and then busting free. So I ought to find those famous passages and read them over. Then I'd see that climbing held a *different fascination* for Muir than it does for me.

You shithead, I wanted to say. Don't you remember how I came for you, the other night? Or how we had *nooky in a nook,* this very afternoon? Whole Stowe valley laid out beneath our feet? But instead I nodded shyly, trying to look *chastened* and *grateful* for his words of wisdom. I said I would try to find those passages, for sure.

Change of subject: I need to avoid *at all costs* going through another bout of serious tendonitis. Strained two fingers yesterday on the final pitch of Elephant Head—up where the rock is loose and crumbly, so you have to dig. Dinged a pinky knuckle, too. Hard to close my left hand all the way, this morning. *Not a good sign.* Anyway, a few days of just working at the store is what I need to set me right. Hopefully set my mind right, too.

Fine line between knowing when to lie back and heal, when to hang tough. Keep focused. Not lose hard-won conditioning, intensity.

I don't like admitting this, but I really wonder what he's doing right now.

9/14—Saturday

I think I have something like a photographic memory. When I did that photo shoot for Kyle on the mountaintop, I wasn't paying *conscious attention* to the way that tower's built. And yet now I keep picturing each detail—they come back to me in vivid, living color. It's become my new obsession.

In fact, I *made a model* at the store today when things were running slow. I used an aluminum tent pole for the tower's shaft, adding on sections till it stood nearly twelve feet high. Then I took some spectra cord to represent the cables—six of them, arranged in pairs so that they fed three anchor points. Three fastened high up on the tower, and three more down low. I used key-chain carabiners for connectors.

But here's the kick-ass photographic revelation. Each pair of cables comes together at a steel bracket fastened to the blob of concrete that embeds its anchor, and there's *only one pin* tying those brackets to their base. Enormous cotter keys are drilled in on either side to hold each pin in place. But they wouldn't be that hard to pull, with the right tools. What I'm saying is, the *entire web* of cables—without which the tower would be *virtually unsupported*—all comes down to three steel pins.

So I think that Kyle lied when he told me it would take explosives to drop that thing. I *ran some experiments* on my working model, and I'm pretty sure it would be totally easy. Unhook those support cables, then stand back. Upsy-daisy.

Just a theoretical plan, but I'm feeling *empowered* by taking time to work it out. I'm not a husky woman. I've never *seen* explosives, let alone worked around them. But I do believe that I could take that tower down.

9/15—Sunday

Cancelled my afternoon of climbing with Corrections kids, on account of I need time to let these fingers heal. *Felt bad* to disappoint them, but we're on for next week.

Okay—time to *kick some ass* in this notebook, write something that will blow Erin away.

AMAZING FACE

. . . Because a rock wall really, truly *is* one. Everybody understands this basic comparison. Never just a blank expanse. Always with unique features. Cracks and chimneys, bumps, depressions, ledges, corners, chicken-heads. Some are tiny, some immense. No two faces, though, are ever quite the same. Like people. Climbing an unfamiliar face is like a Lilliputian crawling over Gulliver. Scaling a cheek, a forehead—not to conquer, but to make an intimate acquaintance. Till you know a rock face like your lover's. Or your own.

HOW STEEP THE GROUND

. . . Which means you have to bring it all of you, offer each face everything you have. But the satisfaction is primordial, prehistoric. Sheer joy. And joy in the *process* of climbing—more so, even, than the moment of topping out. Process, like a bird in flight. Like a fish swimming. This is something we were made to do—a fundamental pleasure. This is what it means to be a primate. Weren't our ancestors apes, gorillas, chimpanzees? This is why our childhood playgrounds all had *monkey bars*. And now that we're grownups, we need grownup versions of the same. Steep ground, amazing face.

THAT SAVED A WENCH LIKE ME

. . . All right, so I never was a total ho. But there was a year or two when I felt addicted to a kind of sexuality that left me feeling disrespected. By myself as well as by those men. Those fuckers. Then a summer in New Hampshire got me onto big walls, and I've spent the last five years climbing to a better version of myself. Building inner confidence. Catlike in a jam. Smart at finding hidden holds. Tough. Muscular. Toned to the bone. And disciplined about the ways I use my body.

I ONCE WAS LOST

. . . As when you're fifty feet above the last fixed bolt, and one false move sends you tumbling through thin air as stoppers you spent twenty minutes placing all zipper out. *Bang, bang, bang.* The World Trade Center coming down. That feeling of being right out of control. Plummeting down the face, gathering speed. Waiting for a bone-splitting crunch that will likely be the last sound you will ever hear.

Lost, as in without hope. Falling, bouncing off random ledges till there's nowhere more to fall. Lost, as in coming to the end of your rope.

BUT NOW AM FOUND

. . . As when at last a nut you placed *does* hold, one last piece hugs firmly where you wedged it in a fissure of the rock. Springy jolt as nylon rope expands to halt your tumbling fall. Harness squeezing tight around your waist, thighs, crotch. It finds you. Oh, does it find you. And sets you free as you take gear in hand to try again.

WAS BLIND

. . . As when you're too close to the face to make sense of things. Clinging to a jumar out of white-knuckled fear. No wider vision, no placing where you are and what you're doing in perspective. Unable to think even one move ahead. Or to go backward, either. Blood draining out of fingers, lactic acid drowning every muscle in your arms. Sewing machine legs. And then the sky dims, scraps of granite right before your eyes become a blank canvas. Blindness. Darkness all around you. Then . . .

BUT NOW I SEE

. . . No way to get higher than the moment when blank rock becomes a face again. Just when you thought it couldn't. Features re-emerge. Amazing moment of *illumination,* miracle of *revelation.* When the mind clears and a pattern of potential moves starts to show up clearly. Possibilities you never saw, until you had to. Jam a finger, hook a heel, lean back and look around. Everything you need is there. Features. On the faces. Of the rock. Touch them. Hold them tight. This is how it feels to experience salvation.

Damn. Now I'm thinking I should maybe write a *climber's hymnal.* Self-publish 500 copies, sell them at the store. I'll bet a lot of our customers would want to own one.

9/16—*Monday*

Most of the others in Erin's group do their writing first thing in the morning. I wish I could be creative at that time of day, but I think I do my best work in this *late-night venue*. Darkness all around. I go with incense, Cuervo, candlelight. I like to get my journal written, then fall right to sleep.

Crack of dawn, I'm ready for *the day* to kick my ass. I don't need to have it kicked by a piece of paper. Trying to be *honest* with the page, writing something true. I need to have the business of the day behind me before tackling work like that.

I think my own standard of *complete honesty* is what takes place between my body and an unfamiliar wall. I know I can't fake out the rock, can't fool it into being something that it's not. But if I am sharp and on my game, the rock cannot fool me.

Kyle told me that his own best metaphor is soaring. He's not just a glider pilot—he's logged many hours flying fixed-wing ultralights. He's a paraglider, too. But it's all the same thing, he said—*doping out* a complicated pattern of currents that you can't really see, then *committing* yourself to choices that reveal who you are. Choices that show what you've got, and show that you'll accept the consequences of being right or wrong.

I wish getting on with people and their prickly egos could be that direct, that simple. That satisfying, too.

9/17—*Tuesday*

I have made an *amazing* discovery. John Muir was something of a psychic, too. He had some *persistent gift* for knowledge that is basically clairvoyant, and he proved his powers time and again. Like when he was in the high Sierras, searching for a glacier, and he got this *wild thought* that one of his college teachers had just arrived at the hotel in Yosemite. How he turned around and made his way back to the valley, and there was Professor Butler from Wisconsin.

Or the time he got a *premonition* his estranged father was slowly dying at his sister's house, in Iowa. How he bought a train ticket, rode east from California, and got there in time to hold his dad's hand as he died.

How he berated himself when one of his Yosemite honeys got thrown from a horse, and he somehow didn't pick up on the mental distress signal she was putting out. A nine-one-one—she needed him. He didn't sense she was in trouble until later on, after she had gotten rescued. But that was *atypical,* and Muir wrote to tell her he was *mortified* about what happened. As if somebody had turned off his psychic beeper.

Kyle was right about the Muir letters. They're a gold mine. And they show that—just like me—this mountaineer who turned his life around to save the wilderness had this *peculiar gift,* and had to find out how to use it. How to see around the rigid corners of the present moment, understand what's coming next but not be *sandbagged* by the burden of that special knowledge. And also not try to *strong-arm* events, not use the psychic gift to make things go your way. Hard to learn to use this tool for good, for worthy purposes.

I look into the future and there's one thing I see clearly. I see Kyle with me—we're together, working side by side as *lovers and warriors* making Earth a better place. Making Earth more beautiful. All around this vision I see shimmering light, too. As if I were staring at an iridescent sky.

9/18—*Wednesday*

So he came into the store today to buy a Petzl Grigri—high tech, virtually infallible belay device. That was his excuse, I mean. We both understood that he had come to see me. It was only 3:00, but I asked Chip if I could take off for the rest of the day. He's no hardass—he will let me catch up on the weekend.

Off to my apartment, taking care of *first things* first. Then I asked Kyle where he'd been and what he had been doing. He's talked Lauren

Blackwood into letting him stay on her farm, in some kind of *rundown cabin* that she has there. Just what he had hoped for, when we looked down on it from the air. Score, he said. A great location.

"So have you been working on the mountain, nights?"

He said that he'd *decommissioned* two log skidders and a front-end loader. Not much, but it was a start. Pig heaven, he called the setup over there at Stowe. Very low security. Heavy equipment parked all over the mountain.

I switched positions in the bed, was about to suck him but he asked me not to. He had some other news. His pal from Oregon—the tower man—really *took a shine* to the pictures on that roll of film. The thirty-two consecutive photographs of me.

I picked up his drift, though it surprised me. "Serious?"

Serious. This guy's an expert, and he is obsessed with *beautifying ridgelines.*

"Good," I said. "But I've been thinking we don't need a specialist. Or dynamite, for that matter. We just need a sledge hammer, and a way to pull out half a dozen cotter keys. It's that simple."

Nothing that big will come down easily, said Kyle. Or safely, either. But this friend of his—he's got a made-up name, "Kung Pao"—is confident it can be done. And Kyle's working on a complicated plan that sounds *totally ingenious.* It involves Lauren's llamas, and a foot-path running up the mountain from near her farm, and some high explosives that he figures can be taken from the Ethan Allen Firing Range. But we'll need the help of several people, since the summit needs to be secured for one whole night. We'll need to seal off all means of intervention, once we get this project going.

I *could not believe* that he was laying all this out for me. "I thought you wanted just to fuck with Stowe Resort," I told him. "You said towers weren't your thing."

Yeah, he said. That's right. And then you called me a wuss.

"Not in so many words."

No? I heard you loud and clear.

"So—wow, Kyle. Do you really want to do this?"

If you're game, he said. And if you'll go on with me, after.

My, my. I had the strangest reaction—and I *still* do. Realizing that *I have manipulated* Kyle Hess. The activist from California. Who was going on, that first night, about how good he was at manipulating others. He came with a modest plan, but now I've raised his sights to tackle a *heroic project.* Take a shot at something major. Something way important. And because of me, or something in the two of us. The way we spark each other. Something in our chemistry.

He told me not to breathe a word, and that he had to go. Lauren has an *annoying habit* of checking on his whereabouts. But he's going to sit in on the writing group again tomorrow, and we're going to keep in touch. On our telepathic line, with *spirit-letters* back and forth.

I am feeling bold enough to use the word *love,* tonight. Because I do think at last I understand its meaning—know what sort of litmus test a bond to someone needs to pass before it's worthy of that word. I'm in love with Kyle Hess. And when it is love, you know because your life becomes just totally empowered. If it's love, you feel like you're able to move mountains.

9/19 — *Thursday Night*

Being in the same room with Kyle at the writing workshop has become *incredibly awkward,* and I'm thinking about dropping out of the group. He is such a ladies' man in that kind of situation, and it seems like all the women there now worship him. I do understand he *has* to be sweet to Lauren, since she's letting him hang out on her farm. He needs that strategic location for his night work. That's his staging ground. But tonight Kiki had that look about her, too. A lilt to her voice when she'd turn to ask him questions about how she had described two hummingbirds. A *nesting pair.* And she wore a short skirt that was totally flirtatious. Marianna Finch, the RE/MAX bitch, left with Kyle after—even though he basically laughed at her insipid writing. Something about a dead leaf being like the suburbs. Erin just sits there like an interested *ringleader,* watching all that's going on but keeping her own counsel. I am like the one woman who has to make believe we're strangers, and it isn't fair. *Not fair.*

We are far from strangers. And I'm sure that keeping up this fiction must be hard on Kyle, too.

9/20—Friday Night

Dear Rachel:

This is an example of what happens when you get angry, skip supper, schlep around the neighborhood, and trudge home with a pint of Cuervo and no one to share it with. This is not the way you want to spend a Friday night. This is also not the way you told yourself—and promised him—that you would manage this relationship. I'm writing to warn you not to do what you've been thinking about doing for the last half hour. Do not get into the car and drive to Pleasant Valley. No reason to suppose he's even going to be there. Not at midnight on a clear, calm night like this. He'll be somewhere up on the mountain, taking care of business. You're a fool to get between him and the work he wants to do.

And even if he is in his rustic cabin, I don't think you want to let him see you in your present state. He has placed his trust in you. He's shared a big secret. He wouldn't want to know you're capable of getting so smashed, you might say anything. Irresponsible behavior. Totally irrational. That's why I am sure you're going to do the right thing.

Love,
Rachel

Now if I could only find my goddamn—ah. My car keys.

9/21—*Saturday Morning*

That was a *godawful mistake* to have blundered into. Found my drunken way over to Underhill, found Pleasant Valley Road and made my way as far as Lauren's long driveway—then I wised up and parked next to her pick-your-own, traipsed up the drive on foot. As if I were bringing Kyle a sweet surprise, a *midnight treat.* His van was parked next to a cottage, sure enough. But the door was locked, and I knocked and knocked with no response. Nothing. Then I saw candles in a window of the farmhouse. Walked in that direction till I heard a *two-note song* whose tune was unmistakable. And I knew the baritone voice pretty damn well. Backed off the way I came and managed to drive home, polish off the bottle, and collapse into bed.

All right, I'm a grownup and I know we both are *free agents.* He can fuck Lauren Blackwood all he wants. I hope she's good. I don't think she'll be good for the movement, though. Or for the mountain. I've got a hunch that woman's going to be *big trouble.*

Long, long day I have to put in at the climbing store, making up for skipping out on Chip the other afternoon.

I'll be better off, I think, if Kyle stays the hell away.

9/22—*Sunday Evening*

Amazing afternoon. Even after getting used to living with a *sixth sense,* I still can't believe what happened. I took the climbing kids—my bad boys, my delinquents—back to Smugglers' Notch and led them up the trail to Elephant's Head. Seemed like the first pitch of that climb would be a good place to work on rope skills, and there is a really solid pair of fixed bolts for anchoring belay/rappel lines. Shortly after lunch we've got our gear in place and Bruce Lepage—this gangly, quiet, kind of *spacey* kid from Essex Junction—is starting up. Twenty feet above me, he gets dizzy and sits back in the harness, like his world is *spinning.* Nothing can go too far wrong, but I talk him down and make him sit over by the backpacks, gather his wits about him while the others practice climbing. And then—this was dumb of me, *really stupid*—I stopped paying attention to Bruce when I saw he'd settled back and gone to sleep.

Well, I had my hands full with the others in my group. But at 3:00 or so, everyone was off the face and Danny Frank, a friend of Bruce's, went over to sass him. But *he wouldn't wake up.* Now a bunch of scary thoughts began to crowd into my mind. Was Bruce doing drugs? Was there a medical problem? Just when I was panicking, *Kyle* came striding up the trail from the parking lot down in the Notch. Breathing hard, black T-shirt soaked with perspiration. He was grinning—he didn't know I had a problem, yet. But *there he was,* arriving just in time to help me.

He said, "I looked down and saw you from the air. Soaring." Then he read my look and saw I had a *crisis* on my hands.

"I can't wake up Bruce," I said. "He didn't fall—he just got dizzy, so I sat him down. This isn't right, though—I think he may be unconscious."

Kyle kneeled down—he was *immediately* on the case. Rolling up Bruce's sleeve, he found a diabetes bracelet. Then he said there had to be some insulin on the kid, and Danny showed us which pack belonged to him. Sure enough, a loaded needle that Kyle knew how to administer expertly. Then he picked the kid up in his arms and carried him down off the mountain, all the way to the van. By then, Bruce was coming around and looking pretty sheepish. He said that sometimes he puts off taking his shot, because delaying it gets him high.

Can't believe Corrections never told me he was diabetic! And I'm thinking, Ohmigod. If Kyle hadn't come along, Bruce might be in a coma.

I had to get the kids back to their parole officer, and Kyle said he had some major errand to take care of, too. But we both agreed we have *some issues to discuss,* and he is coming over later. I have to *fine-tune* the chaos of emotions that now surface when I think about him, which is nearly all the time. One thing for certain, though: *I will not be his cunt* as a matter of convenience, when he's not sticking it to Lauren or some other woman. I have more respect for myself than that. And yet I keep realizing that my spirit *cried for help* today, and Kyle heard me. He came. He was right there.

9/23—*Monday*

Kyle says: I thought you knew the difference between *having sex* and actually *making love*. Can't you tell we touch each other in a way that's off the chart? Who on earth could match us?

So why did you do that, then? If what we have together is so good, why do that with Lauren?

Kyle says: You're acting like a schoolgirl. I'm not proud about it, but there are times when I've used sex to forge alliances. Sometimes people *need to*, if they want to get things done.

I want to get done, damn it. I want you to do me.

Climbing up on top of him and beating fists against his chest. Then our hips began to move in time, till we were making love—yes, I do know the difference. Even if somebody else might fail to see the distinction.

Then he told me Kung Pao is arriving in Vermont, either today or tomorrow. With his girlfriend, Holly. He has some *roving assignment* with the Environmental Protection Agency, and he's also got a solid military background. Decorated hero in the Gulf War. Getting this guy authorized to check out the Firing Range took a few phone calls, but nothing more. There are four things that he wants to study there, produce reports on: waste disposal, toxic fumes, noise pollution . . . and one other. He let the commander know he's *sympathetic* to their needs, not some asshole bureaucrat. So they're giving him some kind of *blanket clearance*.

I told Kyle that sounds great, although I still think we could drop that tower my way. For a lot less time and effort. Then Kyle told me that the plan has been expanded—while we're up there on the mountain, we'll be toppling *every broadcast tower* in a single busy night. Won't that surprise the Champlain Valley, come next morning?

He explained that there are *certain rules* for such an operation, based on years of eco-defense in California. Only one person ever knows the total plan—that would be this Kung Pao character, in our case. Each participant knows *only what he needs to.* And they have to follow each instruction to the letter. There should be as few participants as possible, since every time you add a person you compound the risk. Lastly, everybody has to keep his goddamn mouth shut—not just for a few months, either. Keep it shut forever. Which, he couldn't keep from adding, is a long, long time.

Would you cut this out? I told him. Think of who you're talking to. Have you forgotten that we share the same mind?

He said that he had to go, then. It was getting on toward midnight. He said that the nights apart were hard, but soon we'd be together.

9/24—Tuesday

Kyle stopped by this evening with a couple of six-packs of Long Trail Ale and this pair of West Coast activists, "Kung Pao" and Holly. Or maybe it's "Holly." *Great big bear* of a man, looks a bit like Papa Hemingway without the beard. And with a buzz cut. Bushy eyebrows. Loud voice. Easy, almost raucous laugh. The girlfriend can't weigh ninety pounds—I think she has a lower body-mass index than *I* do, which is saying something. She has guts, though. Long blond hair, *determined* blue eyes. A quiet, cool intensity.

Obviously, Kyle brought these people here to check me out. And I'm almost certain that I didn't disappoint them. Kung said he'd already been up on the mountain, and if this were California that junk heap of broadcast towers would have long ago been *toast.* The smaller ones clustered on the Nose look relatively easy to take care of—unscrew the nuts that attach them to their concrete pads, then blow them off the studs with a well-placed charge. No big deal. But the really tall tower with the cables will be harder.

"I don't see why," I said, proceeding to explain about the steel pins I figure could be knocked out with a sledge hammer. *Whap!*

"First rule of dropping something that size," he told me, "is to know which way it's going to fall. And you *cannot* do that if you disconnect the cables. One thing we don't want is for anybody to get hurt."

"So let's hear *your* plan," I told him.

He spread Kyle's photographs across the kitchen table, then used a felt-tip pen to highlight U-bolts where the cables can be adjusted. Huge, beefy nuts torqued down on several feet of threaded rod. "First we back those lugs off, putting slack in every guy wire. That gives the tower room to move—some play, in all directions. But not enough that it can fall down on top of us. Then we set a charge beneath the base, and blow the tower off it. As it starts collapsing down, the cables govern where it falls. They'll be *working for us,* rather than becoming death traps."

I suppose I saw his point. And he was, as Kyle said, an expert at this business. "Okay," I said. "I guess you're the boss."

"Don't guess about it," said this Holly woman pointedly. Her voice was cold and brittle. "Kung's no amateur. He understands the job."

"Maybe I'm just scared of the explosives."

"So am I," said Kung Pao. "But you get used to them."

"Okay," I conceded. "It's a plan. Where do I fit in?"

Kyle told me maybe I could *do some shopping* for them, once they get a list of tools together. He said I'd be buying things that might tend to raise eyebrows. Better me than them, since I don't have a police record. Yet.

"And something else," said Kung Pao, belching—he was well into his third beer, though he looked built to hold them. "Kyle tells me you're a climber. Are you good?"

"Good enough."

"How good?"

"Well, last month I red-pointed a five-eleven in the 'Dacks."

He looked impressed. "Then what I have in mind ought to be easy for you. I want you to climb around the ski lifts on the Stowe side, think of ways to get them all disabled on a stormy night."

"Why?"

"Wrong question, teammate. You'll figure it out, though."

"How many lifts?"

"All five."

"How much time?"

"Let's say from when it first gets dark till midnight. Do-able?"

"I'll get right on that, see what I come up with."

"Let me know a week from now how you plan to do it."

Holly said she thought it was time they should be going. They had *something else* to do—all three of them together. Not that they were sharing these late-night plans with me. At the door I took Kyle aside, told him I hated to sound *needy* but it's time we spent a night together. Soon. I'm getting sick of all this *in and out the door* stuff, as if we were *dating*.

Thursday, he said. After writing group. You free?

Yes, I'm free, I told him. Obviously I am free, if you want to be with me.

But we can't walk out together, he said. Sends the wrong message.

Message to *whom*? I asked angrily. *Lauren*?

I'll leave early, he said. Do you have an extra key?

9/25—Wednesday

Kyle has given me an article he wrote about John Muir a year ago, for *High Sierra* magazine. "The Reluctant Activist," it's called. Thought-provoking piece. He says modern readers tend to see a *seamless link* between Muir's mountaineering and his public life—the writing, the Sierra Club, the lobbying for wilderness preservation. Actually, Kyle says that nothing could be more untrue. Muir had to be dragged *kicking and screaming* from the private satisfactions of what Kyle calls "Big Nature"—dragged down into the cities and public forums where the work of changing people's attitudes gets done. Once he began that work, though, he kept at it. *Stubbornly.* Even when it kept him from the outdoor life he would have chosen, if the times had not required someone who would take a stand.

Then Kyle extends that sense of *inner conflict* to his own life, and that of the West Coast forest movement. These people never planned to give their lives to such a cause. Given a choice, they would surely choose an afternoon of hiking in the woods to all the dark nights of working to save endangered trees. That kind of activism doesn't "come naturally." It's a *bizarre way* of responding to nature, if you consider the history of the human race. But for a person who is *thoughtfully aware* today, there is no alternative. We are all like John Muir, torn between our private goals and the need for public action—rising up and making a commitment, taking a stand. And if Muir were alive today, he'd be standing with us.

9/26 — *Thursday After Work*

Holly came by the store and handed me a shopping list written in her miniscule handwriting. Don't buy anything yet, she told me. Look this over, start thinking how you're going to get this stuff without a lot of questions asked. Then run your ideas by Kung Pao.

So I glance down this list, and much of it is *not* stuff you can walk into Home Depot and grab off the shelves. Come with me over to the shoe section, I tell Holly. Let me look this over while you check out our new boots.

We find a quiet corner and she sits down, starts trying on a pair of Tecnica Vetta's in the smallest size we carry. That would be a six. I'm going down the list, and some of what they're asking for is *serious shit.* They want a three-quarter inch drive ratchet with a set of deep-wall sockets in *enormous sizes.* Sockets up to two and three-eighths inches in diameter.

Check, says Holly.

A pair of adjustable wrenches with *twelve-inch jaws?*

That's right. Two of them. I know what's on the list, she says.

Heavy-duty, half-inch, rechargeable hammer drill, cordless. Eighteen volts—expensive kit. Masonry bits, chisels, bolt cutters, assorted hammers. This shit's going to weigh a ton, I pointed out.

We're not taking down a house of cards, she tells me.

Let me look around, I told her. See what I can find.

Then Holly asked me how I'm coming with the ski lifts. Look, I said, I've got a day job. Stowe is a good hour's drive from here—*before* I start climbing around on the mountain. Kung gave me a week, remember?

She smiled. Just checking.

Who's going to pay for all these tools? I asked.

We will. Put it on your plastic, and we'll find a way to reimburse you.

I'm not sure I want this on my credit card. It leaves a trail.

True, she said, but nobody suspects you of anything. Paying cash looks *more suspicious,* buying stuff like this. Main thing is to not purchase more than two items at the same place. No shopping yet, though. Talk with Kung first.

Where's he staying? Where are *you* staying?

Lauren Blackwood's farm. We're renting one of her cabins, not too far from Kyle's. I wouldn't recommend you come around there, though.

Why not?

It just wouldn't be smart. When you need to see Kung Pao, let Kyle know. She started putting her street shoes back on, then handed me the boots. I do like these, she said. But they're a size too big. Else you'd have a sale.

That woman may look innocuous from a distance, but she is *a bitch.*

Dear Rachel:

Be yourself with Kyle tonight. You do remember how to. Don't stress about how the unfolding of this project has made life complicated and seems, in the short run, even to have driven a wedge between the two of you. This was your idea in the first place, don't forget. In a way, he brought these people here to make you happy. And events are moving forward— soon this will be something you'll look back on and smile about. An important time that molded how you learned to be together, how to do things with each other.

So many things you've learned to do required being careful, keeping clear about yourself, and sticking with a plan. That is all anyone is asking of you now. That is all I'm asking, dear one. Much love,

Rachel

9/27—*Friday*

Events *are* moving forward, and I have to get my act together to spend a night at Stowe figuring how I can disable all those ski lifts. Kyle says Kung Pao is not an easy man to work for. He can be *demanding*. He wants things done right, on time, and exactly to the letter. But he's had a string of *amazing successes* at making broadcast towers in the Northwest disappear. Eradicating public eyesores— which then raises people's consciousness, and forces giant corporations to *think twice* about where they build that sort of thing. We're lucky to have Kung here, putting in the time to get this job done right.

What's going to happen is, I may start getting calls *out of the blue* to stop what I am doing, drive to the mountain, and take care of some detail or another. Unforeseen problems tend to crop up in this sort of work. Also, *opportunities*.

Talking in bed, sharing a postcoital J in the dark. Red ash-glow, sweet smoke drifting back and forth. I asked Kyle if that Holly woman gets to order me around. Because she's a real pain in the ass.

Yes, he said. You have to do whatever Holly tells you to.

Who's paying for all this? Where does the money come from? Those hand tools alone will run a thousand dollars.

We do have some outside sources of income. Private monies, some donations—

Yeah, I'll bet. What kind of donor writes a check to blow up towers?

You'd be surprised, he said. For example, right now I am working on someone from the writing group. Haven't put the hit on yet, but—

No way.

Way.

Who?

Can you keep a secret? . . . Marianna Finch.

Oh, you're going to screw her, too?

There was a long silence, and then he fumbled with the sheets to find the book of matches. Struck a light and held it up so we could see each other's eyes. Wouldn't *you* screw someone, he asks, to get this project done? If success depended on it?

I blew out the match, but I could still feel his eyes on me. Not just anyone, I said. It would depend.

Many things are asked of people who set out to change the world. This is not a biggie.

Yeah? Well, I wish you'd keep your exploits to yourself.

This isn't a fight we're having, is it?

Not a fight. But it's a—it's an expression of regret. And weariness. I'll be happy when this whole thing's over. When your West Coast friends have gone back to Oregon. What do you suppose will happen to us, then?

What do you want to happen?

I would be with you, I said, if you'd treat me in a way that shows you *value what we have.* We both know you're not doing that now.

He said, Well, I'll work on it. Many things are possible. I'm a believer in the art of possibility.

I want to believe in possibilities, too. Although it isn't easy. It can be damn hard.

So we had a night together and I think I sort of blew it, dumping all this shit on Kyle even though *he did deserve it.* I'm thinking back, now, to the first part of the evening—before he came over here. Sitting in the writing workshop, listening to him read to us from his own nature notebook. Tender, *incredibly sensitive* piece about a sheep that died for no good reason. People had to fight back tears. How can a person with such empathy and deep emotion—this capacity for *really caring* about living things—how can he even *think of using sex* as a way of getting what he wants? As nothing more than a means to achieve an end? A tool? I wish I could understand how he can do that. I wish I could understand him. Complicated, gifted, deeply discontented man.

9/28—Saturday

Phone rang early in the morning, and it's Holly saying, Wake up, get your ass to Stowe, and try to make the gondola stop at half past eleven. Then keep it off-line for as long as possible.

Wait a minute, I said. What if I have other plans?

You change them.

I haven't even been to *see* those lifts, yet. Dammit—I'm not ready. And in broad daylight—

Oh, so we're supposed to let a *golden opportunity* go down the drain?

Opportunity for what?

Not for you to know. So, are you on this? Or will you wimp out, the way I said you would?

Look, I told her, I will go to Stowe and take a look around, see what's up. No promises.

Come on, Rachel. Do your best. Go on out there and impress us.

I don't know what I would have done if Jimmy Paquette hadn't been running the lift this morning. But when I saw who it was, I knew I had *a hand to play.* I remembered all the staring that used to go on back in homeroom, in eleventh grade. Glances back and forth across the band room, too—he played tenor sax, and I was alto. So I brushed my hair back, pushed the door to his control booth open, and said I couldn't get him off my mind since the other day. That chance meeting, when I was *all sweaty* and *weighted down* with climbing gear. I was feeling light today, though. Did they give him time for lunch? Did they give him any time at all, with a job like that? Did he ever get really hungry and just want a snack?

Well, what happened to the lift is not what I would call a *mechanical breakdown.* But it went off-line around 11:35, and I had it decommissioned for the best part of an hour.

Score. Eat that, Holly. And Kyle can eat it, too. Now he's not the only person who can do that kind of thing.

Never did I think that hanging out with Kyle Hess would turn me into a *sexual commando.* But that's what I'd call it—that fits what I did today. And to tell the truth, the whole thing left a *bad taste* in my mouth.

Fortunately, that's what we have mouthwash for. Listerine. I bought a bottle on the way home, had a long gargle.

9/29—Sunday Night

Drove my climbing kids up the Toll Road at Stowe this morning, and we had a great day exploring the mountain's ridge. From the Forehead to the Chin. Nothing really technical, although we did explore some of the crags above the Cliff House, and I even helped them find the mossy cave where Kyle and I made love, the *third day.* Right after I sowed the seed that brought on this whole tower project.

Seems as if for all the time I've spent around Stowe lately, I would have a plan in mind for shutting down the lifts by now. But I don't. And just two days till Kung Pao needs to know what I've come up with. What if I can't find a way?

No, I'm sure that I can do it. Because someone has to.

When I got back home, *sweet Kyle* had left a message on the phone machine. He said that he thought we owed ourselves a real date, a *celebration* just like conventional couples have. Because tonight is our three-week anniversary—it was three weeks ago that I went to Erin's place for supper, and we got together. Smashed into each other's lives. Dinner at the Thai place on Pearl Street, and then a movie—*Losers.* Nothing that I'd recommend, but that doesn't matter. It was the spirit of the evening that was so important. Holding hands and snuggling in the dark, with real people sitting all around us. Paired off. *Coupled,* just like us. Then walking down along the waterfront, listening to the clank of ropes against tall masts. Sailboats bobbing at their moorings, singing to the night.

Kyle says to scratch a couple of items off the shopping list—we don't need those *monster wrenches* with the twelve-inch jaws. Good news, because I've been to several hardware stores and seen nothing even close. He got this simple and obvious idea: They must keep those wrenches stashed away *right on the mountain,* since the cables have to be adjusted with the changing seasons. Routine expansion and contraction of the steel. So he broke into the Summit Station the other night, and sure enough . . . We're golden.

Which still leaves a lot for me to buy, but not too many items that are going to need explaining.

Going back to my place would have changed the evening's character, so we decided not to. We will have *so many nights,* looking ahead to when this business with Kung Pao is over. Then, before we kissed good night in the parking lot, he asked me how on earth I did that number on Stowe's gondola. He said it *raised havoc* with some people at the Cliff House.

You know people who were there? I asked him.

I didn't say that, he said. Just tell me how you did it. Because I would love to know.

No, I said. I won't. You wouldn't.

9/30—*Monday*

I think I have figured out why John Muir is important. Not because he *writes that well,* because he really doesn't—unless you have amazing stamina for *pure description.* It's not that he traveled to so many places, did so many things. It's not even that he founded the Sierra Club and used that group to lobby on behalf of the wilderness. No, the main thing is that Muir came to understand nature in a way nobody had before. He saw that the whole thing is *one giant organism,* and that we're a part of it in *just the same way* as trees or bears or snakes or grasses. Rocks, even. Oceans. Dirt. No better and no worse. Not "above" the rest of creation, just a part of it.

And that's why he writes he has *no fear of dying*—Muir keeps saying this again and again. Because what's important is not his own survival, but the larger project. Nature. Earth. The wonderful and nonstop party.

10/1—Tuesday

NIGHT CLIMB

Unnatural, this march of steel stanchions up a mountainside. Chairs hung swaying from an endless steel braid. Who are we to do this to a proud peak, a soaring summit? Who are we to make this one more *playground* for our selfish pleasure?

Just ahead, the complicated housing of machinery looming at the lift's far end. Three-story *space station,* looking like it just landed. Ramps and ladders, platforms, pods. Lexan observation booth. Horizontal bullwheel where the cable makes its U-turn, wraps around the building and begins its motorized descent.

Endless cable. Endless shame.

Climb it—go ahead, it's nighttime. No one's going to catch you.

Crawling on the roof of this *bizarre* piece of architecture, taking in the sights by the cool light of a gibbous moon. *No one has the right* to build a thing like this on such a mountain. I can see the whole contraption tumbling down the slope someday in a grand finale, like in *Zorba the Greek.* Time, then, to dance. But I am not strong enough to bring this chairlift down. I am just one person.

And yet one person can do quite a lot.

I think: A short length of *two-by-four* jammed between the cable and the bullwheel might unhinge things. Like separating a tire from its rim. Or a few *deft strokes* with a *hacksaw* might weaken the cable enough that it would break apart. Clatter, crash. Hundreds of suspended chairs all dropping to the ground. Now I see boxy concrete counterweights, suspended to hold tension on the line. Without them, the cable would be unsupportable. Everywhere are places I could fuck with this machine.

Hand over hand now, down the greasy cable to the first chair. Drop into it. Sit there, swinging and thinking of disabling plans. Roomy, like a sofa—this is a quad lift, designed to carry four abreast. All around me, night sounds. Autumn. Winter closing in.

Think: *What would you do* to give this mountain back to itself? And how would you actually go about doing it?

10/2—*Wednesday*

It came to me—I knew it would. Again, from putting together a model out of stuff we have lying around the store. A loop of rope with pulleys on either end, hex nuts hanging down to represent the chairs. This will be so easy and effective, I can't wait to do it.

Log chains. One per chairlift. Hung between the side of the cable going up the mountain, and the side descending back to the base lodge. Shackled to itself like that, getting a lift to run would take a motor strong enough to *tear the chain apart*—and I'll bet they cannot do that. Kung Pao agrees with me. Not on startup, anyway. First the engine stalls, and then we win. Every time.

Even Holly said she had to hand it to me. This will work.

Small detail of buying five log chains and stashing them at various places on the mountain, but we're going to do that. As for getting them hung across the cables on a dark and stormy night—well, I have my climbing gear.

Speaking of stormy nights, we have one on our hands right now. Fat raindrops pelting on the window, hurled by *shrieking winds*. I hope Kyle isn't doing something on the mountain. I hope he is safely tucked in bed. All by himself.

10/3—*Thursday (Late)*

I did *something nervy* at the writing group tonight, and now it's coming back to haunt me, but I just don't care. Asked to read a notebook entry when we went around the circle, I picked the one from Tuesday about climbing on the ski lift. Kyle wasn't there, but I gather he got wind of what I did from Erin right after—he came *barging in here* half an hour ago, *furious* at me for doing something that could blow our cover.

Our cover? I asked. Excuse me. Where have *you* been, since Sunday?

Don't change the subject, he said. How could you read such a thing aloud to that group? What were you thinking?

I was thinking, I said, that I might dope out *who else* you've roped in. Based on their responses.

So what did you get?

Nada. I guess you're as good as your word. If others are actually involved—Lauren, Erin, Kiki—they don't have a clue. Way to go, Kyle. Way to manipulate.

I don't think you understand the half of what is going on.

No, I don't suppose I do. But then you're not around that much, to fill me in.

Wow, he said. I really *overestimated* you. I thought you were *tougher* than this—and more disciplined. Can't you see we're having these relationship issues on account of the importance of the work we have committed to? Which was *your idea,* in case you've forgotten.

I want this thing *over,* Kyle. When? I can do my part anytime. Tonight, even.

Kung Pao needs explosives, Kyle told me. And he's got a line on something perfect—antitank mines. But they're *way expensive,* on account of several palms to grease down at the Firing Range.

So get some money from that Marianna Finch bitch. Get things moving, Kyle—get this fucking show on the road. Because I swear to God, things will not be right between us until this is over.

I am doing what I can, he tells me. But you must *be patient.* And no more reading stuff aloud to the writing group—you hear me?

You don't tell me what to do, I told him. That's what I have *Holly* for. If that's her real name.

He shook his head, looking *sadly disappointed* in me. Get a grip, Rachel. Please. Then he started putting on his windbreaker.

Where do you think you're going? I asked, working down the buttons of my blouse. I stripped it off, defiant, and made him stare at me.

I have to see somebody.

At eleven-thirty?

Rachel—you don't know. You're fearful. Someday, though, you'll learn to trust me. When I close my eyes at night, all I see is you.

Get out of here, I said. *Get out.* And keep your damn eyes open.

10/4—*Friday*

Dear Rachel:

This is a time for you to think more with your heart, and less with your head. Do you remember what you felt when you and Kyle met? In your heart, you knew that this was what you had been waiting for. This was why you'd hung on to something pure and innocent inside you all those years. A place you never let a man touch before, so that when he touched it he would be the first. So this person blew into your life, and now you think because that happened everything should always be perfect. Wrong, dear one. It takes many years to learn to move in time with someone. Not just in the bed, but in the daily work of moving through a shared life together. You need to be patient with him. Patient with yourself, too. If you hadn't trusted your heart, you never would have gotten in this deep. So you need to trust it now, when he is doing things that can't help disappointing you. Don't let disappointment cast a cloud over the things your heart knows. Those things are true, dear one. Those are the truths that will get you through these current troubles, all these sadnesses. Those true things will save you.

Take care,
Rachel

10/5—*Saturday*

SHOPPING SPREE:

Sears, South Burlington:
    Craftsman three-quarter-inch ratchet drive: $79
    Socket assortment for three-quarter-inch drive: $119
    ("I have a brother who works as a heavy machinery mechanic.
       Next week is his birthday.")

Home Depot, Williston:
  DeWalt heavy-duty half-inch hammer drill, eighteen-volt
    cordless kit with recharging unit: $289
  Selection of Bosch hardened masonry drill bits: $99
  ("I have to take apart a concrete retaining wall at my family's
    lakeside camp, and the job is half a mile from the nearest
    power line.")

Trowel Trades Supply, Colchester:
  Three standard bricklayers' hammers: $66
  Two assortments of professional cold chisels: $70
  ("My boyfriend's having a work party to build a sauna out of
    concrete blocks. Wood-fired. Lined with cedar.
    Scandinavian design.")

Red Hed Supply, Colchester:
  Thirty-six-inch heavy-duty bolt cutters (two): $114
  Deadblow hammers (two): $56
  ("I'm leading a crew to clean a private cliff where climbers have
    left too much fixed protection. The owner wants it out of
    there. One or two permanent bolts are okay on a wall, but
    things have gotten out of hand here. No climber likes a face
    that's littered from prior use.")

Cost of all this: $892, plus tax. Various salespeople took an interest
in my stories, offered lots of free advice.

10/6—Sunday Night

This was the last day of mountaineering classes for my crew of
juvenile delinquents. I am going to miss those kids, but we agreed to
get together in a few months' time to have a reunion. They have *so
much spunk,* such spirit. Hope from here on out they're able to stay
on the right side of the law.

I took them to the crags at Bolton for our last adventure. Good choice, because you can top-rope that cliff in eight different places. Mostly 5.7 and 5.8 routes that have the right amount of challenge, but no serious risk. Before going up to set ropes, I made them stand back and study the entire face. Chalk marks *everywhere,* as though the rock had broken out with a case of acne. Whiteheads. Or like chicken pox. "See that?" I asked the kids. "Don't you find that *unattractive*? Don't you think the climbers who left marks up there were *disrespectful*?"

Then I gave them each a water bottle with a squirt nozzle, and a palm-sized scouring pad. Over the course of the afternoon, we scrubbed away hundreds of white pockmarks where previous climbers had left holds smeared with chalk. End of the day, as we were packing up our gear, I made them look up and *admire their accomplishment.* Far from truly clean, but those kids had *made a difference.* I think that was a perfect note for us to end on—something they can carry with them. We enjoyed a good time on the crags, but at the same time we had worked to make them better. Restoring them to something like their natural state.

We are not at war with nature, I wanted these kids to see. This is not a contest where we try to prove how strong we are, how smart, how we can "conquer" heights. No. It's a *communion* that we're trying to *participate* in. It's a *celebration,* too. And its name is Earth—our beautiful home, where nature has flourished so bountifully and for so long. Something that was going on before we came upon the scene, and something that *will be going on* after we have left it. While we're here, though, why not do whatever we can to make Earth a better place? Sometimes just a squirt of water and a bit of elbow grease is all it takes to do that. Sometimes it takes more—a lot more. But responsibility begins with simple tasks like what we did this afternoon. I like to think I showed those kids how to be *caretakers.* How each one of them can learn to take good care of Earth.

Kyle called, a couple of minutes ago. *Sketchy invitation* to come spend the night at Lauren's farm—he has maps and things he wants to show me in his cabin. Information that I'll need to disable the ski lifts.

There's a store in Underhill where I should leave my car, he says. So that Lauren won't discover that I am around. He wants to pick me up there at 10:30.

I don't know about this. I said *maybe* I would be there, *maybe not.* Tomorrow's Monday, work—no. That wasn't it. The whole thing smacks of being sneaky, going someplace where you're not supposed to be. I don't want to be with him on Lauren's turf. *It isn't right.* If he's got some maps to show me, he should bring them over here.

10/7—*Monday Morning*

Guess he knew I wasn't really going to turn him down, so Kyle found me waiting at the Underhill store when he pulled in with his van. Up Lauren's driveway with the headlights off, then sneaking into this *surprisingly nice* cottage where he's been living for the past few weeks. Fieldstone fireplace crackling with apple branches—last year's prunings, he said. They put out a lot of heat. Maker's Mark bourbon in brandy snifters, neat. Let's make up, he said. I know that both of us have been under a strain, but now there's light at the end of the tunnel.

Part of me was gearing up to turn *wary and accusing,* like I did before with him—but then I saw on the refrigerator door the photos he had taken of me standing by the tower, that day when we cased the joint. Last afternoon of our Three-Day Event. Held against the metal with some little fruit-shaped magnets. Some of the expressions on my face looked goofy, but others recalled the *sincerity and candor* that we have with each other when we're *at our best.* We do have an *amazing vibe* together—like no other I have ever known. And I really do mean a lot to him, I realized. I never meant to disparage what we have together.

Then he started telling me this *outrageous story* about how naive and credulous Lauren Blackwood is. Kyle had a visit from his editor the other day—the head of Rolling Thunder Books—and as a gag they tried to pass him off as some kind of eco-terror mastermind. Lauren *fell for* this charade—it sounds like she fell for it hook, line, and sinker. They even asked her to attend some *bogus pow-wow* on Saturday afternoon, a "strategy session" with this editor and Kung Pao to decide whether or not to blow up some earthen dams! Lauren was *way impressed,* as though she were really helping shape the movement's policies. She doesn't know which end is up. But she's got these llamas, and they are our secret weapon. Four-footed tanks, he called them. Those llamas are going to pack our demolition gear up Mount Mansfield.

Then Kyle spread out an *incredibly detailed* map that showed where each of the ski lifts comes closest to the ground, which is where I'll want to shackle them. Also, there are markings to show where someone will hide the log chains on the day of the attack. I should scout the territory sometime in the next few days, make sure I can find all of these landmarks in the dark. We are on a *definite flight path* now, he told me. Just sort of waiting on the weather to cooperate. Something about needing a *good shot of rain* to close off the Toll Road, and to obscure what they'll be doing on the mountain. On a stormy night, a few explosions on the summit will be written off as thunder.

Then to bed—*his* bed, which we conquered like a foreign country. So many sweet sensations that we still are learning how to give each other's bodies. Being fondled *there,* and *there.* Taste of nipple, navel, tongue. Making future plans before the first light meant I'd have to leave him, have to drive back home. Kyle has been thinking about going to New Hampshire, next. Many *bad things* are taking place in the presidentials—sprawling theme parks creeping up the base of Mount Washington. Would I ever think of pulling up stakes in Burlington and following him there?

Yes, I said. I would. No question. First of all, that's one of my favorite places in New England. Big wall country. No lack of multipitch technical climbs. And to be there with him—yes. Living, working, *struggling together* on Earth's behalf. Yes, I told him. Yes, I would.

So we made a pact, and sealed it—I'm not going to put down how. But the coming days are going to be about *affirming* our *best versions* of each other. And after that, we'll be *embracing* the shared future our *amazing love* requires. And richly deserves.

Ducked out the back door of Kyle's cabin just in time—Lauren was already out walking in the sheep pasture, calling to her big white dog. One false move on the part of either one of us and there would have been some explaining to do. Fortunately I won't have to feel like I'm sharing Kyle for much longer. When two people just *belong to each other*, anyone who's gotten in the way will have to make adjustments.

10/8—Tuesday Morning

Well, the hair-and-nails babe from RE/MAX came here last night for a little heart-to-heart. I thought the journal entry that I read on Thursday hadn't smoked anybody out, but I stand corrected. Because Marianna Finch was at the Cliff House when the gondola quit running, and she figures I must be the one responsible. On account of what I read. She said that I ought to *come forward publicly,* otherwise for some reason Stowe is going to nail Kyle.

Fascinating piece of news she managed to divulge to me: *Kyle* was at the Cliff House that day, too.

First I tried to stonewall, then I realized I ought to find out *what she thinks* is going on. Even if she thinks she is "in love" with Kyle, or something. So I got her just a teensy bit drunk on Cuervo, then chatted her up. Incredibly, it turns out Marianna is *clueless* about the plan to take down the broadcast towers. Even though, from what Kyle told me, she is paying for it. She's afraid he's going to get the ski resort *pissed* at him for pulling off some minor pranks that made it hard to sell some condos—big fucking deal. As if that had *any importance* in the grand scheme. I think I managed to keep her in the dark, and let her leave here thinking Kyle's not involved with Stowe at all.

Interesting test of wits, and I came out the winner. I give Marianna points for coming here to see me, though. Obviously Kyle has managed to worm his way into her essentially frigid heart. But I can see how she would be a *hopeless sucker* for him—how he could quite easily turn her lonely self-absorption into a major crush. Give her something more than bugs and leaves to contemplate.

Come to think of it, I'll bet Kyle wouldn't even *need* to sleep with somebody like that, to get her all obsessed.

Maybe, then, he hasn't. *I wouldn't,* if I were him. I know what kind of shit these needy, insecure women dump on a man in bed.

Wondering how many bucks he hit her up for?

Tonight will be my dry run on the mountain. Glad that someone else is going to hide the log chains for me, when we do this thing for real. Because I swear to God, the one that I just snaked into my backpack must weigh *fifty pounds.* Plus a coil of climbing rope, my harness, jumars, carabiners. I hope I don't throw my back out from the weight of this adventure.

10/9 — Wednesday (Early Morning)

Lesson in the way *big things* grow out of *small intentions.* How do you hook a log chain to a steel cable hanging twenty feet overhead? You can't toss it up there. You can't put it like a shot, or twirl it around like a lasso and rope the target. But you can fling a weighted length of clothesline upward, wrapping it around the cable and letting the free end fall back into your hands. And you can attach that to a climbing rope, and pull that over. And you can attach *that* to one end of the heavy chain, hauling it hand over hand until it drops in place.

Start small—lightweight, manageable. Narrow gauge. But don't let a small start stop you from *thinking big.*

You can do this in the dark. You *could* do this in a rainstorm. Dark and stormy nights are nothing to a person with a plan.

10/10 — Thursday Evening

This wasn't an easy call, but I decided to bag on the writing group tonight. First of all, at this point it is simply not an *appropriate venue* for me to be with Kyle. Second, after letting down my guard with Marianna I don't want to have to see her, run the risk of having her pursue our conversation.

Third, though—and here's *the biggie*—I am getting just a bit down on Erin Furlong. Maybe I do owe her *something* because she brought Kyle to me, but it seems as if she's put a lot of balls in the air without making much of an effort to juggle them. Let alone managing to bring things to a resolution, back down to earth.

I suppose I mean this in relational terms, considering how so many people in the workshop seem to have had their lives disrupted by her "friend." But I also mean it in terms of just our notebooks, our journals of personal nature writing. She has unleashed forces in people's lives that are destabilizing their whole sense of who they are. And she hasn't got a clue what, if anything, to do about that. So I feel there's an *abdication* of what ought to be Erin's *responsibility*. What good does it do to tell somebody where to put an adverb, when that person's nature notebook is causing her to come unhinged? Making her *lose her grip*, casting her *adrift* from the person she used to be. That is scary stuff.

I need to admit, too, that I'm *dog tired* after spending last night on the mountain. Getting my procedure down, locating various drop points for the chains and gear. If—as Kyle promised me—Kung Pao wants to do this soon, I need to get my body rested for the main event.

What a night it was, though. Billions of starry pinpricks glowing in an inky sky. Hoot owls calling to each other, coyotes gathering to mourn some loss on a distant ridge. Sigh of maples giving up their burden of brittle leaves. I kept looking all around me, thinking, *What a beautiful place* this world is. And *keeps managing* to be. Maybe that is nature's final, ultimate purpose—beauty. Boundless and eternal. Brimming cup that just keeps running over.

Wondering how Kyle will react to my bagging on the writing workshop. But he still has my spare key. I'm going to fall asleep and see if he shows up to wake me—see what we can figure out to do with the night.

10/11—*Friday Morning (Right After He Left)*

So this day began with the *infinite pleasure* of waking to find Kyle sliding into bed beside me, just before the crack of dawn. What a long night, he told me. Running down a dozen last details. Getting everything in place to take down the towers tonight.

I can't even *think* of a time when I wanted more than anything just to be making love, but he kissed me tenderly and said we'd have to wait for that. He just wanted to close his eyes a little while, let him feel my arms around him. Our legs entwined together. I reset the alarm, then snuggled down beside him.

Later, having coffee, I asked what I should do after my work tonight is finished—once the ski lifts are disabled. He said I should *get off the mountain* and drive back here, make sure I keep my normal Saturday schedule. Do *nothing suspicious*. Kung and Holly plan to leave the summit by 4:00 A.M., well before sunup. They're all packed—they're aiming to leave Vermont on the first ferry to Plattsburgh, tomorrow morning. And from there, who knows? As for Kyle, he said I should meet him Tuesday morning in the lobby of the Mount Washington Hotel, in Bretton Woods, New Hampshire. Heart of the White Mountains. Ten o'clock sharp. And come prepared, he said, to start *this new life* we will share.

I'll be there, I said. But why not swing by my place tomorrow?

He said once the last broadcast tower hits the ground, his first goal will be to get the heck out of Vermont. One way or another, he must do that. Any way he can.

I could see a sadness in his eyes, and I told him so. More than just being tired from the night behind him, and facing the night ahead. Why? I asked him bluntly. This close to doing what we dreamed of, why not show some joy?

When he tried to answer me, I couldn't help thinking back over all my wounds and wanting to forgive him. He said he gets torn between *commitment to the cause* at hand—a just and necessary cause, if humans are to learn to live in harmony with nature—and the *intense friendships* that come up along the way, that make the good work possible. He said he was feeling sad because he would miss Kung and Holly. He'd miss getting to spend time with Erin Furlong, and he even—this was hard, he knew, for me to understand but it was still true—he would even miss, in a way, people like Lauren Blackwood and Marianna Finch. People he had met along the path who had shared something, helped advance the project with him. So while he did feel excitement for the night ahead, it would be dishonest to deny a certain sorrow, too.

I told Kyle that he shouldn't be *so hard* on himself—that he'd given gifts to all those people, in return. Things that they would keep for life.

He said, "I wish I could learn to value people more. Try to care as much about them as I do for Earth."

"You can learn to do that," I said. "You can start with me."

4:30 (After Work)

All packed up and ready to head for Stowe. Kung and Kyle waited for a foul night, and they really got one. Wonder if they've got some off-road tires for those llamas.

Nothing left to do except to do it.

11:35 P.M. (On the Mountain's Nose—Warm, Dry Weather Station!)

So I got those log chains hung in record time, then told myself *no way* am I going to be left out of the action that was my idea in the first place. So, here I am. Soaked to the bone and *shivering like crazy,* but I made it up the mountain and even found a way to get in out of the weather.

I hear voices now, outside. Here comes the wrecking crew.

2:30 A.M.

I've been out there doing my bit to help, but Kyle said to duck into this Quonset hut and get dried off, warmed up. He said to take five.

Marianna Finch is here! She was the llama handler, but of course she didn't know the program so she *went berserk,* started to *scream* and *beat up* on people. Kung Pao shoved her in the weather station, barred the door. He has a nifty system, which has gone like clockwork. First remove the bolts holding a tower to its concrete pad, then weaken the concrete with the hammer drill and cold chisels. Then he sets the pressure fuse on one of these antitank mines he got his hands on, and everyone takes cover. When he shoots the mine with his rifle, there's a *quick explosion* and a falling heap of metal.

Three of the smaller towers are already on the ground—just one more to go. Then we're taking down the big one.

10/12 — Saturday Morning (still dark/not quite dawn)

Major screw-up, two hours ago. When the mine went off to bring down tower number four, one of the llamas—*Abelard,* Kyle called it—broke its tether and went charging up the trail to the Nose. And in its saddlebag was the mine we planned on using to take down the final tower. The 200-footer. Kyle and Kung Pao started arguing back and forth, then Holly grabbed the gun and *fucking shot* the llama dead. Which made the mine go off, so Abelard exploded in a wet burst of blood and guts.

That stopped the argument.

Holly said we're not going to risk taking people's lives. We can't have a loaded llama roaming up here on the mountain, like a ticking bomb.

So then it was time for Kung and Holly to get off the mountain. Four towers out of five is not a bad night's work, they said. I watched them set off down the Long Trail, then turned to Kyle and said, Goddamnit, *I know how* to bring down that last tower. And I'm going to do it. Can you stay another hour?

We got the tools and started putting slack into the various cables—one person holding the flashlight, and the other tugging an enormous wrench.

You shouldn't even be here, Kyle tells me. How will you get off the mountain? Soon as someone figures out what's happened, there'll be choppers up here. Filled with *very angry* people.

I'm a climber, I said. I will go down in the crags, and hide there. Find our mossy nook and wait till nightfall. How will *you* get off?

I have a way, he tells me. But I have to move out before the sky turns light.

That gave us time to drive out two of three linchpins—then he kissed me, held me tight, and made me *promise* to meet him in New Hampshire, Tuesday morning. I'm writing this by flashlight, waiting for the dawn so I can see enough to drive the final pin and run for cover.

Is the world ever *more lovely* than by first light? Eerie glow, veiled premonition of the dawn. I love these early moments of a coming day—as if all night long you had been *blindfolded,* then here comes this *gift of sight.*

Cocoon of mist is parting now, and I see—Kyle, up there! Hanging from a sky blue paraglider, floating past the mountain's ridge and down into the valley.

Okay. Time to do this thing.

I am *so privileged* to be alive at this moment, and in this amazing world.

Afterword

Erin Furlong

Three days later, I allowed myself to be coerced into helping out the FBI with Kyle's capture. I still have attacks of panic when I rethink doing this. Was it really necessary? Was it somehow "right"? But with the law breathing down my neck and threatening charges, I had no good options. The lead agent on the case, Steve Chasen out of Boston, was the first thorough reader of the journals here presented—Lauren's, Marianna's, Rachel's—so he was aware that Kyle planned to meet Rachel on Tuesday the fifteenth at the Mount Washington Hotel. Chasen was prepared to put a dozen agents in that lobby, but he made me come along to show I was cooperative and guarantee a positive I.D. of the man they wanted.

He didn't tell me the truth about Rachel's fate, and why she couldn't make it to their 10:00 A.M. rendezvous. He said that after the police had found her on the mountain, they had a helicopter fly her down to Dartmouth-Hitchcock Medical Center in Lebanon, New Hampshire. That she was being held in custody there, as well as in intensive care—unconscious, and with multiple injuries from the broadcast tower's collapse. That when she woke up, she would find herself in big trouble.

On the morning of October fifteenth, Chasen got me at the crack of dawn for the drive to Bretton Woods. On the way he told me there were others involved in what had happened on Mount Mansfield—a pair of West Coast terrorists, plus Lauren and Marianna from my writing group. No way, I told him. You have somehow made a big mistake.

"The Finch woman's probably off the hook," he told me. "She may be criminally naive, but we don't jail people for that. As for Little Bo Peep, though—"

"Leave Lauren alone," I told him. "She is nothing but an innocent sheep farmer."

"She did forty thousand dollars worth of damage."

"How?"

"By washing out the Toll Road. It'll be weeks before they get those culverts back in place."

"Let her make some restitution, then. I'm sure she can. No way could Lauren Blackwood be a real criminal."

Nine thirty in the morning, we pull up to a side entrance of this enormous old resort hotel and I'm whisked into an upstairs parlor that overlooks the lobby. Row on row of wooden columns, and maybe a couple hundred foliage tourists milling about below me. I look and look, but don't see Kyle down there anywhere. Eventually it's after 10:00, so Chasen sends me downstairs to prowl among the guests. Knowing that I'm being watched from thirteen directions. I wanted to explain the way it is with Kyle and women—that just because he promised Rachel he would be here doesn't mean he's going to show. But I do as I am told and cruise the lobby several times. Nothing. And I'm thinking maybe Kyle smelled the trap.

Then, on a whim, I step onto the hotel's wrap-around veranda and see Kyle standing way down toward the end of it, staring up at Mount Washington's summit through one of those scenic view binoculars you put a quarter into. There's a weather station up there and a cluster of antennas—I could guess what he was thinking. "Kyle!" I called even though he was quite far away, down this amazing porch like something out of *Gatsby*. Then I shouted: "Kyle—run!"

He looked up—maybe the scenic binoculars had just shut off. The instant he saw me, he started climbing up onto the heavy wooden railing. But before he'd leaped from the veranda to the ground below, three large men materialized and tackled him. I got to Kyle just as they had put the handcuffs on and were reading him his rights. He stared at me with a look at once enraged and plaintive.

"Rachel couldn't make it," I said by way of explanation. "Sorry things turned out this way."

"How could you betray me?" he asked. "You, of all people?"

I didn't answer that question, and I still can't. But a moment later Agent Chasen came running up, and I thought I'd seize the moment to do Lauren a good turn. "Tell this man that Lauren Blackwood is no criminal," I begged him. "Set the record straight, so that she can go free."

"Anything you say can be used against you," Chasen noted.

"Lauren isn't innocent, exactly," Kyle said in a voice just above a whisper. "But I'll take some blame for how she got in over her head." Then something dropped from his hand, and an agent dove to scoop it up as if it were some kind of high explosive. Wrong, though—it was a wooden ring, hand carved and sanded till its redwood grain might almost pass for metal. "Do what you have to do with me," Kyle told Chasen in quiet resignation. "But I want the ring to get to Rachel."

"I could do that," I suggested.

Chasen examined the meticulously crafted band, debating whether it might have some evidentiary purpose. Then he handed it to me. Only hours later—when they dropped me off in Burlington—did I learn that Rachel would never get to wear that ring. I wept and wept— I still weep, sometimes—but no amount of grieving is going to bring her back.

Now, months later, Lauren is back home in Pleasant Valley and participating in a restorative justice program. She's had to remortgage the farm to pay for damages, but at least she's not in jail. I went to see her just a couple weeks ago, and she seems recovered—more or less—from what she called her five-week flight of fancy. She's cured of men, though, she told me. She is cured for good.

Marianna's testimony seems sure to doom Kyle when his trial date comes up. I went to talk about it with her, but she's unforgiving. She's left RE/MAX to strike out on her own; getting disciplined by the realtors' association was an awful blow to her professional pride. That's not where she's really hurting, though. I don't know exactly what it's going to take to heal her heart, but I was surprised to learn she's riding horses once again and offering to teach dressage. These are positive directions.

As for myself, the most enduring pain came from having to disband the nature writing group. I didn't realize how much our shared efforts had come to mean to me. Nailing down the legal rights to publish this volume became an obsessive project of recouping something that would manifest—and honor—our workshop's vitality and its members' high ambitions. I may find another writing project somewhere down the road, but nowadays I'm feeling silent. And, on my bad days, chastened by the tragedies that befell so many in our circle.

I've kept Kyle's ring for Rachel as my keepsake, though. Beautiful, organic jewelry. And one of a kind, like him. I don't know how fragile it might prove, were I to wear it daily. Ordinary life hands out some terrible abuse. But I do slip it on from time to time, to think and wonder. Wearing it, I can't help feeling that my friend had found his love—a love to match his fiery nature, and determined to serve Nature. I think: What a couple those two must have been, and would have made. I think there is something to be said for dying as she did, riding an infectious wave of hope and energetic joy. Dying as she must have lived—with a capacity for passion and amazement that cannot, when all is said and done, be adequately put in words.

Reading Group Guide

Questions for Discussion

1.   This novel is presented as excerpts from the "nature notebooks" of three of the characters. Why might the author choose this approach? How does this presentation affect your experience of the novel?

2.   The excerpts are framed by the comments of Erin Furlong. How does this framing device function in the novel? How does the frame affect your reading of the story?

3.   The notebooks cover the same period of time, and sometimes the same incidents, from three different points of view. How does your understanding of characters and of events change as you read these different perspectives?

4.   How does your understanding of Kyle Hess in particular change over the course of the novel? To what degree is that understanding shaped by the descriptions and feelings of the narrators who describe him?

5.   How does Hess present himself differently to each of the three narrators? How do their own feelings about him evolve? Is there one "version" of Hess that seems to you more likely or authentic?

6.   What opinions do these women hold of one another? To what extent do you consider those opinions to be well- or ill-informed?

7.   How does the author create distinctive voices for each of the three narrators? How does the author reveal information about the narrators of which even they may be unaware?

8.   Several characters remark on the differing yet possibly complementary attitudes of Vermonters and those "out west" toward both

the environment and the possibility of activism. What is the importance of place in this novel? How is place important to the characters?

9. Each of the three narrators engages in what she considers to be "nature writing." How do their understandings of nature and nature writing differ? What do those differences reveal about the characters? How do they respond to the "models" they have each been assigned?

10. What knowledge or opinions about nature writing did you bring to this novel? What works have you read that might be considered nature writing? How were those opinions either revised or reinforced by the novel?

11. What knowledge or opinions about eco-terrorism did you bring? How were those opinions either revised or reinforced?

12. Kyle Hess claims that "we don't have to make people converts to get them to help us." To what extent does he succeed or fail in securing such unintentional assistance? How do you apportion responsibility for the events of the novel among Hess and the three narrators?

Author's Statement

This novel reflects a wariness—earned, I suppose, by my experience of life—of both ideologues on the one hand and dilettantes on the other. It also means to suggest that when these two types go head to head, the ideologues are likely to have a field day. I also set out to consider where the line is drawn that demarcates the school of "nature appreciation" from the ranks of environmental activists; this question goes, I think, to the heart of an American literary tradition that has long inspired and fascinated me.

It's never easy to tease out the various sources that give rise to something so complex and ambitious as a novel, but I can identify at least three clusters of interest that seem to have coalesced to produce *The Nature Notebooks*. In the summer of 1997, I was well into developing a novel about the commercialization of *southern* Vermont's landscape when I was invited to write a guidebook to the state in the "Compass American" series, whose books tend to emphasize issues in natural history and cultural history. Over the next couple of years I came to know the entirety of my chosen state extremely well, and was forced to ponder repeatedly how and why Vermont was luring tourists by marketing an iconic way of life that was palpably dying all around the cash-laden visitors—and dying, in no small part, on account of the success of tourism. The contradictions inherent in this state of affairs crop up in many places around Vermont, but nowhere more so than in the Stowe— Mount Mansfield—Underhill area.

In October of 1998, I followed with interest news reports alleging that an extremist environmental group calling itself Earth Liberation Front had set fires causing $12 million in damage at the ski resort in Vail, Colorado, in order to stop an expansion that it was believed would threaten critical habitat for the lynx. The event seemed to signal an expansion of West Coast style "ecoterror" activities from such classic targets as protection of old growth forests to entirely new venues, such as discouraging new development for recreational tourism. I asked myself whether such tactics might ever find their way to Vermont, and whether the environmentally attuned culture of this state would tend to make us more susceptible to or immune to such activities.

Finally, for many years I have taught a course on nature-oriented literature at Middlebury College; as part of that course, I often ask each student to choose a place on the campus to visit several times a week and record their impressions in a "nature observation journal" spanning the months of winter through spring. Reading through these notebooks, I discovered early on that they inevitably assume certain qualities of a private diary. I also saw how certain events of universal interest—a major blizzard, say, or a major news event—tended to get recorded again and again through the unique filter of each writer's personality. I realized that such journals might serve as an offbeat but serviceable storytelling device, in which each word would simultaneously reflect the depths of a character's personality while also contributing to a larger storytelling project that would emerge, so to speak, between the lines of the journal entries. Late one night in June of 2000, I challenged myself to try to write a novel in this way—and once I had begun the process, there was no turning back.

An Interview with Don Mitchell

              This is your fourth novel, but the first that you have published in more
              than a decade. In the interim, you have published several books of non-
              fiction. Why the return now to fiction? In what ways has your non-
              fiction writing informed your fiction?

I never really abandoned writing novels, but for several years my interests as
a novelist seemed to be out of synch with those of the surrounding culture.
When that happens, I think all that a writer can do is be patient and keep
developing one's craft. Working in nonfiction—particularly the personal
essay—became a way for me to stay active as a writer, and my approach to
the essay has certainly been influenced by a love of storytelling that is rooted
in respect for the novel. On the other hand, writing nonfiction imposes a
standard of factual accuracy that I've tried to carry over into my recent work
in fiction. A novel's story is—or should be, I believe—a product of the imagination, but it can also unfold in a real-life landscape that is rendered with the
sort of specificity of detail more often associated with nonfiction. That was
one of my goals in writing *The Nature Notebooks*.

              How did the experience of writing this book differ from your earlier
              novels? How have your interests or goals as a writer changed since
              your earlier novels?

I managed to begin publishing fiction three decades ago, at the tender age of
twenty-two, and I fell pretty quickly into the dual traps of writing largely out
of personal experience and trying to become a spokesperson for my generation. Neither of those past strategies as a writer is of any current interest to
me. In fact, my main aspiration in developing *The Nature Notebooks* was to
write a story that would be a work of "pure" fiction—no characters based
even indirectly on people that I happen to know, no plot elements derived
even loosely from episodes in my personal life, and no one in the novel
whose voice reads as a stand-in for my own sensibility or authorial perspec-

tive. I felt that if I could accomplish this, a world of wider possibility would be open to me as a novelist and I would have validated a choice I made several years ago to stop living my personal life with a third eye constantly roving about, trying to scope out material for possible projects in fiction.

     How did you decide on the format of the notebook entries? How did you go about it? What were the challenges in writing the book this way? What were the advantages?

Like any creative person, my conscious mind gets regularly bombarded with ideas that come from somewhere and which seem—for the moment, at least—worth considering. Like any developing novelist, I've been tantalized by the dream of telling a story in a way that no one has ever told one before. When the idea came to me of trying to use several characters' "nature observation journals" as this novel's entire narrative strategy, it became an irresistible and obsessive challenge. It was over a year from the time I conceived this idea to the time when I could devote myself to executing it, thanks to a semester's leave from Middlebury College; by that time, I knew a great deal about the overall shape of the book. Since each of the three journals is comprised of daily entries that span a five-week period, I spent five weeks trying to live within the psyche of each character and drafted an entry for that person each day—in short, I built each person's notebook in the same way that the novel purports that its characters wrote them. In fact, I wrote the initial journal entries longhand, which is not my usual writing practice. After finishing one person's journal, it would take me about two weeks to let go of that character and get into the head of the next one. Of course there was a lot of rewriting and problem-solving to attend to afterward—particularly in trying to make the timelines congruent and not have Kyle Hess show up in more than one place at the same time. But drafting one journal entry per day gave me a steady sense of progress, and imparts to the notebooks—I hope—a feeling of verisimilitude with an actual journaling process.

     What were the challenges in making the several narrative voices distinctive? Were there some key differences among the three principal narrators that you particularly wanted to convey through their language?

Consistent with Erin Furlong's recommending a specific canonical "nature writer" for each person in the group to model his or her efforts after, I was trying to explore some of the differences between the sensibilities of Ralph Waldo Emerson, Henry David Thoreau and John Muir. These are all authors whose works I have taught to college students. Emerson was (in my view) essentially an armchair enthusiast of nature, and Marianna's voice and personality are designed to mimic that. Lauren has a much stronger level of practical engagement with the natural world, as did Thoreau; both also have an antigregarious strain and a mistrust of conformity. Rachel, like John Muir, is fundamentally a person of action who reveres nature particularly for the physical and psychological challenges it offers. Those were the broad lines of distinction I was trying to establish, and which I hoped to demarcate by certain mechanical devices such as varied sentence rhythms and choices in diction and emphasis, but also by the different kinds of natural phenomena each character turns her attention to and the different sorts of interactions with nature that each seeks.

You are a farmer yourself. Can you say a bit about that aspect of your life? How did you come to that life? How does that experience inform your writing in general and this novel in particular? How has living in Vermont shaped your perspective and your fiction?

Flush with money earned in Hollywood in my early twenties, my wife and I bought a farm in Vermont in 1972 at the height of the post-hippie "back to the land" movement. We were escaping urban environments that we had tried out and grown tired of—Los Angeles, San Francisco, Philadelphia, Boston. We didn't become serious about farming, though, till after the birth of our children several years later; caring for livestock and making hay and managing a large garden became a wonderful project to bond our family together with a sense of shared purpose. Obviously, agriculture keeps a person grounded in natural cycles and attentive to patterns of weather, changing seasons, shifts in the land's state of health. Like Lauren Blackwood, I find it ironic that farming has come to be seen as suspicious in contemporary "Green" circles because it involves the flagrant manipulation of ecosystems. This is an accurate criticism, though it's hard to imagine a way of life that fosters a greater sense of engagement with and responsibility to the natural world than farmers enjoy.

❧   *Do you consider yourself an "environmentalist"? What do you under-*
     stand this term to mean? In what ways has this term has been abused
     or misunderstood?

I think of myself as someone who tries to be cognizant of the ways in which my personal lifestyle choices have specific impacts—both positive and negative—on the integrity and sustainability of both the local ecosystems that surround me and the health of the planet as a whole. Without excessive self-denial and/or self-flagellation, I generally try to make choices in the conduct of my life that I believe are environmentally responsible; in my understanding, people who do so have earned the right to call themselves "environmentalists." It's not a term that particularly quickens my pulse, nor do I want to proclaim it from some rooftop as central to my identity. I happen to dislike what I take to be a preachy and self-righteous strain among environmentalists who wear their values on their sleeves. Environmentalism will have a better chance of succeeding, I think, when people adopt its perspectives simply because they make practical sense, rather than to satisfy the quest for a surrogate religion.

❧   *Terrorism of all kinds has been a topic of much discussion in recent*
     years. Did you have any special concerns or considerations in taking
     on the topic of eco-terrorism in this novel? What did you find most
     challenging or rewarding or surprising in treating this topic?

I date my interest in "direct action" to my first day of kindergarten when, after an hour or so, I quietly got up and left the building and walked home. No one had told me I couldn't. Certainly the experience of coming of age in the late 1960s—when civil disobedience (a Thoreauvian term) was widely embraced by the young as a means of achieving social justice—reinforced my fascination with the idea that breaking civil laws could at times be justifiable and even necessary in order to obey "higher" ones. Consequently, I followed with philosophic interest the extension of this outlook into the realm of environmental action during the 1980s and 1990s. The issues raised by spiking trees or setting lab rats free seemed worthy of consideration in a novel, and the people who undertook such actions promised to be lively characters. For better and for worse, I was smack in the middle of drafting

The Nature Notebooks on September 11, 2001, and since then—obviously—
all forms of terrorism have come to be seen in an altered perspective. For a
time, I felt that my novel was dead and unrevivable. But then I gradually saw
that its story could be shaped to ponder a newly relevant question: How *do*
individuals of reasonable intelligence and generally promising lives get caught
up in this sort of activity? Perhaps the novel's characters, with their diverse
and at times conflicting strands of motivation, can help to shed light on a
wider phenomenon that is so troubling and so much on our minds.

    *Your novel contains a certain implicit critique of the genre of nature
    writing. Why do you think that such a critique is necessary or timely?
    What examples of this genre have you enjoyed or found useful?*

I tend to admire examples of nature writing that begin with a clearly stated
philosophic question and then attempt, in a roundabout but conscientious
way, to answer it. For Thoreau, I take the question to have been, Is life fundamentally sublime, or mean? and I take his answer to be—after hundreds of
pages of nature meditation in *Walden*—Wrong question, since it is generally
both at once! For Annie Dillard, the question was Is the existence of the
natural world a matter of caprice, or not? and I take her answer to be—after
hundreds of pages of nature meditation in *Pilgrim at Tinker Creek*—Not!
But nature writing as a genre strikes me as a jug of milk in which very little
cream has risen to the top—because so little cream is present. To make matters worse, very few readers seem able to distinguish the cream. I'm particularly annoyed by a histrionic strain within this genre that tends to be self-
absorbed, self-congratulatory, and vaguely autoerotic. The roots of this
school go deep into our literary history, but its modern practitioners strike
me as exploiting nature for their own selfish purposes, just as surely (although
admittedly more benignly) as loggers, miners, whalers, and oil drillers.

    *Obviously these three women each regard nature in different ways. Is
    there one whose views reflect your own?*

I do think I'm closest to Lauren Blackwood's point of view, because she's
torn between efforts to appreciate nature along traditional romantic lines
and the practical (i.e., unromantic) realities of trying to run a farm opera-

tion. It's a contradiction with which I can easily sympathize. But every character a novelist creates is an emanation of some dimension of the author's personality, and I certainly have at times regarded nature through the lenses that Marianna and Rachel do.

꙳   *In addition to fiction and nonfiction, you have also written several screenplays. How is the experience of writing for the screen different from writing a novel?*

For me, the hardest aspect of writing for film is to portray the content of a character's thoughts, since only in rare circumstances can they be filmed directly. The modern novel's greatest accomplishment, I think, has been the variety of strategies that its practitioners have discovered for accessing the human psyche, even in its most intimate and personal areas; in this respect, telling a story by means of several characters' private journals afforded satisfactions that screenwriting would be hard-pressed to match. On the other hand, writing for film forces one to foreground visual turf as the primary locus for a story's conflict. When I realized that central to *The Nature Notebooks* was the cluster of large, ugly broadcast towers atop Mount Mansfield, I was arguably thinking like a screenwriter.

꙳   *You teach writing at Middlebury College. How has teaching informed your own writing? What are your goals as a teacher of writing?*

First of all, teaching college students has kept me directly in touch with the perspectives of people on the threshold of adulthood, a life-stage that energizes much of our cultural life. That's a real plus. On the other hand, much of the work of teaching creative writing involves carefully reading and editing other writers' manuscripts, and in doing so a teacher is directly flexing the muscles he would be using, under different circumstances, to accomplish his own work. That's a definite drawback. I like to think that talking through a wide variety of creative ideas—and trying to identify and solve their hidden problems—with so many students, day in and day out, has helped me to better sort my own best creative ideas from those that should be discarded. The main skill I try to teach students is to become resourceful at problem-

solving, which involves learning to read one's own work critically and ac-
quiring a stamina for the processes of revision.

> *Can you tell us a bit about your own writing practice? Do you write*
> *every day? In certain circumstances? What draws you to a particular*
> *story?*

When I'm at work in the drafting and revision stages of a writing project, I
do try to feed it for a least a few hours every day. When I have full flexibility
to schedule my time, I like to embed two working sessions of three to four
hours within each twenty-four–hour day, separated by a long nap. But when
I don't have a writing project developed to the stage where it can absorb that
kind of attention, I don't show up at my desk to stare in frustration at a blank
computer screen. While I'm always testing various story ideas in my mind,
the one element that consistently draws me into a writing project is a deep
psychological response to a particular setting, whether it be a natural landscape or an architectural creation. When I'm moved in this special way by a
sense of place, an inner voice pipes up and asks me: "Why not set a story here?"